DON'T TELL A SOUL

TIFFANY L. WARREN

Kensington Publishing Corp.

http://www.kensingtonbooks.com

DAFINA BOOKS are published by

Kensington Publishing Corp.
119 West 40th Street
New York, NY 10018

All Kensington Titles, Imprints, and Distributed Lines are available at special quantity discounts for bulk purchases for sales promotions, premiums, fund-raising, and educational or institutional use. Special book excerpts or customized printings can also be created to fit specific needs. For details, write or phone the office of the Kensington special sales manager: Kensington Publishing Corp., 119 West 40th Street, New York, NY 10018, attn: Special Sales Department, Phone: 1-800-221-2647.

Dafina and the Dafina logo Reg. U.S. Pat. & TM Off.

First trade paperback printing: February 2013

ISBN-13: 978-0-7582-8057-2
ISBN-10: 0-7582-8057-2

10 9 8 7 6 5 4 3 2 1

Printed in the United States of America

Acknowledgments

First, giving honor to God, who is the head of my life . . .

Ha! Don't get me started testifying, because I will absolutely get to hollering and singing in my deep voice. Seriously, I thank God for the opportunity to bring you the sequel to *What a Sista Should Do.*

Thank you to Selena James at Dafina for understanding my vision for this story and for being an advocate for me! Also, I don't know about other authors, but I have the coolest, most down-to-earth editor in the business. Mercedes, you are a gift, and don't let anybody tell you different!

Thank you, Brent, my love, for continuing to support my writing career after all these years. I know that it's not always easy having an "artist" for a wife, but I thank you for understanding me. You have my heart (and my cooking)!

Thank you to my little chickadees, Briana, Brittany, Brynn, Brent II, and Brooke! You guys are a well-oiled machine! Thank you for being wonderful children and only making me fuss a little (well, maybe more than a little). I love you!

Everybody knows (ha) that I rely on my girls! Y'all get all my drama, prayer requests, testimonies, and victories during rush-hour drive time. Please . . . let's go on vacation this year. I shole is tired! I don't have to list y'all by name, but I think if I don't, y'all might beat me! So thank you, Shawana, Kym, Robin, and Tiffany T. Love y'all!

If I start naming book clubs, I'm gonna get myself in trouble, because I know I'm gonna forget someone. But here goes. Doing Something Different, SistahFriend, Sista to Sista, Driven Divas, OOSA, Women of Character, Virtuous Women Book

Club, and every Glory Girls chapter that's still in existence! Thank you to all the book clubs that have supported me since 2005!

I want to thank all my writer buds for your encouraging words and support. ReShonda, Eric, Lolita, Rhonda, Dee, Bonnie, Kim, Sherryle, Stacy, Booker (White Shoes), Pat T., Pat S., Pat W., Pat B. (I sure know a lot of Pats), Tia, Shelia, Vanessa, Michelle, Vivi, Shewanda, and Victoria! Thank you all!

To my pastor, Bishop T. D. Jakes; The Potter's House family; and The Potter's House Choir, I love you and thank you for feeding my spirit and praying for me! Yellow flower is in the building ☺!

And last but definitely not least, to every reader and reviewer, I appreciate you. This book is for you, and I pray it is a blessing.

And now . . . without any further ado . . .

Don't Tell a Soul.

PROLOGUE

One hundred eighty-seven breaths in ten minutes. Eva couldn't stop herself from counting them. She'd been taking note of each inhale and every exhale since the phone call last week from her manager, Leo.

He'd said only one sentence. "You need to get tested, babe."

Eva had dreaded hearing those words since her very first adult film at the age of seventeen. But when Leo spoke the fear-inspiring words over the phone, Eva hadn't panicked. Not then. She'd hung up the phone with Leo and called the clinic. The one that all the film stars used. The one that would keep her results private. The one that didn't require insurance, because porn didn't pay benefits.

Although Eva hadn't suddenly come undone in that moment, she'd started to unravel second by second—breath by breath. She'd started counting when it occurred to her that her days might be numbered. If she was HIV-positive, then was it full-blown AIDS yet? And if it was full-blown AIDS, how many years did she have left? Or was it months?

Sheena, the clinic nurse, had called Eva, telling her to come in and receive her results, because they couldn't be given over the phone. That was this time yesterday. Now Eva was sitting in the clinic. Waiting . . . and breathing.

Eva breathed sixteen times in a minute when she was re-laxed, but thirty when she was near hyperventilation. Would breathing faster make her time expire quicker? That thought occurred to her as she gripped the sides of the metal card table chair in the clinic's waiting room. She could feel the moisture of her nervous sweat beneath her thighs and wished that she'd worn a longer skirt. But Eva wore skirts only in the summer months. It was her favorite season, and skirts made her feel in-credibly feminine.

Why couldn't it be winter? Getting this kind of news is a gloomy, gray downtown Cleveland, January kind of thing. Not a mild Midwest summer thing. If Eva turned out to be HIV-positive, summer wouldn't be the same. She'd have to pick a new favorite season.

Eva stared at the clock in the clinic's waiting room. It said ten past noon, but it was wrong. It was more like seventeen after ac-cording to Eva's watch. Eva had to fight the urge to take the step stool out of the corner and correct the clock. If she was somewhere else—a friend's house or her home—she wouldn't have been able to let the small time discrepancy remain.

Amanda, known in the industry as Princess Mandy, had gone in right before Eva. They'd spoken to one another in the wait-ing room. It made sense for them both to be there; they'd both filmed an orgy scene four months ago. Eva remembered Amanda asking the film producer if they were using condoms. He'd said no. Amanda had protested, but not loudly enough. Her rent had been due, and she'd needed the money.

Eva hadn't complained at all about using protection. They were all professionals on set. Everyone took their once-a-week test, so it was all good to her. Plus, her fans online told her that they didn't like the safe-sex scenes. They wanted edgy.

Did it really take this long to give a negative result? Eva's nerves sent her into a near frenzy. She scooted to the edge of the chair, gripped it as if it was a roller coaster safety bar. Her breaths were fast and shallow and tears streamed down her face as the feeling of inevitable doom engulfed her.

Eva prayed a sinner's prayer. *God, I know I don't deserve to ask for anything from you. I don't even know if I'm allowed to. . . . Well, I'm just gonna ask. God, please don't let me have HIV. If I get a negative result . . . I—I promise I'm gonna quit doing this and work a real job, no matter how much it pays. And, uh, I'm gonna go to church, too. Please, please, please, please . . .*

Then it dawned on Eva that the results were already there, in an envelope or on a chart, just waiting to be read. Her prayer and her promise wouldn't change the outcome—at least she didn't think they could—but her grandmother was always shouting and dancing over a miracle. Maybe this would be one.

Amanda walked out of the results room. Her face was tear-streaked and pale. The test results were confidential, but to Eva it was more than obvious that Amanda hadn't received good news.

"It was Alfonzo. I know he's the one that gave us the package. We were both with him, and now we've got it," Amanda said.

Eva was unable to respond. The lump in her throat wouldn't allow her to speak. Amanda was right. They were both with Alfonzo that night. Although the evening was a drug- and alcohol-induced blur, she did remember him, because he was new to the group. It was his first scene.

"W-what are you going to do?"

"You mean other than die? I don't really know. It's not like I have a job anymore." Amanda's voice was void of emotion. Empty.

"They have drugs now, Mandy. It's not a death sentence anymore, right?"

Eva's words were more for herself than Amanda. She had moved past her friend's pain and had started living inside her own, which seemed inevitable.

"Call me later," Amanda said. "We can go to Jamaica or something. Meet some hot guys and share the happiness and joy."

When Eva gasped, Amanda threw up one hand. "I'm joking, Eva. I didn't mean that." Then she burst into tears. "I-I'm afraid."

"Me too."

Eva didn't know what should come next. Should she hug Amanda? Promise to contact her? She couldn't do the former and wouldn't do the latter. Hugging was not an Eva thing, and she never, ever contacted anyone from the industry in her real life.

The awkward moment passed. Amanda composed herself and wiped her tears with the crumpled-up tissue in her hand.

"Maybe I'll wake up tomorrow, and this will have been a nightmare."

"If it is a bad dream, what would you do? Would you quit the business?"

Amanda lifted an eyebrow and then sighed. "I don't know. What else am I gonna do?"

Sheena emerged from the results room with a solemn expression on her face. "Eva, I'm ready for you now."

Eva stood on wobbly legs; Amanda helped her get her balance.

Amanda pulled her close and whispered, "If you're positive, too . . . we could be there for each other, you know?"

One side of Eva's mouth twitched. Amanda's tone dripped with seductiveness. How could she be thinking of anything sexual at a time like this?

"Call me," Amanda said, her hot breath feeling damp on Eva's ear.

Eva cringed. She didn't mean to do it, but she did.

Amanda chuckled. "You can't catch HIV from a whisper, silly."

Eva walked—no, stumbled—toward the nurse, loosening herself from Amanda's grip.

"Right this way, Eva."

Eva had been in the results room before. She knew Sheena's life story—how many kids she had, where she went to nursing school. They'd had too many conversations, but none this serious.

There was the chlamydia outbreak of 1995, when Eva had gotten burned on her very first film. Then they shut an entire set down in Parma because of a hellacious round of staph infections. Once Eva contracted an E. coli infection after putting something—she had no idea what—in her mouth that didn't belong there.

Through all these Eva had managed to remain relatively unscathed. She hadn't come across anything that antibiotics couldn't cure, not even herpes. She had been luckier than most.

"Don't beat around the bush, Sheena," Eva said. "Don't try to make it pretty. Just tell me."

"You're negative."

The relief that washed over Eva was so utterly complete that her tears flowed like faucets at full blast.

"I'm okay? I'm okay!"

Sheena cleared her throat. "I can't clear you to work until you have two more negatives, spread over two months."

"You can't clear me to work? But I need the money."

Sheena's chest heaved up and down in a frustrated exhale. "How many bullets are you gonna dodge?"

Eva closed her eyes and shook her head. Sheena, of all people, knew what Eva was going through. Sheena had gotten into porn as a teenager and had worked until a group scene turned into a brutal rape that left her unable to have any more children. After Sheena's body had healed, she had gone to college and hadn't looked back.

"Everybody isn't like you, Sheena." Eva stared at the floor, embarrassed about her revelation. She wished she was more like Sheena.

"You know, Eva, you could always work a real job . . . no matter how much it pays."

Eva's head snapped up and her eyes widened as the words of her quickly forgotten prayer echoed from the walls. This was uncanny. This was unsettling.

"I could."

"If you want, I can give you some numbers. I have some friends that will give you a job, no questions asked, if you're ready to leave the industry."

"What kind of job?"

"Something that doesn't degrade you or make you have to

come talk to me in another six months, after the next outbreak. You could leave the business while you're still young enough to do something else."

Eva shook her head and stood from the table. "I don't know about the job thing yet, but thank you, Sheena, and thank God I'm not gonna die."

"Go ahead and thank God, because He was the one that did this for you."

"Why'd He do it for me, huh? Why not Amanda? I don't even go to church, and she does. She even goes in the middle of the week. Why would He save me?"

"He must have a purpose for you that you can't fulfill if you're sick."

"That's a joke. God don't want nothing from me."

Sheena smiled. "You can't know what God wants until you ask Him."

Then Sheena came from behind her desk and hugged Eva before she could escape the office. Eva endured the unheralded affection but didn't participate by hugging back.

"Thanks again, Sheena. I gotta go now."

"Take my card. Call me when you're ready to change your life."

Eva took the card from Sheena's hand and read it. The top said NO LONGER BOUND—BREAKING THE SHACKLES WOMEN'S MINISTRY.

"You're a minister?"

"No. I just help women who've lost their way."

Eva said her good-byes and saw herself out of the office and into the balmy summer day. She turned the card over in her hand and then slipped it in her purse. She didn't feel lost, but she had no idea what she should do with herself. After Sheena regurgitated that piece of her prayer, she was scared to ask God anything else. If He answered her directly, she'd probably just pass out in the street.

But now that Eva knew He was listening, she *did* have a few things and a few people that she wanted to discuss with God.

In her opinion, God had some explaining to do.

CHAPTER 1

PAM

Isn't it weird how the very best things can happen to you at the very worst times? I just got off the phone with an editor at Gideon Publishing. Her name is Carmen, and she wants to give me a book deal. It's for my second book, a fictional version of the story of Jesus and the woman at the well. I never sold the first one that I wrote, which is probably a good thing, because there is too much of my own life in its pages.

My second book, called *The Chance Meeting*, took me only a year to write, but it took another year for me to get replies back from my query letters. Now, finally, eight years into my publishing journey I'm being offered the opportunity of a lifetime.

It is the best thing that could happen in my life, but I hate that it's happening when Troy is at absolute rock bottom with his music thing. He's lost nearly every penny of the three and a half million dollars he earned after discovering a powerhouse vocalist named Lisa with an incredible voice.

"Hey, babe. Logan is coming over in a few. Are you gonna cook something?"

Troy's voice pulls me from my thoughts, and I gaze directly into my husband's ruggedly handsome face. That very appealing face, those incredibly sexy light brown eyes, and his undeniable swagger caused me to postpone every single last one of my dreams while he pursued his music career.

Not anymore. I feel God moving me in a different direction, one that doesn't include feeding his friends. I've got to write a proposal for my *next* book. Carmen wants to offer me a two-book deal, but I've not given any thought to another project.

"I think *you* should cook something or order out," I say.

He blinks, as if blinking will help him hear me better. "Come on, Pam. This is important. He's going to collaborate with me on some music. He's really well connected, and I think he can help get Aria's project off the ground."

I roll my eyes. I should've stopped myself from doing that, because it makes me seem like an unsupportive wife. But I've been hearing that singing harlot's name for the past eight years.

Aria is Troy's big project. He's spent almost a decade trying to blow up with this girl. She's in my home so much, she might as well be my sister-wife, except I can't ever see that chick lifting one of those acrylic-nailed fingers to do a dish or a load of laundry.

"Pam?"

I shake my head and the negative thoughts about Aria. "No, Troy. I can't do it tonight. I've got something really important to do, and then I have to go to a Sister to Sister meeting."

"What can you *possibly* have to do that's more important than handle my business? Your job is to take care of home. Me and the kids, Pam. You been chilling for the past eight years, so the least you could do is be hospitable when I have guests."

I know he did not just reduce everything I've done in the past eight years to "chilling." I didn't know raising three children was chilling. I didn't know that the upkeep of a five-thousand-square-foot house was chilling. If I was chilling, then what was he doing in all the years before he made the three million dollars? Sounds like if I am in chill mode—which I am not—then it's my turn.

Besides, Troy knows dang well that if something doesn't give in the next six months, then I definitely am going to have to go back into the corporate workforce. He hasn't even asked me about my writing career—not since he bought me a journal when I was pregnant with our son, TJ. I'm starting to wonder if he even meant anything he said about supporting my dreams.

I close my eyes and sigh. "What do you want me to make, Troy?"

"I can make some wings and salad, Mom. Do you want me to?"

That is my surprisingly capable fourteen-year-old Gretchen. She's been obsessed with cooking since the age of ten, and she can probably cook a better meal than I can. A month ago, I let her handle Easter dinner, with me supervising, of course, and she really did a wonderful job.

"I'll give you an extra ten in your allowance if you do, honey. I sure appreciate you," I say and give Gretchen a kiss on the cheek. Then I give Troy a dry peck. "Gotta go."

"Your Sister to Sister meeting is not until seven. It's only five o'clock. What are you doing between now and then?" Troy asks.

I was wondering when he'd ask what I had to do. I almost thought he wouldn't. Troy barely notices anything that doesn't impact him directly.

"A publisher offered me a book deal, but I have to come up with a proposal for my second book."

Troy's eyes widen, and he hugs me tightly. "That is great, Pam! When were you going to tell me?"

When you stopped making requests. "I wanted to make sure I'd be able to come up with a second book proposal."

"That shouldn't be a problem. All that gossiping y'all do at those women's meetings, you ought to have plenty of story ideas."

"I'm not going to write about my friends."

Troy shakes his head. "I don't know why not. They would if they had the opportunity. How much money is the publisher offering you?"

"Um, she said seven thousand dollars for two books."

Troy frowns and scratches the back of his head. "Is that all? I

thought publishers were handing out six-figure deals and what-
not. That's what we talked about when you were sending out all
those letters."

"I did some research, and what they offered me is pretty standard for a brand-new author."

"So when do you get the money?"

"I-I'm not sure."

"You're not sure? Pam, if you don't know the right questions
to ask these people, you need to put me on the phone."

"I'm sure I have to sign a contract first."

"Well, we could sure use those thousands, Pam. We're getting low on funds, just so you know."

I lift an eyebrow and fold my arms across my chest. "How
low?"

"We've got about two hundred thousand left, but it won't last
long if we don't get some additional funds up in here."

See, this is exactly what I'm talking about with him. I'm sick
of Troy living from one gig to the next. We've got about two
hundred thousand dollars left out of the three and a half million. That's barely enough to get us through another one of
Troy's ventures.

First, there was the Aria record project. He finished that one
and sold about twenty-two copies. Okay, it was more like ten
thousand. But he spent more money marketing and creating
that record than he earned in profits.

Then there was the Aria tour. I guess Troy thought since he
had all those CDs stacked in the garage that they should probably go on the road and try to sell them. Yeah, that wasn't such a
good idea, either. The concerts—mostly in shopping malls and
hole-in-the-wall clubs—didn't move many records. Just money
from the assets to the liability column of our family balance
sheet.

Finally, there was the Aria video shoot. Get the pattern here?
The singing harlot and *her* career have sucked our blessing dry.

"And by additional funds, you mean the money from the
book?"

"That and some more. I was wondering if you'd mind getting a part-time job, just until we get done with this project."

"You're kidding, right?"

"No, I'm not. I mean, it's not like I'm really marketable in corporate America, and you know I can't do no factory work. You were a VP at Ellis Financial. They'd give you something."

Anger simmers in the pit of my stomach, like a tea kettle full of near-boiling water. Troy told me I'd never have to go to work again. That I could take care of our family and that he'd take care of me.

"I've been out of the workforce for eight years, Troy. It won't be easy for me to get a job, either. Plus, I'd like to see where my book career could go."

"Both of us can't be starving artists."

"You're right, Troy. One of us has to be *responsible.*"

Troy touches my arm lovingly, but I snatch it away. "Pam, baby, it's only for a while. Just until Aria's new record takes flight."

"Don't you think you should find a new artist? You've been trying with Aria for years, and she's not a young twenty-year-old anymore. I think her time has passed, and you need to move on."

"You always want to give up before we break through."

"That's the problem, Troy. There's no *we* in this conversation. It has always been about you."

"You'd think that after all these years with me you would've learned something about teamwork."

Teamwork? Teamwork! I can't believe what I'm hearing. Troy is on a team, all right. Only I'm not on it, too. Aria is his partner and has been for eight years.

The teapot is on full boil now, and the whistle is ready to blow.

Then the doorbell rings. Troy looks as if he wants to say something else to me before opening it, but then he gives me a soft look and turns the knob.

"Logan! Man, it's about time!" Troy exclaims as he gives Logan a one-armed hug and fist bump.

"What do you mean? I'm early," Logan says.

"No, man. I mean, where have you been my whole life? It's time to get this thang popping."

I suppress the urge to cringe at Troy's slang. He keeps forgetting that we're almost forty years old, and that it sounds a lot better for grown-ups to use standard English.

"Man, God's timing is always perfect. This is our time!" Then Logan looks at me. "You must be Pam. You look exactly how Troy describes you."

In my opinion, there's nothing more handsome on a man than a smile, and Logan's smile is contagious. I can't help but give him one in return. His pretty white teeth seem to gleam in contrast to his blackberry-tinted lips and ebony skin. I can't believe he's standing here in our living room. He could be on a movie screen.

"Nice to meet you, Logan. Troy speaks highly of you," I finally say as I shake Logan's outstretched hand.

"This is my wife, the *writer*," Troy says. "Doesn't she look like a writer?"

Logan chuckles. "Sure, she does."

"Yeah, well, she needs to write some song lyrics or something, 'cause that's how we're gonna get to stack the dough. Nobody black is about to get rich off writing books."

"I only know music, not books," Logan says. "And this sounds like a discussion I wouldn't touch with a ten-foot pole."

"Troy doesn't know, either," I say, hoping Troy can hear the venom in my voice.

I spin on one heel and grab my purse. I storm out of the house, knowing that this isn't over. As a matter of fact, it's only just beginning, because if Troy thinks he's going to throw my dream away like it belongs to him, he's got another thing coming.

This dream is mine, and God opened a door that no man can shut. Especially Troy.

CHAPTER 2

PAM

"Sister Pam, can I talk to you for a minute?"

One look at Carmisha's puppy dog eyes and quivering bottom lip and I know what this conversation is going to be about. Carmisha gets on my nerves. She's new to our church and our Sister to Sister group, but already she's hip to the one-woman benevolence fund. Ever since Troy got paid, it's like the entire broke people's party adopted "Can You Pay My Bills?" as their theme song.

I give Carmisha my Sister Pam smile. The one I save for the folk at the church that I really would be cursing out if I wasn't saved.

"Sure, girl. What's going on?"

Carmisha glances around the community room, where we hold our meetings. Her baby blue contact lenses distract me. Even though they perfectly match her weave, they look completely ludicrous next to her dark brown skin.

She says, "Sister Pam, I was hoping that I could . . . well . . . borrow a few dollars from you, just until I get my food stamps at the beginning of the month. Me and my babies don't have nothing to eat except raminy and peanut butter sandwiches."

"What's raminy, Carmisha?"

"You know, those little Oriental noodles."

"Ah. You mean ramen noodles. Those aren't really all that healthy."

"Yes, I know. My baby girl and baby boy need some fruits and vegetables."

"And protein," I add. "How about some ground beef?"

"Oh, yes, Sister Pam! They would love some hamburger meat."

I lift an eyebrow at her enthusiasm. "Did you know that we have a food pantry right here at the church? Let's go grocery shopping in there after the Sister to Sister meeting so that you and your babies don't go hungry."

Carmisha's excitement evaporates. I guess she's figured out that I won't be writing her a check today. Even if I had the means, I wouldn't. Not when there's perfectly good food that the church collects weekly for just this very purpose.

"Sister Pam, I know about the food pantry, but I was also hoping to get some personal hygiene products."

I sigh, open my purse, and pull out a twenty-dollar bill. I can't really spare it, but I can't imagine not being able to purchase tampons or deodorant. That's just pitiful.

Carmisha frowns but takes the money, anyway. I mean, how much was she expecting for some hygiene products? She should've thought up a better story if she wanted me to dig deeper in my pockets.

"Thank you, Sister Pam." I hear the words, but the girl's bitter tone makes it sound more like an insult than gratitude.

Yvonne, one of my best friends, sashays into the meeting, looking incredibly fresh for her forty-seven years. I guess the single life does that for a woman, because her looks definitely improved when she divorced her abusive and cheating husband, Luke. There's not a wrinkle on her smooth chocolate brown skin, and the few grays that she does have, she's deftly covered with dye.

"Pam! How are you, honey?" She hugs me tightly and kisses my cheek.

Yvonne and my other best friend, Taylor, are the only ones in the entire church that know about my money issues, and even they don't know the whole story. Even with the part that they do know, they're constantly hugging me and asking me how I'm doing. Sometimes, such as on a night like tonight, when I could choke the life out of Troy, their incessant checking up on me is irritating.

"I am doing okay," I say.

Yvonne gathers her eyebrows and gives a little head shake. "You are blessed and highly favored, Pam."

I nod and smile, unable to repeat Yvonne's words. Maybe I used to be highly favored, but not anymore. Not since Troy lost a fortune. Not since I got a book deal I don't know if I'm going to be able to pursue. I went to Starbucks and tried to write a book proposal, and nothing would come out. Maybe Troy is right. No black person ever got really rich writing books.

"What's going on with you, Yvonne?" I ask, trying to take the focus off of me.

"Nothing but work, work, and more work. Those kids are driving me right up the wall."

Yvonne's mini-rant evokes a real smile from me. She can complain all she wants about being a seventh grade English teacher, but I know she loves it. She never got to have children when she was married to her ex-husband, Luke, so she adopts every single last one of those babies like they are her very own.

"You love it!" I tease. "But I wasn't talking about work. What's going on with Kingston?"

Yvonne rolls her eyes. "Nothing! I'm too old for a knight in shining armor."

"You ain't too old for a man, Sister Yvonne," Carmisha chimes in. "And Brother Kingston is all that, if you like old guys."

"Oh hush, Carmisha! Nobody asked you!" Yvonne fusses while wearing a smile.

Carmisha pokes her lips out and nods while waving her hips from side to side in a little dance. She snaps her fingers and says, "Look at you smiling. You know you want to get with him."

"As much as it pains me to say this, I agree with Carmisha, Yvonne. You need to stop playing hard to get."

"Next topic!" Yvonne says. "Why is everybody always late to these things?"

"Taylor is not coming. I don't think," I reply. "Joshua has a soccer game tonight, and Spencer couldn't make it, so she's doing Mom duty."

"Well, what about Rhoda and Rochelle?" Yvonne asks.

Carmisha sucks her teeth. "I *hope* they don't come."

Sometimes Rhoda and Rochelle are the only things lively about the Sister to Sister meetings, even though they are full of drama. Outside of their gossip sessions, the group has gotten rather dull over the years, but we keep it going because it's ministry and every now and then someone really gets the help they need.

The door to the community room swings open, and a woman that I don't think I've ever seen before marches right inside. She's a little on the thick side. Actually, she's probably beyond thick to extra healthy, but she's got on a nice velour jogging suit and a pretty short wig with a bang that covers her eye. I give her my friendliest smile, my *real* smile—the one I save for new folks that visit the church who just might need to meet the Lord.

"Is my girl Taylor here yet?" she asks.

Oh, wait. I remember her. She's Taylor's old friend. I can't quite place her name, but she started attending our church with Taylor many, many years ago. She never came back after Taylor had an affair with Yvonne's husband and had a baby with him.

I wish she had returned. She would've witnessed a stone-cold miracle that only God could've orchestrated. It's hard to believe that a scorned wife could be reconciled to the mistress, but that's what happens when you put God in the mix.

"No, I don't think she's coming tonight," I reply as I walk over with an extended hand. "But do you remember me? I'm Pam. You're welcome to stay and join us, even if Taylor can't make it."

She looks down at my hand and then up at my face. "That's okay. I'll just come back when she's here, but I do remember you, Pam. I'm Shaquan."

"Yes, that's it! Shaquan! Welcome back to New Faith."

"I wouldn't say that I'm back," Shaquan says. "Taylor just wanted me to meet her here. You know, she stays on me about coming to church."

It's all coming back to me now. Shaquan was a member of New Faith for about five minutes, and she dated Deacon Wallington. Seventy-year-old, arthritic Deacon Wallington.

As Shaquan heads to the door, Yvonne swoops in like the prayer warrior that she is. "Are you sure you don't need some prayer?"

The woman takes a step back. "Y'all are awfully aggressive up in here. I'm just coming to catch up with my girl. I'll let you know if I'm trying to pray."

"I'm sorry. I didn't mean to come across that way. I just want you to know that you're welcome, whether Taylor is here or not."

Yvonne gives Shaquan a warm and genuine smile and then takes her seat in the circle of chairs. Carmisha and I follow her lead.

"Carmisha, do you have any prayer requests?" Yvonne asks.

"Yes, I do, Sister Yvonne. I need a financial blessing."

While Carmisha tells Yvonne all about her newest trial, I glance over at Shaquan out the corner of my eye. She lingers at the door, as if she's not quite ready to leave but unsure if she wants to stay.

She takes one step toward the circle when Rhoda and Rochelle burst through the door and scurry over to the circle in a rush. Shaquan stays by the door and watches with her arms folded. I smile over in her direction, but she remains firmly stuck in place.

"I tell y'all, it's only the blood of Jesus that keeps me from going slap off on some people," Rhoda declares.

Yvonne sighs. "Who are you going *slap off* on now?"

"Are you mocking me, Yvonne? Huh? Is that what you're doing?"

Yvonne chuckles. "No, Rhoda, not at all."

"Because you know what the Word says. It says God's

anointed ain't to be mocked. Whatever a heffa is sowing, that she's gonna reap tenfold, heaped together, until she can't contain all the vengeance of the Lord."

"Ooh, Sister Rhoda, I felt that down in my spirit," Rochelle, Rhoda's gossip in training, says.

If the two of them spent more time actually reading the Bible, they probably wouldn't have time for all their perpetual drama. I'm just saying.

"Well, your spirit is broken, then, because that is not in the Bible!" Yvonne says.

Shaquan bursts into laughter at the door and finally walks over to the circle and slides into a seat. "Okay, y'all are entertaining. Maybe I will stay."

"Anyway!" Rhoda continues. "Like I was saying, some people in this world are blessed that I know Jesus as my Lord and savior."

"Tell 'em, Sister Rhoda!" Rochelle cosigns.

I shake my head with irritation. Why does Rhoda have to build all her stories like this?

"Rhoda, what exactly happened?" I ask.

"I turned in the final draft of the Sister to Sister announcement for the Sunday bulletin, and that old evil heffa Lucille said that because I got it in at two sixteen instead of two o'clock, she wasn't going to be able to accommodate us."

"Lucille is just jealous because we're selling dinners on Sunday and we know how to cook, unlike her and those raggedy nurses that don't know the difference between hot water corn bread and Jiffy mix," Rochelle says.

Yvonne stares at me, and I stare back. These meetings are a joke. Rhoda and Rochelle are either gossiping or requesting prayers of revenge, and they are the only regular members besides me, Taylor, and Yvonne. Maybe it's time to end this group and move on to the next ministry.

Shaquan says, "Y'all have got to be kidding! This is the prayer group that Taylor rants and raves about? This is a mess."

"See, Yvonne, I knew once we start letting these hood rats into our meetings that the quality of discussion would decline," Rhoda says while cutting her eyes at Shaquan.

Typically, I'm the one that gets everyone back on target—back to the "praise the Lord" place. Back to the "bless the Lord, oh, my soul" place. But right now I feel like screaming at the top of my lungs.

"Hood rat?" Shaquan asks. "You know what? I'm gonna let that slide. I am not trying to violate my probation dealing with y'all churchy heffas."

Yvonne says, "Rhoda, apologize right now. You've run away almost every visitor to our meetings. I'm telling Pastor Brown about this."

"Oh, whatever. I'm sorry, okay? I hope you stay and enjoy yourself *in the Lord.* Come on, Rochelle. Let's be out."

"Where are we going?" Rochelle asks.

"To a place where they honor the anointing."

Rhoda storms away from the circle of chairs, and Rochelle follows at her heels. I keep wondering when Rochelle is going to grow up and find a friend other than Rhoda. I guess some people are just made to be followers.

I feel something inside me snap. I think Troy started this. He caused the first crack in my armor before I left the house.

"I'm sick of them," I announce.

Yvonne's and Carmisha's eyes bulge with shocked expressions. I know they're not used to me telling it like it is, but that's the place I am in at this very moment.

I go on. "And you know what? Carmisha, I'm sick of you, too. Coming to these meetings, always talking about a financial blessing. When are you going to get a job?"

Yvonne jumps out of her seat and plops down next to me. "Pam . . ."

"No, I'm serious. McDonald's and Wal-Mart are both hiring last time I checked."

Carmisha looks at the floor. "I . . . I have a special needs child."

"Just because you took that boy to the doctor for some Ritalin so you could collect a check does not mean he has special needs," I reply.

Yvonne locks her hand around my arm and pulls me away

from the circle. I open my mouth to say more, but Yvonne whispers in my ear. "No, Pam. Don't do that."

Yvonne continues to pull me until we are outside and standing next to her little black Ford Focus.

"Get in," Yvonne says.

"I'm fine, Yvonne. You don't need to do an intervention."

"This is not an intervention, Pam. You've got something on your chest, and clearly, you need to get it off. I'm just gonna let you vent. In a safe place."

"I don't want—"

"Get. In."

Since I know that Yvonne is not going to leave me alone, I get in the car. Yvonne gets in on the driver's side and slams her door.

"Spill it, Pam. I know the money is not right, but y'all have had this issue before."

I swallow hard. I don't know if I'm ready to share this struggle. "Yvonne, I'm just stressed."

"It's more than that. How are your book proposals going?"

"I got an offer from Gideon Publishing. A two-book deal."

"Then why are we not celebrating?"

"Why do you think? Mr. Dream Killer himself, Troy didn't even congratulate me. He was mad that I didn't get offered more money, because he's got yet another trick up his sleeve for that Aria."

"You have got to be kidding me, Pam. What is his problem? You've been praying about this open door for years."

I let out a long, weary sigh. "Tell me about it. He had the audacity to tell me I need to get a job!"

"Oh, my Lord. Come on, Pam. Give me your hands, girl. We have to pray about this."

Yvonne grabs both my hands and begins her supplication, which I promptly tune out. She's praying for the book deal to pan out, for opportunities, and saying all the right things. Yvonne is a prayer warrior; I learned this about her when she was going through her divorce.

While Yvonne pleads the blood over Troy's ignorance and

names and claims open doors and windows of heaven, I watch a woman emerge from her car in the church parking lot. She looks down at a piece of paper, as if checking the address, and then back up at the church.

The woman has on a business suit and heels, and her hair is pulled back into a bun at the nape of her neck. She has a pretty, exotic look, and curves that I would kill for.

Yvonne has worked herself into a prayer frenzy by the time she hollers out, "In Jesus's name!"

"Amen," I quickly say, trying to match, but not quite capturing, her intensity.

"Who is she?" Yvonne asks as she notices the woman, too. She looks as if she's trying to decide whether or not to go in.

I open the car door and get out. "You know, if God brought you this far, you should probably go on in."

The woman laughs. "You're right. I—I just . . . well . . . I'm not a b-beggar."

She breaks down in tears, and her body shakes with violent sobs. I take a few more steps until I'm close enough to embrace her. Yvonne jumps out of the car and joins me. She rubs the woman's back until she calms down.

Then the woman looks embarrassed. "I'm so sorry. I didn't mean to do that."

"We all cry sometimes," Yvonne says. "Today it was your turn. Tomorrow it might be mine. How can we help you? What is your name, honey?"

I hand the woman a tissue from my purse, which she uses to blow her nose and dab her eyes. "My name is Eva Jacobs. I lost my job, and I've spent just about all my savings. I was told that there is a food pantry here. Is that true?"

I stare at Eva in wonder. She doesn't look like someone who needs to use our pantry. Her makeup is carefully applied, especially her eye makeup, which showcases her striking doe-like eyes. Eva could've been one of my coworkers at Ellis Financial or maybe even a pastor's wife. Usually the women who come here for help look more like how Carmisha did the first time she walked through the church doors, high on some kind of drug and dragging her toddler son in tow, begging for food and money.

Yvonne takes Eva's hand and pulls her toward the church. Eva looks so shocked at Yvonne's aggressive manner that I almost let out a chuckle as I follow them.

"Do you have somewhere to stay?" Yvonne asks.

"For now I do," Eva says.

"That's good. Let's get your kitchen stocked, then."

When we walk back into the church, Yvonne leads Eva to the food pantry. Carmisha's eyes lock with mine, and Shaquan, who is texting someone, looks up at me and smiles.

"Well, Ms. Keepin' It Real is back," Shaquan says. "Let me get up out of here before you read me, too. I ain't all the way saved, so I can't say things would turn out the same way if you start telling me where I can go."

"Sister Shaquan, what you saw tonight was totally out of character for me. I assure you this never happens. I'm . . . having a bad day."

Shaquan gives me a skeptical head nod. "Sure it doesn't. I just know Taylor didn't tell me y'all get down like this. I mean, if she had, maybe I would've come sooner. This is pretty entertaining."

I shake my head and ignore Shaquan's response. I already feel bad enough; I don't need her rubbing it in. "Carmisha, I'm sorry. I didn't mean to say those things to you in that way. It wasn't Christlike at all. Will you please forgive me?"

After a long pause, Carmisha sighs and nods. "I do forgive you, Sister Pam, but did you mean what you said?"

"Well . . ." I clear my throat, trying to bide my time and think of the best response. "I would like to see you become self-sufficient. If you had a job, you would have such a better quality of life."

"I know you don't believe my son is special, but he is. He is not successful in day-care facilities. If I just had someone to take care of him, I would get a job."

Carmisha stares at the floor, but not before I see the look of shame on her face. She can't be feeling lower than me, though.

I'm supposed to be the leader of this group, and here I am, letting my emotions get the better of me.

Shaquan finishes her text and stands. "Will you please tell Taylor that I was here, Pam? I sent her a text, but she doesn't believe me."

"Why wouldn't she believe you'd come to church?" Carmisha asks, looking genuinely curious.

"Well, I had an issue with one of the deacons here. He started tripping when I broke it off, and I didn't want any drama," Shaquan explains.

"But now that Deacon Wallington is in the nursing home, it's safe for you to return, right?" I ask.

Shaquan laughs. "Yeah, girl. I didn't want ole deacon salting up my game, in case there's anybody else up in here I might want to meet. A sista is always looking for a husband."

"I know that's right!" Carmisha says. "You should really come back to this group! It would be nice having someone on my level."

Shaquan gives Carmisha a tiny smile and a squint, which, in my opinion, says, "We are not on the same level," but I don't think Carmisha gets this message, because she's grinning from ear to ear. Something got lost in the interpretation.

Yvonne and Eva emerge from the food pantry with several heavy bags of groceries. Eva's face is tear streaked, but she's wearing a smile. Leave it to Yvonne to make Eva feel okay about her situation.

It wasn't always that way with Yvonne, though. She wasn't really the warmest sister in the Sister to Sister group. Well . . . she was actually the most judgmental of us all. But life taught her a lesson I wouldn't wish on my worst enemy.

"Eva's going to come to service on Sunday!" Yvonne says.

Eva glances quickly at each of us. "I haven't been to church in a really long time."

"That's okay," I say. "God isn't keeping track of attendance."

"Thank you all for being so friendly. I didn't know what to expect," Eva says.

"Now, why wouldn't we be friendly?" I ask Eva while giving her the most welcoming smile I can muster with Troy and his chicanery still lingering in the back of my mind.

Eva gives me an intense stare that sends a chill right through me. She seems to shrink before my eyes, her eyes blinking and the corners of her mouth twitching with uncertainty. It isn't a look of someone redeemed.

She looks broken.

She'll fit right in here.

CHAPTER 3

TAYLOR

"**S**pence, honey. Put the belt away."

Spencer steps out of his walk-in closet and looks at me like I'm crazy, but I do not care. He is not about to hit my son with that belt.

"The Bible says, 'Spare the rod, spoil the child.'"

He is not changing my mind by quoting a Scripture. I know all about not sparing the rod. My mother never spared the rod on me, and it just made me angry. She was beating my tail until I was seventeen years old, when I finally had enough and took the belt away from her. I don't want my son angry.

"You're not hitting him with that, Spencer. You'll have to find another way to discipline him. He is eleven years old. You should be able to get through to him without putting your hands on him."

"He should not have hit that boy."

"Maybe if you'd been at the game—"

"You are not going to make this about me working on Saturday. Taylor, you know I have to work weekends during month-end close!"

"I'm just saying."

Spencer throws the belt onto the bed and sighs. "Why do we keep arguing about this, Taylor?"

"Because you are not listening."

"Every time I get ready to spank him, you act like he's *your* son. But when it's time to spend some money, he's *our* son."

I look away from Spencer's demanding glare and shake my head. He knows this is not true. He *is* Joshua's father, even though he's not his biological dad. We don't use the terms *stepfather* or *stepson* in this house. And I know that he loves Joshua.

But when it comes to laying hands on him, I just cannot get with it. I've heard too many stories about boyfriends and husbands killing a woman's kids, by accident or worse . . . on purpose. That's not about to happen in this house.

Every time we have this conversation, it makes me feel like I have to choose between my son and my man. I don't want to do that.

"Joshua is out of control, Taylor. He punched a boy in the face on the soccer field. Are you getting that? He knocked the boy's front teeth out, for heaven's sake. Is he going to pay for that boy's dental work?"

"And you think the way to show him not to hit someone is to beat him with a leather belt? That doesn't make any sense, Spencer. You're just angry because it's going to cost money."

"My father whipped me when I was a child, Taylor. He did it out of love, not anger, and I am the same way. I love Joshua. But if we don't teach him right from wrong, the world is going to teach him."

"I want you to teach him right from wrong. Without hitting him."

I fold my arms across my chest and stretch my legs out on the bed in front of me. In my opinion, the conversation is over. It's a done deal.

"You know what? You handle your son. When he winds up dead or in jail, I won't say I told you so."

I jump up from the bed and stand to face my husband. "Seriously? You're calling down curses on my baby!"

"No, you are. Because you're not letting me be a father to him. You're spoiling him."

"He is not spoiled."

I know he did not just say that. He is really trying to take me there. If my son wasn't two doors down, I'd cuss Spencer out, and I stopped cussing a long time ago.

Joshua spent the first five years of his life with nobody but me. He struggled as I struggled. He never had birthday parties and big Christmases and Easter baskets overflowing with goodies. I was too busy trying to keep a roof over his head and clothes on his back. My mother helped me try to make his life normal, but a grandmother is not a daddy. Not even close.

When Spencer and I got married, Joshua finally got to start living like a normal kid. He started getting clothes that weren't hand-me-downs and toys that were brand new and out of the box. But even with all that, he's had too much hurt in his life to be classified as spoiled. Never that.

Spencer paces back and forth across our bedroom, looking like a caged lion ready to pounce on some dang body. I change gears a little bit, because while I do want to protect my son, I don't want my husband to turn on me. I don't want to go back to raising Joshua by myself.

I grab Spencer by the hand and pull him into an embrace. "I know that it's hard raising Joshua, and I appreciate everything that you've done for us. But can you please just handle this my way? Let's be on one accord, baby."

I plant tiny kisses on Spencer's neck and feel him relax. Finally, his strong arms embrace me back. This man can't resist me. I'm all that and—*boom*—he loves me!

"We'll try it your way for now. But if I don't see a change in Joshua's behavior, we are using my strategy."

"Okay, honey. I hear you." My work here is done!

If nothing else, I've bought some time to deal with Joshua on my own. I don't know how long I can hold Spencer back if Joshua keeps tripping. He got suspended twice last year for fighting. I don't know where he gets this anger from, but I do agree with Spencer on this. It has to stop.

I leave my husband relaxing in our bedroom to have a chat with Joshua. His bedroom door is locked, so I pound on it a few times.

"Open this door, Josh."

After a few long seconds, Joshua finally opens the door. Standing there, still in his soccer uniform, he is the spitting image of his biological father, Luke. He's tall for eleven, with muscles bulging in his arms, legs, and abs. That wild head of curly hair, he got from me. We have twin Afros, since I decided to give up the weaves and embrace my natural hair.

"Tell me again why you hit that boy."

"I told you. He said something about you, and I didn't like it."

I put my hands on my hips and say, "Boy, how many times have I told you that it doesn't matter what people say?"

"He said you were hot."

I crack up laughing. "Boy! You punched him in the face for that? You are just gonna have to get used to the fact that your mama looks like Beyoncé."

Joshua balls his hands into fists. "That's disrespectful. Ain't nobody 'bout to talk about my mama like that."

"Calm down, honey. I have Spencer to protect my honor. You just practice being a kid, okay?"

Angry tears pour down Joshua's cheeks. I have no idea what to do with all this turmoil in a little boy.

"I'm quitting the soccer team," Joshua says.

"Why? Because of the fight?"

"No, because everyone laughed when Braydon said that about you. I hate them."

I let out a long sigh. "Baby, just think on it. Don't make a rash decision. Tomorrow it might not seem as bad. Maybe I'll get Uncle Tee to come over and take you out for lunch."

Uncle Tee is my big brother Tyrone. He seems to get along with Joshua a lot better than Spencer these days. My brother is a thug, but he loves Joshua to pieces. He can usually get through to his nephew.

Joshua's eyes light up. "Uncle Tee! Yeah, I want to hang out with him."

"Okay, go ahead and get a bath and chillax. We'll talk about it tomorrow."

Joshua laughs. "Mommy, nobody says chillax anymore."

I stick my tongue out at him. "I do! So get with it!"

As I close the door to Joshua's room and head downstairs for a snack, I wonder why he can't have that type of relationship with Spencer. I know they love each other, but something is hindering them from being close.

My phone is ringing on the counter. The caller ID says that it's my homegirl from way back—Shaquan. *Oh, shoot!* I had asked her to meet me at the Sister to Sister meeting this afternoon, and I totally forgot. She's probably mad.

For a second I consider not answering, but knowing Shaquan, she's just going to keep calling me back until I answer.

"Hey, Shaquan."

"What's up, girl?"

It always tickles me the way Shaquan says "girl" as if it has two syllables. It sounds like "gu-ruhl."

"Nada. What's up with you?"

"Nothing here, but your little church friends are off the chain."

I cringe involuntarily. "What happened? Was it Rhoda and Rochelle? I already told you not to pay attention to them."

"Well, Rhoda did call me a hood rat, but that wasn't even all that bad compared to Pam."

"Pam?"

"Yes, honey, she brought the drama with a capital *D*. Told that girl Carmisha, who I like, by the way, to get a j-o-b and stop begging the Lord for money."

My eyes widen, and my jaw drops. "No, she didn't."

"Yes, she did. I thought Pam was about to swing on her, until Yvonne dragged her out of the meeting."

"Pam does not fight, Shaquan. Stop exaggerating."

"I don't know Pam all like that, but I promise she was about to get rowdy, rowdy, okay?"

"She was not!"

"You weren't there, Taylor. You might need to go holler at your girl."

I was going to see Pam, to ask her to pray with me about

Joshua and Spencer. Shaquan might be my oldest friend, but Pam is my rock. She's the one who prayed me through disappointment, shame, and helped me to learn how to love myself again. Pam is a true intercessor.

What on earth could she be going through that would make her act this way? I hope Troy's not drinking again. Sometimes he's a straight-up buster! I've been Troy's cheerleader from day one, but he needs to man up for real.

"I think you're right, Shaquan. I do need to holler at her . . . and pray for her. I'll call you back, okay?"

"Okay."

I hang up with Shaquan and dial Pam's number. She answers on the fourth ring.

"Hi, Taylor."

I listen closely to see if there's anything out of sorts in Pam's tone, but all I can hear is lots of noise in the background. It sounds like music.

"What is all that noise, Pam? Is it a bad time?"

"You know when Troy got rid of the studio, he brought his productions back home, to his study. It gets kind of loud in here. It is what it is."

Got rid of the studio is Pam being nice. Troy lost that warehouse that he had turned into a studio. He couldn't afford the upkeep and the taxes on that commercial property. Luckily, they still have the home they purchased.

"Do you need me to call you back?" I ask, the music starting to irritate me a little.

"Let me go to another room."

I hear Pam's heavy footfalls as she leaves the room, and the noise finally fades. "So what's going on?" Pam asks. "Something wrong?"

"No. Everything's good over here. I'm just checking on you. Everything okay over there?"

Pam pauses for a long moment and then chuckles. "Let me guess. Shaquan told you about the Sister to Sister meeting."

"She did mention something about you going slap off on Carmisha."

"Did she tell you I apologized? Some folks love to carry a story back and leave out the important parts."

"She didn't mention your apology, and I promise Shaquan wasn't trying to be mean-spirited. She thought the whole thing was kind of funny."

"It really wasn't. I think I hurt Carmisha's feelings."

"Well, she does need to get a job, so you told her the right thing to do."

"Thanks for trying to make me feel better, but I was awful to her. Did Shaquan tell you about Eva?"

"No. Who's she?"

"Someone told her about the food pantry at the church, and she just happened to stop in during the Sister to Sister meeting," Pam explains.

"Oh, so she's not a member?"

"Not yet, but Yvonne is on a mission. She's already started in on her."

I laugh out loud. "Then she doesn't have a chance. Yvonne won't quit until she's baptized, filled with the Holy Ghost, speaking in tongues, and healing folk."

"I know, right!" Finally, Pam starts to sound like her usual cheerful self.

"So what are you doing today? Want to go get pedicures or something?"

"That sounds wonderful, but I can't. Cicely has cheer practice, and Gretchen has soccer. Then TJ will be up under me for the rest of the day, because Troy and his new producing partner, Logan, are working with Aria."

"So you're on Mom duty today."

"And then some. Does Joshua have a soccer game today?"

"He had one yesterday, but he's hanging out with my brother today, so I'm gonna get a breather."

"Enjoy, girl. I am incredibly envious of you."

I laugh out loud. "Ain't nobody tell you and Troy to keep popping out babies left and right!"

"I know, girl. Enjoy your peace and quiet."

"I'm about to enjoy those ladies rubbing my feet and a glass of Moscato, too!"

"Go ahead and rub it in! I'll see you at church tomorrow. Yvonne is singing a solo, so don't get there late."

I do have a reputation for getting to church just when the preaching begins, but I would love to hear Yvonne's singing. Joining the choir was something she did after she divorced Luke. No one knew she had such a wonderful voice. It was almost like she didn't even know.

"Talk to you later, Pam. If you get a free moment today, let me know. Maybe we could get some coffee or something."

"Oh, wait! I forgot to tell you! I got offered a book deal."

"You *forgot* to tell me that? Girl, what is wrong with you? Did you accept it? When do we celebrate?"

"I haven't accepted it yet, because I need a proposal for a second book. The offer is contingent on me having more than one book idea."

"That's easy, girl! Why don't you write about a single mom with a bootleg baby daddy who finally finds her Prince Charming? That sounds like something I'd read!"

Pam laughs out loud. "That sounds like a Tyler Perry movie! But maybe I will write a romance! I'd have to do some research, though, because Troy hasn't romanced me in forever."

"Who knows, maybe if you start writing a romance, you'll feel more romantic. Just don't have no more babies."

"I rebuke that in the name of Jesus!" Pam shouts. "Girl, let me talk to you later!"

"Okay, bye."

There is absolutely something going on with Pam. This book deal has been the most important dream she's had since we became friends. For her not to be screaming it from the rooftop tells me that something ain't right. And usually when there's something wrong with Pam, it can be traced to one person. Troy. I've talked Pam out of walking out on him more than once. But if he's hurting my girl *again,* he's gonna have to deal with me, too, and I do not play.

CHAPTER 4

YVONNE

After getting married at nineteen and staying married for twenty years, I never thought I'd enjoy being alone. I never thought I'd get used to sleeping alone, to not making dinner for someone, to not having to ask permission for the simplest things.

But I have become quite accustomed to this single life. Solitude does not have to equal loneliness, and I am just fine not having a man in my life. I hear women talking all the time about their *needs*, but I am not having a problem at all being saved and single.

"Just one?" The hostess at the restaurant has a bit of pity in her tone, as if a beautiful black woman can't dine alone on a Saturday night without being desperate.

Obviously, she doesn't know me very well. I've got a taste for P.F. Chang's, and there's no way the lack of a man is going to keep me from those delicious lettuce wraps.

"Just one!"

"Would you like to sit at the bar?"

"No, honey. A booth would be nice."

No, she did not try to seat me at the bar, like that's where single women like to eat their dinner. This poor child has got me confused. If I wasn't saved and sanctified, I'd give her a piece of my mind, but I'm about to get my relax on and read my novel.

I follow the girl over to the big leather booth. She probably had hoped to seat a party of five here, but I got here first! Here's to me, good food, and the single life.

I ease into the booth and relax. Since no one is here with me, I kick off my shoes under the table. I never would've done that eight years ago. Luke would've embarrassed me and called me country. Well . . . so what if I'm country? I'm doing me.

I open my novel, *An Inconvenient Friend,* by Rhonda Mc-Knight. Talk about drama! Enjoying fiction is another new thing about me. Who knew a story could be so much fun and teach me a lesson, too? To think I'd spent all my time reading Bible concordances and devotionals.

As I read, I think about Pam. My best friend is going through something. I have never seen her act so ugly toward anyone. And poor Carmisha! It is true that she needs to get a job, but the child is the product of three generations of mothers on welfare. It's going to take some time, prayer, and effort to break that cycle. Pam knows that. Pam has prayed for that girl, *with* that girl.

"Good evening, ma'am. Will someone be joining you, or would you like to order now?"

I beam a smile at the waitress. "I would love to order now. I will have the lettuce wraps and a water with lime."

"Coming right up. My name is Sharday, if you need anything."

"Okay. Thank you, honey."

It annoys me, just a little, that Sharday called me ma'am. Something about the term just makes me feel old. And I know that I'm not. Forty-seven is far from used up. I keep reading that fifty is the new thirty! I'm inclined to agree. I sure would like to relive my thirties. I'd do a lot of things differently.

The first thing I'd change is staying married to Luke. I *knew* he was cheating on me, even before he seduced Taylor. I'm sure she wasn't the first young lady at our church to fall under his spell. I should've left him the first time he went away for the

weekend and came back with laundry that smelled like perfume. But back then I thought it was godly to suffer in silence.

I hear my phone buzzing away in my purse, so I pull it out.
I've received a new text message.

**Thinking of you this evening. Wishing we were
spending time together. Let me know when you're
ready. Kingston**

I can't stop the smile from blossoming on my face. Kingston
is persistent! He's been asking me out on dates for the past two
years, ever since I joined the choir. I've politely declined, not
just because he's the choir director, but because he's just too
fine. His caramel-colored skin, hazel green eyes, and deep,
wavy hair take my breath away. He thinks that I'm playing hard
to get, and so does everyone else. But I'm afraid I wouldn't be
so hard to get if I started seeing him. My Lord, what if I'm *easy*?
Folk gone be calling me a choir groupie.

Even if I was interested in getting to know Kingston better, I
think it would be strange to be married to another man. I can't
even think about learning another man's intimate habits or
subjecting myself to someone new. And letting another man
see me naked when Luke is the only man I've ever known? The
thought of it makes me shudder.

I close out of the text without responding. While I am flattered by Kingston's pursuit, I am not ready for another relationship.

Sharday walks by and leaves my water on the table. The lime
gives it a kick and keeps me from ordering some sugary bever-
age that I shouldn't have. That's the other thing that's changed
about me. The new Yvonne is fit! I've never had a weight problem, but my body looks better now than it has ever looked.

I turn my attention back to my book and try to wait patiently
for my lettuce wraps. My stomach growls as the wonderful aro-
mas in the restaurant tease my nostrils.

"Hello, Yvonne."

The familiar voice rips open a wound in my heart that I
thought was healed. Slowly, I drag my eyes away from the page

and look into the face of my ex-husband. Without thinking, I slide my feet back into my shoes and sit up straight.

"Luke."

He chuckles. "That's all? Just Luke? After twenty years of loving each other, I'd think we could be a little more cordial than that."

I spent twenty years loving him. He did *not* spend those years loving me. Not the way I needed to be loved. I really can't believe he went there.

And Luke's got the nerve to look incredible. He is aging well. The salt-and-pepper hair is now more salt than pepper, but his nearly white goatee against his dark skin is very attractive. Unless he's wearing some kind of girdle for men, he's taken care of his physique, too—not even a sign of a beer belly. The only thing that's different is the eye patch over his left eye. I wonder if it's real or a fashion statement.

"It's been a long time, Yvonne," he continues. "It's good to see you looking well."

It has been a long time. Nowhere near long enough. I could've gone the rest of my life without ever seeing him again.

"Same to you, Luke. I didn't know you were back in town."

"I am. I moved back to be closer to my son."

My Lord. This almost makes me burst into laughter. Taylor's husband, Spencer, has raised Joshua, and he's the only father that boy knows.

"That's good news, Luke. May I ask what happened to your eye?"

Luke sighs. "This is a consequence. Got into a fight when I was locked up."

Now, this almost makes me feel good, even though I know it shouldn't. God wouldn't be pleased with that evil thought. But since Luke decided to use me for a punching bag, I can't make myself feel sympathetic. Looks like he finally stepped to someone his own size and got his eyeball handed to him.

"I am sorry to hear that," I lie.

"Since you don't seem all that happy to see me, I'm going to let you enjoy your meal . . . and your book. Have a wonderful evening."

"You do the same, Luke."

I don't know why Luke thinks I'd be happy to see him. He spent a year in jail after nearly killing me with a beating. I'm supposed to be ecstatic when he walks in the room? I don't think so. It took every bit of Holy Spirit to keep me from grabbing my Mace and spraying him as a precaution.

My eyes follow Luke as he walks away. I try to look back at my book, but curiosity has always gotten the best of me.

Luke stops at his table and kisses a woman on the cheek. A beautiful black woman with hair flowing down to the middle of her back. A young woman. I can't tell for sure from where I'm sitting, but she looks about half his age.

He says something to her, and she throws her head back and giggles. I don't remember giggling when I was with Luke. As a matter of fact, he would've told me that I was loud and I was embarrassing him if I had.

The woman is gorgeous and vibrant and free.

So why is she with Luke?

I force my eyes away from them and back to my book, but the words are now a blur. I am surprised when a tear splashes down onto the pages. I thought I was done crying.

Luke is living life. He looks . . . joyful. But I'm sitting here, alone, and crying over something that should be left behind. It is not fair that he should be happy with another woman. He does not deserve another relationship after what he did to me! He should suffer alone in retribution for his sins.

I am fine with not seeking my own revenge as long as he reaps what he's sown. Isn't that what the Bible says? I know what he's sown. The reaping shouldn't be a beautiful woman.

Why isn't God punishing him?

CHAPTER 5

EVA

Eva slid into the pew and folded her hands in her lap. She didn't want to draw any attention to herself, so she looked at the floor and tapped her foot, waiting for the service to start. She'd wanted to sit in the last row, but the usher wouldn't let her. She told Eva that the last rows were reserved for latecomers. She'd remember that if she ever decided to come back.

Eva wasn't sure why she'd come to church. She did feel a little obligated after they gave her the food that she so desperately needed, but that wasn't the reason she'd gotten up and put on another nice outfit. Eva bit her lip, trying to figure out her own motives.

One thing she knew was that she didn't need another handout, because that night she was supposed to start a new job. At a strip club.

Eva told herself that it was a step out of the porn industry. She wouldn't be having sex with anyone, and she'd shown her body to strangers for years. At least they couldn't touch her. And she'd have rent money. As twisted as it might sound, she thought the call from the Gentlemen's Den was a blessing.

Eva glanced from right to left at the families and churchgoers. She felt that they could see right through her St. John's Bay suit and six-dollar panty hose. She smoothed her hair over her eye and straightened her glasses on her nose. Eva was in disguise with her schoolgirl look. It was a necessity. She never knew when she'd run into a fan or, worse, a porn addict.

Luckily, she looked a lot different in her films than she did in real life. When Eva went onto the set of an adult movie, she wore wigs and a ridiculous amount of makeup. She was so undercover that it would be hard for her own mother to recognize her. Like every other star in the industry, she didn't use her own name. X-Stacy was her porn handle—like the drug, and what the viewer was supposed to feel when they watched.

Eva's leg shook nervously as the other attendees filled up the pews around her. Soon she was lost in a sea of worshippers and their children. She breathed a sigh of relief when the service started and no one had tried to start a conversation with her. A few people had said "Good morning," but none had gone the extra step to engage her.

On the pew in front of Eva was a very shapely woman wearing a skintight dress that showed every curve. Eva caught herself fixated on the woman and quickly took her eyes away. Eva wasn't gay—she loved men, in fact—but she'd done so many films with women, that either sex could cause her to feel lustful.

Eva swallowed hard and shook her head. Why were these thoughts invading her mind during a worship service? Wasn't this supposed to be God's house? So why was the devil tormenting her here with his demonic presence?

That was what her grandmother had always called Eva's precocious sexuality—demonic. A trick of the enemy and a curse. Eva always agreed with her, because it did have roots in evil. It was just that the evil had a name—Uncle Parnell.

He'd started touching Eva before she even knew the names of her body parts. He upgraded to full-fledged intercourse by the time she was fourteen. His abuse didn't stop until she ran away from home at the age of sixteen. A few months later she did her first adult film. If nothing else, she had experience in mentally taking herself to another place during sex. It made her a rising star in the industry.

Eva closed her eyes and listened to the music coming from

the choir stand. They were singing a song about saints coming to worship. Yvonne was leading the song, and her voice sounded so pure and angelic that it brought tears to Eva's eyes. But it wasn't just the good music that touched Eva's spirit. The words echoed through her mind and landed in her conscience. Eva felt like she was the very opposite of a saint. It made her remember her grandmother's pastor, Reverend Wells, who always used to differentiate between the "saints and the ain'ts." Reverend Wells would say, "The ain'ts ain't trying to live right, ain't asking God for forgiveness, and they ain't going to heaven."

Yes, Eva would put herself in the "ain'ts" category. If there was a heaven, she probably wouldn't get anywhere close to it. So much wrong had been done to her, and she'd done so much wrong, that heaven would probably repel her at the gate. Even still, the music was soothing and encouraging. The lyrics promised that if the saints worshipped, the King of Glory would come in.

Well, she remembered praying that her uncle would never touch her again. She'd asked God to strike him down. She didn't know if that was worship, but no one ever showed up. No one stopped him.

Tears streamed down Eva's face. Everyone around her seemed to be caught up in some form of worship. Hands were extended; shouts of praise were going forth. Something in the music seemed to fortify their faith. Eva searched her heart for faith but couldn't find any.

After the music came the sermon. The message was about trusting God. The preacher said something about not worrying about your situation, but trusting God to see you through.

Eva thought about her situation. She was down to her last five dollars, and she had tried to do the right thing. She had applied for jobs, but since she didn't even have a high school diploma, she thought she'd get only a few calls back. She hadn't gotten any. Well, she'd gotten one, and it was from the strip club, not any of the jobs that didn't require her to be naked.

Eva sighed heavily and wiped the tears away. She finally knew why she was in church. She was there looking for a miracle. She wanted to have a job that she wasn't ashamed of, but her physical needs were getting the best of her. Food, clothing, and shelter were essential, and five dollars wasn't covering any of that.

The preacher said to have faith. Was faith required for a miracle? Eva wasn't sure if she had any—at least not in anyone other than herself.

CHAPTER 6

YVONNE

I am the last choir member in the choir stand after service. I always take it upon myself to straighten the chairs and pick up any stray trash. We have a cleaning service to take care of the church during the week, but I don't mind helping out.

Lord, let me stop lying to myself. I stay afterward so that I can chat with Kingston as he collects his music and locks away the extra musical instruments. He sure looks fine today. I'm not quite sure I should be enjoying his good looks so much right up here in the sanctuary, but I most certainly am. The Lord truly knew what He was doing when He constructed this man.

"Yvonne, you sang beautifully today."

Kingston's voice snaps me out of my daydream, and I have to look away from his penetrating eyes. "Thank you, Brother Kingston. I just wanted to let God use me."

"Well, He did, and I think you pretty much retired that song from any other soloist. If we sing 'When the Saints Go to Worship' with any other singer, it's going to sound crazy."

Now I do look up at him and smile. "You are a mess, Kingston."

"I am a mess. And I'm hungry. Why don't you let me take you to brunch at Phil the Fire?"

"Oh, I can't. I've got . . ."

"What? You've got what?" Kingston asks. "Another date? If you've got another brother wrapped around your little finger, then let me know now."

I almost say something cliché, like "I'm married to Jesus," but Kingston's playful facial expression melts away all my objections. Why shouldn't I, anyway? He's single, and so am I. Plus, it's just brunch, not a marriage proposal.

"Well, I guess it'll . . . Wait a minute, Kingston. I'll be right back."

I dash out of the choir stand and up the center aisle of the church to catch up with Eva right before she leaves the sanctuary. I wondered if she'd come out to service. Sometimes when people want a free meal, they come to New Faith and then we never see them again until the next time they're hungry. It's a shame, because most of them need Jesus more than some canned goods and powdered milk. Eva is waiting around after service, so maybe she has another need.

"Eva!"

She spins around with a look of shock on her face. "Oh, hi, Yvonne."

I give her a hug and feel her entire body stiffen. She doesn't hug me back but stares at me when I release her. "Did you enjoy service?"

"I did. I'm glad I came," she replies.

"Do you think you'll come back?"

She winces. "I don't know. I've got to go back to work."

"You got your job back?" I hug Eva again. "That's wonderful news, right?"

Eva looks at the floor. "It is. Um . . . thank you for helping me and praying with me. I appreciate it."

"You're so welcome! Do you need anything? Are you waiting for someone?"

"N-no, I'm not waiting for anyone. I was just . . . Well . . . it's silly, but I was waiting for a sign from God. I asked Him something during service, and I was waiting for an answer or something."

"Hmm . . . you didn't get your sign?"

"Nope. Nothing."

"Well, sometimes when God is quiet, He wants us to use what He's already given us and then trust Him."

She nods. "I'm not sure I've figured this out."

"None of us can ever hope to figure God out, so don't feel too bad about that."

I quickly take a piece of paper and pen out of my purse and scribble my telephone number down. "Here. Take this. Call me if you need anything. Anytime. I hope you come back and visit us."

Eva stares at the piece of paper like she doesn't know if she wants to take it or not, so I fold it and tuck it into her open purse. Then I hug her once more. This time she hugs me back, holds on for dear life.

When she releases me, there are tears in her eyes. She is a pitiful sight, and I can't just let her leave like this. My mama didn't raise me to let the wounded suffer, and God wouldn't be too pleased, either, I don't think.

"Thank you." Eva says again before turning to walk away.

"Have you eaten yet today? My friend Brother Kingston is taking me to brunch. I'm sure he wouldn't mind if you came along."

The side of Eva's mouth twitches, the closest thing she gives me to a smile. "I'm sure he *will* mind."

"Well, I don't care what he thinks. If he doesn't want both of us, then he can just eat his brunch alone. You and I can find something to eat without him."

Eva cocks her head to one side. "Why are you being so nice to me? We just met."

"Because you seem like you could use a friend. You should be glad you didn't show up here years ago. I wasn't nearly as friendly then. God's been working on me."

"I wish I had come here years ago," Eva says.

"Better late than never."

"I guess."

"So are you going to brunch with us?"

She shakes her head. "Not this time, Yvonne, but I promise you I will soon, especially if your friend is paying."

This time when she turns to walk away, I can't think of anything else to stop her. I notice how well she's dressed, in another nice suit and expensive-looking shoes. She looks like a corporate professional. It makes me wonder how she fell on tough times. But then again, our food bank has serviced everyone from drug addicts to ex-VPs. Down and out doesn't discriminate.

Kingston walks up behind me and touches my back. "You ready to go?"

"I guess so."

"Don't sound so excited, Yvonne."

I chuckle and run a hand through my thick shoulder-length bob. "I'm sorry, Kingston. I was just thinking about something."

"Do you want to do this some other time, then?"

"No, I'm fine. Let's go. Are you driving, or are we going separately?"

Kingston's eyes light up, and a smile spreads across his face. "Well, we can ride together, but I'm not sure what people would say. Maybe we should drive separately."

"You've been trying to take me out for the past two years, Kingston. Everybody knows!"

He winks. "But not everyone knows you've said yes! Meet me there in thirty minutes."

I watch Kingston skip and hop out of the sanctuary. It tickles me that he's so happy to go on a date with me. My ex-husband, Luke, never acted this way. Luke always thought *he* was the prize and that I should be grateful to have him.

Pam walks up to me with her arms outstretched and TJ in tow. I give her a hug and the miniature Troy. We all know how bad Troy got on Pam's nerves when she was pregnant with that baby, so it's no wonder he's the spitting image of his daddy.

"Hi, Auntie Vonne. Can I come over your house for some banana pudding?"

I laugh out loud. "What makes you think I have some banana pudding at my house?"

He shrugs. "I don't know. But if you don't, can you make some, like you did on Easter?"

"Are boys born with the ability to sweet-talk us?" I ask Pam.

She chuckles. "Well, this one sure was. TJ, go over there with Gretchen and Cicely. I'll be there soon."

When the boy is out of earshot, I ask, "You spoken to Troy yet?"

"No. I haven't said two words to him since he embarrassed me in front of his friend."

"How long do you plan on keeping up the silent treatment?"

"Until he apologizes, Yvonne."

"Did you finish your proposal at least?"

Pam nods and smiles. "Yes, I did. I'm going to turn it in tomorrow."

"Well, that's good."

"Let me go, girl. I want to feed these kids and get some writing done on my new novel before Troy comes home from golfing with Logan."

"Since when did Troy golf?"

Pam purses her lips together and rolls her eyes. "Exactly. He doesn't. He's probably making a fool of himself as we speak."

"But this Logan guy is rich? He can help Troy, right?"

"He is rich, and he's a really nice guy, Yvonne. Maybe he'll rub off on Troy."

"Maybe so. Call me later, okay?"

Pam gives me a hug. "I will. Maybe we can get together tomorrow for pedicures or something."

"Okay."

Pam collects her children, and they exit the sanctuary, leaving me in a nearly empty church. I don't know why I'm stalling. I'm sure Kingston is almost to the restaurant by now.

I was going to ask Pam what she thought, but I already knew what she'd say. She and Taylor have made their thoughts pretty clear on me getting back into the dating pool. They're all for it.

I start walking toward the door, still contemplating standing Kingston up and taking myself on home. It might be the best thing for both of us. I'd have no idea what to do if he thought we were an item after one meal.

What if he tries to kiss me?

I don't think he'd do that this soon, but what if he did? I wouldn't know how to fight him off. I've never had to do anything like that. Luke was the first and only man I'd ever been alone with, and he didn't do anything to steal my virtue while we dated.

Then a vision of Luke and his new woman comes to mind. Him whispering to her and her giggling flirtatiously. The thought of it makes me sick to my stomach.

I take in a deep breath and exhale slowly. My stomach growls, and it seals the deal for me. Whether it's a date or not, a woman's got to eat. And food always seems to taste better when a man is paying for it.

When I get to the restaurant, Kingston rushes to my car to open my car door before I have the chance to do it myself. His hazel eyes smile at me as I swing my legs out of the car. He closes the door and then holds his arm out for me to hold on to.

"It is a beautiful day, isn't it?" I ask when I can't take another second of Kingston gazing at my face.

"Yes, it is. A beautiful spring day to spend with a beautiful lady."

I laugh out loud and give Kingston a playful slap on the arm. "I don't know how many more compliments I can take from you."

"Well, I can't help you there. I finally talked you into going out with me, so I'm going to shower you with compliments."

As we walk into the restaurant, I scan the parking lot for familiar cars. I don't know why we picked this spot for brunch. Their food is really good, but everybody, and I do mean *everybody,* from our church comes here on Sunday afternoons.

"I can't wait to eat some of that French toast. They have the best maple syrup I've ever had," I say as Kingston opens the restaurant door.

"It is sweet, but not as sweet as you," Kingston says.

"You are pouring it on thick now!"

"I can't help it, Vonne! I've been storing this up for a while. You should've said yes a long time ago."

I take in a sharp breath when Kingston calls me Vonne. That was the nickname Luke had for me. I heard him call me that for twenty years before we divorced. I can hear his voice in my head. *Vonne, get me something to eat. Vonne, you need to fix your hair, around here looking like a slave on a plantation.*

"Is something wrong?" Kingston asks when I freeze up and pull my arm away.

"Could I ask you not to call me Vonne?"

Kingston nods slowly. "Did I take you someplace with that?"

"You did, and it wasn't to a good place. I'm sorry. I didn't mean to expose you to my baggage so soon."

"You wanted to ease it on me?" Kingston's smile tells me that he understands my issues.

"I wish I didn't have it at all! But yes, I wanted to ease it on you."

"It's all right, Yvonne. I can take it. Let's go eat."

I'm feeling really good about this date now. It was a good idea to finally say yes to Kingston. He is a good man. A good, *patient* man!

We choose a table, and of course, he pulls the chair out for me.

"I don't even need a menu," Kingston says. "I know exactly what I want. The brunch buffet."

"I always get the buffet, too," I say.

The waitress comes to the table with a huge smile on her face. Her name is Rosa, and I see her all the time when I'm here with Pam and Taylor. We're regulars.

"Hey, Ms. Yvonne! I see you aren't here with your girls today, huh?"

"No, I'm here with a friend. Kingston meet Ms. Rosa, and Ms. Rosa meet Kingston. He's the choir director at our church."

"Oh, for real! You kicking it with the choir director, Ms. Yvonne?"

Kingston and I burst into laughter. "I hope she'll kick it with me!" Kingston says. "Can we kick it at our age?"

"You can kick it at any age!" Rosa says. "Y'all want the buffet, or do you need menus?"

"We will have the buffet. Thank you," Kingston says.

"Okay, well, I'll bring some juice and coffee. Holla if you need anything," Rosa says.

"Let's eat!" Kingston says as Rosa walks away.

Oh no! No. No. No! The last people I wanted to see on my first date with Kingston are here at the restaurant. Rhoda and Rochelle. And they haven't had a good piece of gossip to chew on in a minute, so they're chomping at the bit!

"Well, what do we have here?" Rhoda says as she and Rochelle approach the table.

"What *do* we have here?" Rochelle echoes.

I roll my eyes and shake my head. "You have two people about to get some brunch. Excuse us. The buffet is calling."

Rhoda says, "Wait a minute, Sister Yvonne. You don't have to be all like that. We just came over here to say hello. We saw our sister and brother in Christ, and we wanted to extend the right hand of fellowship."

The right hand of fellowship? I don't believe this. They are worse than the paparazzi. My and Kingston's date is going to be in the church bulletin next week. Or worse, we'll be on the prayer list.

"We had a long service today, and we're really hungry, sisters," Kingston says. "Maybe we can chat after we eat."

Rhoda looks Kingston up and down and then turns to Rochelle. "Is he trying to dismiss us?"

"I think he's hungry," Rochelle replies.

"Oh, for goodness' sakes! Can we please go to the buffet?" I say as I take Kingston by the hand and step around those two nosy heffas.

"We're watching you," Rhoda says.

I frown deeply as we approach the buffet. Why do they have to be here today to ruin our date? Rhoda and Rochelle always show up at the most inconvenient times.

"Don't worry about them," Kingston says.

"I'm not worried about them, but they get on my nerves. They'll have our business all over the church by next Sunday."

"It's okay. I don't mind people knowing that we're friends, Yvonne. You're a great woman. Plus, I plan on this being the first of many outings, and it isn't like Cleveland is New York City. Someone was going to see us at some point."

I grin as I scoop the delicious-looking food onto my plate. "What makes you think I'm going to say yes to a second date?"

"Because I am a good catch, and you are a smart woman. That's one of the things I admire about you."

Every time he opens his mouth, Kingston surprises me. For my age, I am severely inexperienced with men, and I definitely have no frame of reference for romance.

"Well, you are persistent. That is one of the qualities I admire in you."

Kingston leads the way back to the table. This time we completely ignore the persistent gaze of Rhoda and Rochelle. I wonder if they plan to eat or if they're just going to watch us all afternoon.

"You didn't grow up here in Cleveland, did you?" Kingston asks.

"No. I grew up in the South."

"What brought you up north?"

I look down at my plate and reply, "I moved here with my ex-husband."

"Well, it's a good thing you didn't move back after you divorced! I wouldn't have gotten my chance if you had."

This conversation has taken an uncomfortable turn. It's like Luke is casting a shadow over this date.

"Are you going to get like this every time we talk about your ex-husband?"

I look up at Kingston and sigh. "I don't know. I've never talked to any men after him, so all of this feels strange."

"If you're not ready to go out with me, I'll understand."

Am I ready to go out with him or anyone? I do enjoy the single life, but I know I don't want to spend the rest of my life alone. That means that at some point, I'm going to have to put the strangeness aside and take the plunge. But I don't know if I can do that today.

"Would you really understand, or would you think that I'm silly for not wanting to date after eight years of being single?"

"I wouldn't think you were silly. Marriage is meant to be for your entire lifetime, so I would be concerned if you didn't take your divorce seriously."

I swallow a few more bites. "You can't be this good."

"I'm not," Kingston says with a snort. "I'm patient, but not good. I have designs on you, Yvonne, and I'm biding my time."

"Should I be afraid?"

"No, you should be excited. This is going to be a wonderful ride."

There is an undeniable sparkle in Kingston's eyes as he stuffs his mouth full of French toast. My mind tells me that I should be cautious—no man's ever been this interested in me. But another part of me says to go on with this and see what the end is going to be.

CHAPTER 7

TAYLOR

"You've got twenty minutes, Luke."

"This doesn't have to be a hostile visit, Taylor."

Luke's Cheshire cat smile makes me sick to my stomach. Actually, just thinking of the man who once fooled me into loving him makes me nauseous. He kills me with this whole "I've changed" routine. Luke is one of the devil's main children, for real. I don't care what he says. Demons don't change; they have to be cast out.

"My husband is waiting on me. We have a date."

I don't know why I felt the need to say that. Luke doesn't need to know any information about my life, and I sure as heck am not trying to make his trifling self jealous. Luke wanted to take me to lunch at the Cheesecake Factory, but I chose Starbucks instead. Number one, this is not a date, and number two, how can he afford lunch when he can't even take care of his son?

"Why didn't you bring Spencer with you? I am a part of your extended family. Spencer and I need to get to know one another and bond. Maybe we can go on a man-cation."

That demonic smile on Luke's face tells me that he is messing with me, and I shouldn't allow him to make me mad. That's

giving the devil room, as my mama would say. But whatever. I
am angry. I can't stand this fool.

"The devil is a lie," I say. "You are not my family."

Luke clasps his hands and places them on the table. "I didn't
come here to fight with you. You don't have to consider me
family, but Joshua is my family. He's my son. He's got my DNA."

So he gets out of prison and sends me a grand total of six
child support checks in eight years, and now he wants to call
my baby family. He can get the heck out of here with that. He's
about to make me go off on him, and I gave up those rowdy
ways a long time ago.

"I want to spend time with my son," he says when I don't respond to his first offensive comments.

"You've gone too far now, Luke. You think I'm about to let
my son spend time with a convicted felon?"

"That's one description of me. Another one would be redeemed man of God. A third description would be *his father.*"

"Let me get up from here right now, before some lightning
comes through the roof of this building. Man of God? You
need to stop playing."

Luke reaches in his jacket pocket, and instinctively I flinch.
He is the man that nearly killed Yvonne. There's no telling
what he might do. That's why I've got 9-1-1 on speed dial. But
he doesn't pull out a weapon. Instead he hands me a business
card.

I read it out loud. "Redeemed of the Lord Worship Center,
Luke Hastings, senior pastor." I burst into laughter. This man
has completely and utterly lost his mind. Pastor? Who in their
right mind would follow him?

"You've got to be kidding me, Luke. It was hard finding a
real job with that felony on your record, so you start up a
church?"

"I've been operating in ministry since I was in prison, Taylor.
You may not believe it, but that experience changed me. For
good."

I purse my lips together in a skeptical tight line. "You've got a lot to prove before I let my son spend any time with you. Why don't you raise a love offering and start paying your back child support?"

"You got jokes, I see."

"Actually, I'm being serious. It's time for you to help share the load for Joshua, especially if you're trying to be a part of his life."

Luke shakes his head. "You are all about the money, aren't you? You and Yvonne robbed me blind while I was in prison, but that still wasn't enough for you."

"We did not rob you. Yvonne took money from your joint account to help with your son. It's a good thing she stepped up to the plate, 'cause you sure weren't there."

Luke sighs and runs his hand over his mostly salt and kind of pepper hair. I can see he's frustrated, but this has no effect on me whatsoever. "Listen, Taylor, I forgave you and Yvonne for everything. Why can't you forgive me? You've got a man that's taking care of you and the boy. Why you gotta kick me when I'm down?"

"Luke fall down, so Luke get up!" I sing. He's getting on my nerves right now, so I'm being pretty ignorant. I'm sure Donnie McClurkin would not be pleased with my remix of his song.

"Since you're in such a jovial mood, I might as well tell you all of it. I'm getting married."

Now my laughs are coming so quickly that I can barely catch my breath. Luke is getting married? Luke is getting married! This cheating, wife-beating, deadbeat father has found some other woman to capture in his web, like a spider ready to snack on a gnat.

"Well," I finally say when I get my breath back, "I would certainly like to meet her. Why don't Yvonne and I take your blushing bride out to lunch? Or, better yet, we can throw her a bachelorette party! I'm sure you're still sowing your royal oats."

Luke sits back in his chair, folds his arms, and stares at me. "I've apologized to Yvonne, but you've never given me the opportunity to apologize to you."

This catches me off guard, and since I don't trust Luke any farther than I can throw him, he gets the "Sista girl, I wish a brotha would" face. "I don't want your apology, Luke."

"I know. You don't want or need anything from me. But in order for me to be right with God, I have to say this. I'm sorry about what I put you through, and I am going to try to do better by you and Joshua financially."

So that's it? I'm supposed to forget that he lied to me, said he was going to leave his wife for me, got me pregnant, and then asked me to have an abortion? I'm supposed to forget that he's let another man raise and take care of his son?

I. Don't. Think. So.

"I don't accept your apology."

Luke's astonished expression almost makes me want to smile. I'm not letting him get off this easy. If he wants my forgiveness and reconciliation with *my* son, then he's gonna have to do a whole lot more than recite two sentences. God might not require penance, but I do.

I stand to my feet, and Luke's shock changes into a frustrated frown. "You're going to make this difficult," he says.

Did he really just say that I'm making this too hard for him? Really? Difficult is showing up pregnant at your church and then trying to convince everyone that your middle name isn't Jezebel. Beyond difficult is trying to take care of a baby on barely over minimum wage, when his daddy lives with his wife in the suburbs. Dang near impossible is convincing another man to raise a child that he didn't create.

Seems like Luke has had a cakewalk to me.

"Listen. I'll think about letting Joshua have one supervised visit with you, and then we'll take it from there."

"I am entitled to more than one visit with my son."

"You don't want to start talking about who's entitled to what, Luke. One supervised visit. Take it or leave it."

"I'll take it . . . for now."

Without giving Luke a good-bye or a "See you later," I storm away from the table and out of the Starbucks. I'm not even in the mood for this high-priced coffee drink anymore. I just want to get away from Luke. It's like he's covered in slimy filth and just talking to him gets it all over you.

I'm still wound up about Luke's half-baked apology and his announcements when I get to Chicago Deli, my favorite lunch spot. I see Spencer's car, so he's already here. He hates to be kept waiting, but I'm late, so I'm going to have some explaining to do.

When I walk into the restaurant, I beam a huge smile in Spencer's direction. His lips only twitch slightly from the deep frown as he looks down at the watch on his arm. I put a little extra sway in my hips and a pout on my lips and watch Spencer's icy expression melt. He can't resist me when I turn on the charm, even when I'm late.

Spencer stands up from the table and pulls out the chair for me. He kisses me on the neck as I sit. Crisis averted, and it's a good thing, too, because I have to tell him about Luke.

"So how's your day going so far, babe?" I ask.

"Good. What have you been up to on your day off? Shopping?"

"Um . . . no, not quite."

The waitress walks up to our table, and she's smiling hard at Spencer. Chicks these days are bold. Someone needs to teach these heffas a lesson in etiquette. I mean, if you're going to flirt with someone's man, you at least wait until they go to the restroom. Before God had His hand on my life, I could've taught a graduate course in man stealing.

"What would you like?" the waitress asks Spencer.

I clear my throat. "I will have a corned beef sandwich on rye, light mustard, and a pickle. My *husband* will have the fish and chips. We'll have water with lemon to drink. Thank you."

I slam both our menus shut and hand them to her. Spencer chuckles as the waitress skulks away with her tail between her legs. She doesn't want it with me. I don't play when it comes to my family.

"You are mean, Taylor. That poor girl was just being friendly."

I lift my eyebrow and grin. "What? All I did was place our order. Had you made friends with her before I came?"

"It was harmless. She asked me where I worked, and we chatted a little."

"About what?"

Spencer laughs out loud. "Her studies. She's in Case Western Reserve's nursing program. You can't possibly be jealous."

"Not jealous. Observant. I know a sideline wannabe when I see one."

"I'm a man of God, baby, and plus, why would I go for a hamburger when I've got a rib-eye steak at home?"

"Mmm-hmm. Every now and then, you might have a taste for a burger."

"Not me. I like the finer things in life. Now, are you going to tell me how you've spent your morning?"

"I met with Luke."

I let the words sink in for a moment and watch Spencer's eyebrows come together in a frown. "What does he want? And why didn't you tell me you were seeing him? The man is a felon, for God's sake."

"He wants to see Joshua."

"I knew this was going to happen at some point. How are we going to handle it?"

I know this is a real messed-up situation, but it makes me feel so good to know that Spencer thinks this is his problem, too. This is the type of thing that makes me know I married the right man.

"I told him he could have one supervised visit a month."

"You gave him an answer without talking to me first?"

"I didn't think you'd have a problem with that, Spence. It's barely any time at all."

Spencer inhales deeply and forces the air out of his nose through flared nostrils. "That is not the point. You thought that you could make the decision because in your mind, Joshua is your son. I don't know if Luke should be around him at all."

"I—I don't think that! I didn't think we could tell him no. He has parental rights."

"That he needs to go through the courts to initiate. And they'll force him to handle his responsibilities, in addition to granting visitation rights."

"I guess I didn't think about that."

"Obviously, you didn't."

My phone buzzes in my purse, slowing Spencer's verbal assault. He's tripping like I signed a joint custody agreement with Luke. I look at the caller ID on my phone, and it's Joshua's school. My stomach flips every time I get a call from there.

"Hello. This is Taylor Johnson-Oldman."

I hear the principal's voice, and what she says causes me to tremble all over. Tears start flowing down my face as she keeps giving me unthinkable news about my son. She can't be talking about my Joshua. Not my son.

"W-we're on our way," I say. "We'll be right there! Don't let them take him until I show up!"

"What is it?" Spencer asks as I sob and disconnect the phone.

"My baby has been arrested. They've arrested Joshua!"

I run out of the restaurant, not waiting for Spencer to follow. I've got to get up to that school and make sure this thing doesn't get out of hand, 'cause if somebody hurts my baby, there's going to be hell to pay.

CHAPTER 8

PAM

"**H**ow long are you going to not talk to me?"

I look up from my laptop at Troy's pitiful-looking face. No, I am not talking to him. Haven't spoken a word since he tried to embarrass me and dismiss my writing career in front of his friend Logan.

"Look, Pam. I'm sorry. I didn't mean what I said. I don't even know why I said it. I'm happy about your book deal."

I bite my lip and twirl a pencil between my fingers. "You're not happy about it. You want me to get a job."

"I want you to be happy. You should do the book thing, see how it turns out."

"What are we going to do about our shrinking bank account?"

Troy shrugs. "God will make a way, right? Isn't that what you always say? All the prayers you send up, it's going to happen."

Wrong answer. Wrong, wrong, wrong! This is not Troy taking the burden of our family off my shoulders. This is him making everything my and God's fault if it falls apart.

"Well, I am doing the *book thing*, as you call it."

"Good. But can you do it somewhere else? Aria and Logan are on their way over here. Logan called in a favor with a producer who just did some incredible work for Beyoncé. We've got some tracks that will make number one songs."

"So you want me to leave my home while you work?"

"It's going to be noisy. That's the only reason I ask."

"I think I'll stay tonight. Maybe I can write a song lyric or two."

Troy runs his hand over his head and sighs. "Pam, you don't have to do that."

"No, really, Troy, it's no trouble at all. Let me get some snacks together, and I'll be right in to join you. I wouldn't want you saying that I'm not a supportive wife."

Troy looks confused but doesn't try to persuade me any further. I snap my laptop shut and leave him in the living room. I wasn't going to get any writing done with Aria in my house, anyway, so I might as well see what they're up to.

I open the refrigerator to see what I can scare up in a few minutes. I have thawed-out chicken tenderloins, vegetables, and flour tortillas that are about two days away from going bad. Couple those with some sour cream and cheddar cheese and we've got chicken fajitas.

My son, TJ, peeks into the kitchen as soon as he hears pots and pans. Gretchen and Cicely tiptoe in, as well. They don't have to sneak, but I guess things have been so tense around here for the past few days that even my babies are walking on eggshells.

"Are you making fajitas?" Gretchen asks. "Can I help?"

"Of course."

Gretchen's face lights up, and she goes to the sink to wash her hands and put on her apron. Cicely, who couldn't care less about cooking anybody's meal, plops down on one of the bar stools.

"So, Mommy, have you talked to Auntie Taylor?" Cicely asks.

I realize that it's Friday and I haven't talked to Taylor since last week at church. Yvonne, either, for that matter, and I need to get the details on her date. I've been so consumed with writing my new book proposal that I've lost a few days in my friends' lives.

"I haven't talked to Taylor. Why?"

Cicely's eyes widen. "Oh, so you don't know about Joshua?"

I stop chopping the bell peppers and put the knife down on the cutting board. "What about Joshua?"

"He got arrested at school on Wednesday."

"The blood of Jesus! Arrested? By the police?"

"Yes, ma'am. They came up to the school and put handcuffs on him and everything. Then they put him in the back of the car. Auntie Taylor was up there crying like somebody died."

"Why did they arrest him?"

"He punched Ms. Golden in the mouth and knocked out her dentures," Cicely explains.

"I don't believe that!"

I wipe my hands and fumble for my cell phone. Gretchen takes over and heats oil in the big skillet for the chicken pieces. She really doesn't need me for this at all. Thank God, because I need to talk to my sister. I step into my study and close the door.

The phone rings three times. "Hi, Pam."

"Taylor, what is going on? Cicely just told me about Joshua. Why haven't you called?"

"I did call, but your phone went right to voice mail," Taylor says in a quivering voice. "I spent the last couple of days trying to get my baby out of the juvenile detention center. Spencer was finally able to get him released a few hours ago."

"Why did they arrest him? The story Cicely told me can't possibly be accurate."

Taylor sighs, and there's a long and pregnant pause. "Cicely was probably close to the truth. He's got this teacher who doesn't care for him, and she just won't leave him alone. I guess he didn't turn in an assignment, she chastised him, he talked back, and then she snatched him out of his seat. He doesn't like people putting their hands on him, so he kind of lost it."

"What do you mean, he lost it?"

"He hit that old bat and knocked her dentures out, but she wasn't hurt."

I let out a gasp just thinking about what I'd do to any of my children if they raised a hand to one of their teachers. "I can't believe Joshua did that! You've raised him better than that."

"Well, that witch shouldn't have put her hands on my son. They did away with corporal punishment for a reason. So that these racist teachers can't put their hands on our kids."

Now, I know Ms. Golden. I worked on the PTA with her, and both Cicely and Gretchen had her for fifth grade. She is a tough-as-nails woman who is somewhat old school. She doesn't tolerate back talk, and she makes the children say "No, ma'am" and "Yes, ma'am." She is a great teacher and is not racist at all. Even though she works in our well-to-do suburb, she volunteers every year tutoring reading students in the urban school districts.

"I never thought Ms. Golden was racist, Taylor."

"Well, she is. She doesn't like black boys. You have girls, so maybe that's why you haven't experienced it yet. You better hope TJ doesn't have her when he gets in fifth grade. Hopefully, she will have retired by then."

"They haven't filed any charges, have they? He's just a little boy."

"Girl, they talking about assault, but we're going to fight it. Right now we've got to worry about where Joshua's going to go to school. They expelled him."

"Oh my Lord, Taylor, I'm so sorry. Do you think if he apologizes to the teacher that they'd overturn the decision?"

"Apologize? He didn't do anything but defend himself. She shouldn't have put her hands on my son."

I can't believe what I'm hearing. I know that Taylor overindulges Joshua a little bit. I thought that it was just because it was only the two of them for so long. I hoped that once Spencer came into their lives, she would be a little bit more balanced about that boy.

"What are you gonna do, then?"

"For now I'm going to homeschool him."

"What about your job?"

"I'm taking a leave of absence. Spencer makes more than enough money to take care of us, and we've been stacking most of my checks for years. We'll be fine if I take some time off to get my son back on track."

"What did Spencer say about you leaving work?"

Another loud sigh from Taylor. "He basically said that all of this is my fault. He's wanted to punish Joshua for his other outbursts, but I don't allow that. He's not hitting my son. So he said I might as well handle it."

This is a touchy subject, and I don't even know if our friendship can withstand me telling Taylor how I really feel about this. I think Joshua could've used a good spanking a couple of times, but I don't think she believes in spanking. I can understand why she doesn't want Spencer to touch him, but I also know how much Spencer loves them both.

"Maybe Spencer's method is not such a bad idea."

"You sound like Yvonne."

"See . . ."

"Neither of you has been a single mother, so you have no idea what I'm going through."

"But you're not a single mother anymore."

Taylor clears her throat. "You just worry about getting that book published, huh? We're all looking for a reason to celebrate, so let's get it poppin', girlfriend."

"Okay, Taylor, you can avoid the issue for now, but we're not done with this conversation."

"I'm not avoiding anything. I'm just done talking about it. I didn't ask for advice, Pam."

"You're right. I'm sorry."

"Don't be. It's what you do. I know where to find you when I need you."

I can hear the smile in Taylor's voice, and I know she doesn't mean to hurt my feelings. "All right, girl. You want to get lunch tomorrow? Maybe Yvonne can come, too."

"Yes. We've got to grill her about Kingston."

"Okay! She thinks we forgot."

"She needs to go on ahead and get back on the horse. Luke is sure riding into the sunset. That loser is getting married!"

I chuckle. "Wow."

"He claims he's changed. He's started a church."

"Shut the front door!"

Taylor giggles now. "Yes, child."

"Well, I guess anyone can change."

"Mmm-hmmm. Anyone can start a church!"

I hear Aria's loud, shrill giggle in my home and decide it's time to end this conversation.

"See you tomorrow, Taylor. Troy and I have company."

"Okay. Text me the place tomorrow."

"Okay."

After I disconnect the call, I walk back through the kitchen, where Gretchen has got everything under control. The chicken is sautéing with the onions and bell peppers, and she's added slices of chili peppers to the mix.

"You need any help?" I ask.

Gretchen smiles. "I got this, Mom. Daddy's *friends* are here."

Gretchen knows me so well. She's been my shadow ever since she could walk, and she has discernment when it comes to my feelings. She knows that I do not like Aria, even though I've never said it out loud.

I put a fake smile on my face as I stride into the living room. Aria sees me and runs over to me. She gives me a tight hug and air kisses. I feel my body tense from this unwanted affection.

"Hey, Ms. Pam! Or should I say authoress Pam?"

"Um, Pam is fine."

Logan hands me a colorful bouquet of mixed flowers and a gift bag. "I was a rude guest the last time I came by. This time I come bearing gifts."

Now, this makes me smile for real. I inhale the sweet fragrance of the flowers and then open the gift bag. There's a small box with a beautifully decorated cupcake inside.

"Troy said you like baked goods," Logan explains.

"I do, but I'm not sure if I need it. I'm on a diet." A fact I am very much reminded of right now with Aria prancing around, wearing skinny jeans that hug her ridiculously large bottom. How can a woman even have that big a behind with those skinny legs? I thought big behinds came with big thighs. Mine does!

"You look great," Logan says. "A grown man isn't afraid of a grown woman's curves. Isn't that right, Troy?"

Troy laughs out loud. "Don't discourage her, Logan! She's doing great on her diet. You are looking good, babe."

I narrow my eyes at Troy and take a huge bite of the strawberry and cream cupcake. The sweet, creamy frosting gives me a sugar rush, which immediately lifts my mood.

"Enough kissing up to my wife!" Troy says. "Let's get started on this music. I can't wait to hear these tracks."

Not knowing quite what to do with myself, I sit down on the couch and wait to see what happens next. Aria takes her usual place on the stool in front of Troy's keyboard. She always looks like she's posing there to me, with her head thrown back and her weave flowing over her shoulders. Troy and Logan go to the computer and load the flash drive.

The next thing I hear is a pounding, almost disco beat, but with a melody on top of it. It sounds like something you'd hear in a club or one of those rave things that teenagers have.

"That's hot!" Aria says. "But what am I going to sing to that?"

Logan holds up one finger, as if he's waiting for something. Then he sings, "I came for the party. Now, leave me alone. You didn't bring your boys. I didn't bring my girls. I came to get my party on. Baby, I'm grown. I'm gone keep on dancing till the break of dawn."

After hearing Logan sing it a few times, Aria starts singing it in her rich voice. Even though I can't stand her, I never could deny that Aria could sing her butt off.

Logan kills the music. "See the vibe we're going for? Strictly club and a couple of really melodic mid-tempo ballads. You want songs that people learn by heart. That's the only way you go from being an aspiring artist to an artist that's making bank."

I've never seen Troy speechless, but when Logan talks, my husband—the self-appointed big dawg in charge—gazes at him in awe like he's looking at a deity. I don't know if what Logan is saying makes sense or not, but Troy and Aria are lapping it up with a spoon.

"How many songs do you think I should do?" Aria asks.

"I think you should start out with five or six, almost like a mix tape, build the public interest, and then take it from there," Logan replies.

Troy says, "And I get songwriting credits on the record?"

"Absolutely. On the songs that you write, you get credit."

"So if she goes platinum, Troy is a millionaire again?" I ask.

Logan turns his attention to me. It's like he forgot I was there and just now noticed me again. "Well, that's not exactly how songwriting credit works. The songwriter gets nine cents per song, per album. So, for every song on a platinum record, Troy gets ninety thousand dollars. I know it's confusing."

"It's not confusing," I say with a tight head shake. "It's really simple math."

Logan laughs out loud. "Troy, you ought to hire your wife to mind your books. It sounds like she'd do a great job of it."

"Maybe she would. Or maybe she'd spend up the money getting her nails and hair done," Troy says.

"No, Troy, that would be me," Aria says. "I think Ms. Pam would do the right thing."

"I'm sorry. I didn't mean to get y'all off track by asking business questions. I was just curious," I say.

"You were just counting my money," Troy says.

"I thought when you got married, it became the both of yours," Logan says with a chuckle.

I give Troy an unblinking stare, wondering how he's going to get out of this one. "You're not married," Troy says. "So you wouldn't know."

"I'm not married, because I haven't found a great woman like the one you have."

I feel myself blush, so I look away from Troy and at the floor. I don't think I've ever had a man say such nice things about me, not even Troy. Thank God Gretchen comes in with her tray of fajitas before I have to respond.

"Troy, I'm going to get out of your way now, so y'all can do your thing. I need to work on my next book," I say.

Troy walks over and gives me an extremely intimate and embarrassing hug. "Good. 'Cause I think you're distracting my homeboy here."

"Boy, stop playing!"

On my way out of the room, I lock eyes with Troy and he gives his eyebrow a slight lift, which lets me know we're not done talking about this. Well, he can talk all he wants; it'll just be noise. He can't get mad at me because another man looks my way. I *still* got it. He needs to recognize.

CHAPTER 9

EVA

Loud music filled the dressing room, where dozens of dancers scurried back and forth in scant lingerie. It was almost eleven o'clock, the time when the club really started jumping. It was when the ballers came through to make it *rain* dollars on the dancers as they gyrated away their dignity and every good lesson their mamas ever taught them.

Eva sighed as she stared at her tear-streaked face in the mirror. The fake mink eyelashes, which were supposed to make her look glamorous, just made her seem more melancholy. The red lipstick and glittery eye shadow couldn't hide the turmoil in her heart.

Earlier in the week, she'd tried her hand at a square job. An employment agency sent her to a collections call center site to make harassing phone calls to people who owed money on their credit cards. She didn't know who she was fooling trying out that job. She couldn't compel anyone to pay their bills. Heck, she was one of those people that hid from those collectors' calls herself.

So here she was at the Gentlemen's Den strip club, trying to decide if she should go and make her money for the evening. Rent on her apartment was due in a few days, and even though she could find a church to give her a free meal, her only other option for somewhere to stay was a homeless shelter. Eva didn't have any family or friends that she felt comfortable contacting.

Eva took two steps toward the stairs that led up to the dance floor. *God, forgive me please.* As she walked up the stairs, the music got louder and the beat was so intense that the walls shook, but it still wasn't enough to drown out the sound of her conscience and a small, quiet voice.

Eva stopped at the top of the steps and sighed as the last few dancers ran past her and out into the club. It was packed. Wall-to-wall men and a few women, all ready to toss their money at her. Money that she'd use to pay her bills. Money that she'd put on the offering plate on Sunday. It was dirty money, but it was still spent the same.

Eva envisioned herself stooping to pick up the money from the floor as every part of her body was exposed. The thought of it made her stomach churn. She didn't want to do it, but what choice did she have? She couldn't pray about it, either. Eva had promised God she'd leave the business for good if her HIV test was negative. And she wasn't doing films anymore, but even if there was no sex, stripping was still part of the sex industry.

The song changed, and Eva didn't move. She stayed planted in her spot through another song, and then another. Every time she tried to will herself to move, she just couldn't do it.

One of the girls walked past Eva and said, "Girl, you better come on out on the floor. I just got all my bills paid for the month. The ballers are being generous tonight."

"For real?"

"Yeah, girl. They paying for lap dances and everything. If you go in the back room, you could probably get your bills paid for two months."

Eva frowned. The back room was where all the rules of the club disappeared and men paid for extra favors that they couldn't get out in the open on the dance floor. Eva wasn't going anywhere near the back room. It was too much like the set of one of her adult films.

"Well, are you coming?" the girl asked.

"I'll be out there," Eva said.

As soon as the girl left, Eva walked back down the stairs to the dressing room area. She got dressed quickly, before she could change her mind or think about a bill that needed to be paid.

Just as she was about to go out the basement exit door, the owner of the club, a guy named Roe, walked into the dressing room. He frowned at Eva as she tried to make her exit.

"Where you going? You trying to keep my cut?"

For a second, Eva didn't understand what Roe meant, and then she realized that he wanted his percentage of her tips. "I didn't dance at all. There's no cut."

"I advertised that you were gonna be here. Film stars make a lot of tips."

"I'm a former film star," Eva said, eyeing the door warily. Roe was standing between her and the exit.

Roe licked his lips slowly and stared lasciviously at Eva. She pulled her jacket tightly around her midsection and started to shift her weight from one leg to the other. She knew the look that Roe had on his face. She'd seen it on the faces of countless johns when she was a teenager. It was a look of lust multiplied by evil.

"If you ain't gone dance, you gone have to do *something*. You losing me money, girl."

"Look, Roe, this was a mistake. I just wanna go to the house."

Roe rubbed his hands together as he walked toward Eva. "You gone undress, or you want me to undress you?"

"Neither. Why don't you just let me go?" Eva didn't plead, because she wasn't afraid. She'd fought off bigger creeps than Roe. But she wasn't in the mood this evening. She wanted to go home and erase the entire night from her memory.

"I will. After." Roe stopped in front of Eva and snatched open her jacket. That was the only move he got to make.

Eva stepped in close and gave Roe a swift knee to the groin. When he doubled over from the intense pain, Eva delivered a roundhouse kick to his jaw, which took his consciousness.

As Roe lay in a crumpled mess on the floor, Eva picked up her handbag and rushed to the exit. She didn't want to be anywhere nearby when he woke up. Men were always meaner and more vengeful when they were taken out by a woman.

Eva opened the exit door and stepped out into the chilly spring night. Her career as a stripper was over before it even started. Once Roe told every club owner in a hundred-mile radius that she'd flaked out on him, she wouldn't be able to get a gig to save her life. But then . . . not getting a gig probably would *save* her life.

CHAPTER 10

YVONNE

Pam and Taylor forced me into having this lunch. I do not feel like being interrogated about my date with Kingston, but by the way they are both staring at me across the table, I know their nosy behinds want to know all my business.

"I think I'm going to order the coconut shrimp," I say as I look back down at my menu and away from their demanding stares.

"Me too," Pam says. "I want some dessert, too. The bread pudding sounds good."

Taylor says, "A dessert, Pam? I guess that means the diet is over, huh?"

"No one asked you to remind me about my diet. You could stand to lose a few, too," Pam says.

"I know it, girl. That's why I'm eating a salad."

I shake my head at both of them. "Why can't we ever enjoy a meal without you two wondering which thigh is going to get fatter?"

"You hush, Yvonne!" Pam says. "You've never been plump, and you aren't ever going to be plump."

"I'm thick. I ain't plump," Taylor says.

"Thank you for reminding us, Taylor. You're vixen-like," Pam says with much attitude.

"Yes, baby," Taylor says. "Yvonne, you could end this bootleg conversation at any time by telling us all about your new boo, Kingston."

"He is not my new boo. He is the director of the choir and a very good friend."

"Well, how was your date?" Pam asks.

"I don't know if I would call it a date. It was more like two friends sharing a meal."

Taylor throws her hands up in the air and groans. "Would you please stop? Kingston has been drooling over you forever! I mean, if I didn't know any better, I would think you wanted to get back with Luke."

"No, you didn't!"

"Yes, I did, Yvonne! Yes, I did! And that woman-beating, no-child-support-paying fool is getting married."

It feels like Taylor just knocked the wind out of me. When I saw Luke out with that young girl, I had no idea he was planning to marry her. I just thought that she was his new flavor of the month.

"Who would marry him?" Pam asks. "Women just don't do background checks these days."

"Probably a woman who wants to be the first lady of a church, because he's calling himself a pastor, too," Taylor says.

My jaw drops, and I stand up from the table. I just can't stay seated on this one. "He's a pastor now?"

Taylor nods. "Yep. You know that was always part of his game. That's how he traps the honeys, talkin' 'bout they gonna be in ministry together."

I shake my head and walk back and forth in front of our table. Taylor knows all about Luke's *game* and the come-ons that he has for his women. She was one of them. But when I met him, he was just starting out in ministry. He was truly impressive in the pulpit, and he charmed me from day one. I didn't know until after we were already married that he was an abuser and a cheater.

"I bet she's young too!" Taylor says. "He likes 'em young!"

I give Taylor an evil glare, and Pam says, "Can you *stop?*"

"Stop what? She knows that Luke is a hot mess! I 'on even know why she trippin'! I'm the one that needs to be trippin'! He probably taking up tithes and offerings and everything else. I wonder if they can put a child support order on an offering."

Now Pam and I both are glaring at Taylor.

"What? Luke is a super villain. Can we at least agree to that?" Taylor says.

I plop back down in my seat. "He is a villain, but I used to be married to him."

"You *used* to be married to him, and God has taken the shackles off!" Taylor exclaims.

Pam chuckles. "I do have to agree with her. You are free of Luke, girl. Free to see someone else if you want."

"Someone like Kingston!" Taylor says.

I let out a big sigh. Kingston is so nice. He is a gentleman, and he is very much interested in me. And to top it all off, he's incredibly sexy.

I'm so glad that Pam and Taylor can't read my mind! I wouldn't ever want them to know that I thought of Kingston, or any man, that way, but I can't even pretend that the attraction between us is happening only in the spirit realm. Something carnal is definitely taking place.

"Well, Kingston is fine," Taylor says. "You better be glad I'm already with Spencer, because I'd definitely let him chase me."

"And what makes you think that you're his type?" I ask.

"I am every man's type. But why you getting all touchy, Yvonne? I am in love with my man. I don't want your boo."

"Stop teasing her, Taylor."

"Okay, I'll tell you," I say. "I enjoyed myself with Kingston. He is a lot of fun. Rhoda and Rochelle were there."

Taylor scrunches her nose into a frown. "All bad."

"I know."

"So are you going to go out with him again?" Pam asks.

I shrug. "Maybe. I haven't made up my mind yet. He's already asked me to dinner after Bible study on Wednesday."

"First brunch and then dinner?" Taylor asks. "He sounds very interested."

"He is, but like I said, I haven't decided yet to take him up on his offer. How do you know about Luke being engaged?"

"He asked me to have coffee with him. He wants to see Joshua, but I don't know if that's even a good idea."

When Luke first went to prison, he called me collect and sent letters declaring his love. I suspected that he wanted me to take care of his money while he was gone and not give it over to Taylor for Joshua's needs. But I stopped reading his letters after the first one and gave Taylor twenty thousand dollars out of our joint account. Then, when I finally decided to divorce Luke, I got half of what was left—a piddly thirty thousand. I had always thought we were better off financially, but Luke had mortgaged our home and he'd blown lots of his money on his various mistresses.

Not once, with all of Luke's begging and pleading for me to stay by his side, did he ask about his son or the grown daughter he'd left behind. He acted as if Joshua didn't even exist, but now he wants to be in his life? If I were Taylor, I'd tell him to go somewhere that is extremely hot and smells like sulfur.

"How is Joshua? Have you figured out what you're doing about school yet?" Pam asks.

Taylor says, "He's fine, but I am definitely going to have to homeschool him for a while. There's no other convenient solution."

When Taylor called and told me about Joshua's problem at school, alarm bells went off in my mind. Immediately I started praying, because I couldn't think of anything but Luke putting his hands on me.

"Joshua sounds like he picked up something from Luke other than his looks," I say. "I've got the scars to prove Luke's anger management issues."

"Well, that's why I've got y'all, right?" Taylor asks. "Y'all gonna help me pray?"

Pam and I answer by each taking one of Taylor's hands and bowing our heads. Praying is what we do when we have no idea what else to do, and I surely don't know what to do about Taylor's situation.

CHAPTER 11

PAM

I've discovered a secret about my writing. If I do it outside of my home, I'm a lot more productive. Maybe it's because the kids and Troy can't bother me, or maybe it's because I hold myself more accountable at this booth in Starbucks than at home, in my bed, with my feet propped up and the TV playing in the background.

My new story is about a struggling single mother of two who finally meets her dream man but is too caught up in her baggage to see that he's a great guy. Admittedly, I got some of the inspiration from Taylor, who almost didn't end up with Spencer. She broke up with him until she found herself, and then she was lucky that he was still available.

I take a sip of my Chai Latte and type a few words. Then a couple sits down at the table next to me, and the writing stops. They are so into each other—he's telling her how his life has changed since he found her, and she's giggling and cooing at every word. I try to remember if Troy and I were ever like that. We weren't.

Not that we haven't had some great times together, because we really got along great when we were younger, before the children. But this goo-goo gaga type stuff? I don't remember

Troy and I having that type of thing, and I don't know if I would've wanted it.

Since I can't even think about writing anything with all this mushiness going on, I play solitaire on my computer and hope that they finish their coffee quickly. Then they can take their romantic selves back to the house or wherever else they gaze into one another's eyes.

"Pam?"

I look up from my computer, and Logan is standing in front of me with a huge grin on his face and a cup in his hand. His jolliness is infectious, and I can't do anything but smile back at him.

"Hey, Logan! Getting your caffeine fix?"

He nods. "Yep. Are you working on a book?"

"I'm supposed to be writing, but I'm playing on my computer right now."

He helps himself to the seat across from me. "It's okay to play for a while, but don't get too off track. That book isn't going to write itself."

Logan stares at me over his coffee cup as he sips, and darn it if I don't have to look away from him. The intensity of his gaze feels too intimate; it makes me feel like we're sharing a moment when we shouldn't be.

"You're right. I need to get to work, but I guess I just got a little distracted."

Just as I say that, the romantic couple decides it's time to take their party on the road. Now I can get some work done.

"I admire writers," Logan says. "It's as if you can tap into something that most of us normal people can't even touch."

This makes me laugh. "You're not normal, Logan! According to Troy, you're some kind of musical prodigy or something. He has nothing but great things to say about you."

"I'm just doing what I'm called to do, you know? Music is the thing I'm most passionate about. I can't imagine my life without music. I can imagine myself without money, but I never want to think about a world without music. I wouldn't want to live there."

I feel myself sigh. It sounds like the kind of noise that young girls make when they meet their musical idol in person. Like, if I had met Ralph Tresvant as a teenager, I probably would've made that sound. When it dawns on me that the noise I made was in response to Logan's love of music, I'm a little embarrassed.

"I'm the same way about writing and books," I say. "I am so glad to finally get the opportunity to share my writing with the world. I got offered a book deal a long time ago, and then I had my son and couldn't focus."

"It's your time to shine, then. I'm sure Troy is going to be happy once you get out there and start doing the book signings and everything else. It's exciting."

I take a long pause before replying. "I'm not sure that Troy is happy about anything other than Aria's singing."

Logan sets his coffee cup on the table and folds his arms across his chest. His handsome face becomes serious. "You're his wife, not Aria. If he's not excited about this, then there is something wrong with him."

"No, no, no. It's not like that." Suddenly I feel the need to defend Troy. "He's just, you know, frustrated about the music. He used to be very supportive of my writing. It's only recently that he's changed a little."

"You want me to talk to him?"

My eyes widen. "Oh, dear God, no! He'd hate that I even shared any of this with you. As a matter of fact, I beg you not to mention it. I was just venting, and I shouldn't have."

Logan's face relaxes, and his smile returns. "Your secret is safe with me, Pam. I'd never want to see that pretty face frowning because of something I did."

Darn him! Now I'm looking away again. He makes me so dang uncomfortable, but in a good way. In a way I don't want to stop.

"I should probably get back to my writing now," I say.

"You should. I'll be quiet so you can concentrate."

I shake my head and laugh again. "I can't work with you sitting here!"

This seems to tickle Logan. He gives a good and hearty laugh and then sips more of his coffee. "Now I'm the distraction."

"Yes, you are! You're even more distracting than the couple that just left."

"I think I like that. I don't believe I've distracted a woman in a long time."

Okay, now I'm giving him my "Yeah, right" face. There is no way this man has problems with the ladies. In fact, the only issue Logan probably has with women is which one to choose. He's got to be beating them off with a stick.

"Get the heck out of here, Logan. I know you've got women lining up to be with you."

"I'm more interested in quality than quantity. The great women out here are few and far between. As a matter of fact, I think that great women are an endangered species."

"Well, what is your definition of a great woman? You keep saying that. I hear women looking for a good man, but you are looking for a *great* woman."

Logan stretches his long legs out in front of the table and grazes my leg in the process. I jump like I've been electrocuted by a live wire.

"A great woman is someone who knows she's beautiful, even if she doesn't look like a movie star. A great woman knows her worth and is confident enough to support her man and chase her own dreams."

"Wow."

"Yeah. I meant it when I told Troy he had a great woman. He needs to recognize it."

"Well, I'm sure you'll find someone."

He shrugs and then lets out a long sigh. "You'd be surprised at how many times I thought I'd found the one. Then, when I tell a woman I want to be celibate until marriage, it all falls apart."

Now *this* is interesting. Actually, this is book material! I've got to hear more about this. Writing can wait.

"Come again? A celibate man? That's a new one."

"You've never heard of a God-fearing man being celibate? I don't think it's that unusual, and if it is, it shouldn't be."

"The only men that I know who are celibate are either virgins or they couldn't get it even if they paid for it. I go to church with a lot of single brothas, and the majority of them are *not* celibate. That's just real talk."

"So if there aren't any celibate men, how are the women living saved and single? They can't be celibate by themselves."

"Right. They are celibate because they are by themselves!"

This makes Logan roar with laughter. He literally has tears in his eyes, he's laughing so hard.

"Pam, you are funny!"

"I'm telling the truth, and you know it."

He clutches his side and laughs a little more. "Okay, okay. Let me clear something up. I am *not* a virgin, and obviously, I could get it if I wanted it."

"It's not that obvious," I say with a deadpan look on my face that makes Logan laugh some more.

"Anyway! I can get with a woman if I want. I just want the next woman I connect with on that level to be my wife. I spent my twenties and half of my thirties having random encounters with women. It's not what it's cracked up to be. I'm ready for something real."

"And you know what? God's gonna bless you with someone incredible. I can feel that."

"You got any friends? Wanna hook a brotha up?"

I scan my mind and try to think of a single friend who'd fit his description of a great woman. I don't have one friend who's anything like what he's looking for. And the ones that come close would probably think he's gay for not wanting to have sex.

"If I think of anyone, I'll be sure to let you know."

"You could just clone yourself, and that would be perfect."

Why does he keep saying these things to me? I feel like he's crossing some invisible line that's drawn in the atmosphere. Maybe he's ignoring the line, or maybe I'm not making it clear that there even is a line. Either way, there's a twinge of guilt in the pit of my stomach that makes me question this entire exchange.

"Logan, I will be praying that God sends the woman you're waiting for. In the meantime, as much as I'm enjoying chopping it up with you, I really, *really* need to get some work done."

Finally, Logan stands, and a wave of relief washes over me. "Okay. I'll let you get to your work. You just make sure you don't put any of my business in that book you're writing."

"You didn't know? Anything you say to me is liable to end up on the page. I come with a disclaimer."

"I'd be honored to be in your book. Just make sure you embellish a brotha a little bit. Talk to you soon."

I wave good-bye to Logan as he leaves the Starbucks. Half of the women in here give him second and third looks as he exits the building, taking all that swagger with him. I let out another long sigh and type a few more words.

Who knows? Logan just might end up in my book. But he doesn't need any embellishment at all. In this case the truth is better than any fiction I'd ever create.

CHAPTER 12

EVA

Eva looked at the little piece of paper with Yvonne's number on it. She had considered calling more than once but couldn't think of what she'd say if Yvonne answered.

She set the paper down and picked up the ragged Bible she'd pulled out of a box in her closet. It had been her grandmother's Bible—it was the only thing Eva took from the house when she died. While everyone else argued over Grandma Susie's jewelry and furs, Eva took the thing her grandmother had cherished most.

Eva hadn't been close to Grandma Susie right before she died. The adult film industry had alienated Eva from her entire family, but especially from her grandmother. Grandma Susie wouldn't speak a word to Eva, and every time they were in the same room, Grandma Susie would just start praying.

Eva had loved her grandmother more than anything. She'd sat in Grandma Susie's lap until she was ten years old, listening to all the stories she told about growing up on a farm in Arkansas with her nine siblings. No matter what any of her cousins said, Eva knew she was her grandmother's favorite.

But everything had changed when Eva's Uncle Parnell had started touching her. He would lure Eva into his room at

Grandma Susie's house with a treat or a pretty toy and then touch her in places no little girl should be touched.

Eva remembered hating the touches, but she loved her uncle and didn't want him to be angry with her. She'd kept the abuse secret for years before she told her mother, who was by then already on drugs.

When the secret was revealed, everyone was angry with her and not with Uncle Parnell. Grandma Susie had called her a little harlot for letting it go on for so long. Her mother told her she was fast and always had been.

Eva shivered and felt her eyes water at the memory of that ordeal with Uncle Parnell. She clutched Grandma Susie's Bible, trying to conjure up a good recollection to counteract the bad. She missed her grandmother—not the mean and hateful Grandma Susie that had cast Eva out of her own family, but the one who had rocked her in her arms and had read her stories from her Bible as if it was her own personal storybook.

Eva felt so alone in the world. Even though the other adult film performers weren't really her family, they were all she had. They were the only other people she'd connected with since the time that she was sixteen. Eva couldn't believe that she'd been in the industry for over twenty years.

Eva opened Grandma Susie's Bible and just started reading wherever her eyes landed. She read a story in the book of Mark about a woman who wanted a demon cast out of her child and asked Jesus for help.

Jesus's reply was, "Let the children first be filled, for it is not meet to take the children's bread, and to cast it unto the dogs."

Eva kept reading. She felt like that woman. An outcast on the outskirts of everyone who seemed blessed. All Eva wanted was a little thing from God. Nothing big. She just wanted a friend and the assurance that she wouldn't be homeless for keeping her promise to Him.

In the next verse, the woman said, "Yes, Lord, yet the dogs under the table eat of the children's crumbs."

And then Jesus did something miraculous for that woman.

He healed her daughter of her demon possession, though she wasn't one of the precious children. Even though she was an outcast.

Another tear trickled down Eva's face and landed on the page. Something told her that if she would just ask God, He would help her with what she needed, despite the fact that she hadn't done everything right. Even if she had been touched by her uncle for four years.

She felt so small, like she imagined the woman in the Bible felt. But Jesus had done a miracle in that woman's life, and Eva wondered if the same could happen in her situation.

Eva's rent was due, and she had one hundred dollars to her name. She hadn't been smart like some of the other film stars she'd known over the years. Eva hadn't saved a penny, but had spent most of it partying and living like a rock star. It had never occurred to her that one day she'd leave the industry.

Eva put down the Bible and picked up the phone. It was dinnertime for most people, but Yvonne had said to call her anytime.

"Hello?" Yvonne said when she answered the phone.

"Um, hi, Sister Yvonne. It's Eva."

There was a long pause. Eva thought it was because Yvonne didn't recognize her voice. Then finally Yvonne replied, "Oh! Eva, how are you?"

"Well . . . did I catch you at a bad time?"

"I was just on my way out to Bible study, but it's not a bad time. You want to talk about something?"

"I do. Maybe I'll just come up to the church and see you face-to-face. Is that okay?"

"Of course it is, honey! I'm looking forward to us talking again."

This made Eva smile. She couldn't think of anyone else right now who'd be looking forward to seeing her or talking to her. A feeling of warmth filled her body.

"I'm looking forward to it, too."

"Well, come on, then. It's funny you called me just now. I

think God must have a Word for both of us tonight. What do you think?"

Eva looked down at the Bible on the table and said, "I think God already gave me one Word today, but I sure wouldn't pass up another one."

Yvonne laughed into the phone. It was a melodic laugh, which Eva enjoyed hearing. "Ain't nothing wrong with being greedy over God. See you at church!"

"Okay, Sister Yvonne."

Even after Yvonne disconnected the call, Eva sat there holding the phone, in awe of what had just happened. She thought that maybe she'd found a friend for the first time since she was a teenager.

But she wondered, would Yvonne want to be friends with one of the dogs?

CHAPTER 13

TAYLOR

"**M**a, I don't want to go to Bible study. Why can't you and Spencer just leave me here?"

This boy is really about to get on my last nerve. He just started this mess calling Spencer by his first name instead of Daddy. It hurts Spencer's feelings, but it just makes me mad.

"Your father and I aren't going to leave you at home, Joshua. You are only eleven. You can't take care of yourself."

"Yes, I can. Those kids in the youth Bible study are lame. I'm not feeling that tonight."

I put my hand on my hip and frown. "Even Gretchen and Cicely? They're lame, too?"

"They're girls. Plus, they be snitching."

Spencer walks into the room and kisses me on my neck. "What's going on in here?" he asks. "You arguing with your mother?"

Joshua says, "No, I'm not arguing. I'm just saying that y'all can leave me at home and it'll be okay."

Spencer points to the couch. "Sit down, Joshua. We want to talk to you about something."

"Now?" I ask. I knew that Spencer wanted to have a conversation with Joshua about Luke, but I was trying to put it off until the very last second. I want to give Luke plenty of time to change his mind about being in Joshua's life.

"Whatever it is, I didn't do it," Joshua says. "I swear I haven't done anything since I got into it with my teacher."

"Don't swear!" I say as I sit down next to Joshua.

Spencer continues to stand. "You haven't done anything, Joshua, and you're not in trouble."

"Oh. What's this about, then?"

I take my son's hand in mine. "Well, son, your biological father wants to meet you and spend time with you."

Joshua looks alarmed as his mouth drops open just wide enough for me to feel his breath on my face. "Why does he want to meet me?"

"Well, because he's made some changes in his life, and he thinks that now he has something to offer you, I guess," I say.

Joshua looks at Spencer and asks, "Are you cool with this?"

"Yes, as long as it's okay with your mother."

"Well, what if I'm not cool with it? Who is he, anyway? I don't even know his name."

I clear my throat and drop Joshua's hand. I knew this day was coming, ever since I first decided to keep the secret of Joshua's paternity during my pregnancy. When Joshua was little, he asked me all the time what his daddy looked like and who his daddy was. The questions stopped when he was five, because that was when Spencer became a permanent fixture in both our lives.

"His name is Luke," I say. "Luke Hastings."

"Hastings? Like Auntie Yvonne? Are they related?"

I look to Spencer for a rescue, but he doesn't say anything. He nods at me like I should just continue. Should I tell Joshua the truth? I don't know if he's old enough to understand what happened with Luke, or if he'll ever be old enough to understand it.

"He used to be married to your auntie Yvonne. He's her ex-husband."

Joshua is clearly confused now. He looks from me to Spencer

and then back to me again. "You hooked up with Auntie Yvonne's husband?"

I let out a huge sigh. "It's hard to explain. Yvonne and I weren't friends then, but it was still a mistake. The only thing I don't regret about it is you."

"Ma! I can't believe this! This is some ho type stuff you talking 'bout!"

Joshua jumps up from the couch before I have time to lay hands on him, but he's not quick enough for Spencer. Spencer grabs him by his arm and snatches him up, suspending him in midair.

"Apologize to your mother right now, or by God, I will beat the mess out of you."

"My mama ain't gonna let you hit me!"

Spencer looks at me, as if for permission, and I nod. Spencer smacks Joshua three times across the backs of his legs, and Joshua falls to the floor, wailing in agony.

"You ain't my daddy! Keep your hands off me!"

"Get up! Go wash your face, and get ready for Bible study. But first, apologize to your mother."

"I'm sorry," Joshua sobs.

I nod my forgiveness, because I'm still too shocked to speak. Did my son just call me a ho? Did that really just happen to me? This is worse than anything that ever happened while I carried him in my belly with no ring on my finger.

Joshua scampers out of the room just before my tears fall. "Spence . . ."

My husband sits down next to me on the couch and wraps me in his arms. "He didn't mean it, babe. He didn't. You just shocked him."

Now my tears are sobs that make my entire body shake. I feel that the only thing holding me together in one piece is Spencer's hug.

"We'll get through this," he says. "But I don't think that he should meet Luke."

"No. Let him meet him. Let him see for himself how Luke is

rotten to the very core. He wants to think I'm a ho? Well, let him meet his ho daddy."

Spencer doesn't reply with words. He pulls me in closer and strokes my hair as I continue to cry.

Maybe everything that's happening with Joshua—his anger, getting expelled, and everything else—is my fault. Even after repentance and after forgiveness, consequences are still coming into my life. I'm still paying for my sins with Luke.

While my husband holds me, I talk to God. *Lord, I know you've forgiven me. I know it, but I am still reaping. Please, God, don't let my baby reap, too.*

CHAPTER 14

YVONNE

I got flowers today at work. For the first time in my life, I got a bouquet of roses delivered to me. I was excited and happy about it, until it occurred to me how pitiful it was that I'm forty-seven years old and I'm just now getting flowers from a man.

Of course, they were from Kingston. He keeps smiling at me, when he should be paying attention to Bible study. He seems so proud of himself, but I'm not sure how I should respond. I know what everyone is telling me, but I still don't know what to do.

I always thought that if I found out Luke had moved on, I'd be free of our marriage and all the things that happened to me at Luke's hands. But I don't know if it's freedom that I feel.

When Taylor told me about Luke getting married, I felt . . . jealous. Why would I feel jealous over that man? I know that I don't still love him. What kind of fool would I be to love some-one who beat me within an inch of my life and slept with church members? A big fool, and if I messed around with Luke, probably a dead fool.

Eva walks into the gymnasium, where we hold Bible study, and I see her scanning the room, probably looking for me. I wave at her, and she takes a few hesitant steps in my direction. I'm in the front row. Maybe she doesn't want to sit up here, on display.

I quickly gather my things and walk back to where Eva is stand-

ing, and I see relief all over her face. I must've been right. I
haven't been a new member in a long time, so sometimes I forget what that feels like.

Eva's two-piece jogging suit and gym shoes are a little bit on
the casual side for our congregation, but she does look nice
and neat with her long brown hair pulled into a ponytail. It
gives me the opportunity to really look at her extremely pretty
face. She's got a tiny nose that's sprinkled with freckles and nat-
urally thick and perfectly arched eyebrows. Her eyelashes are
long and thick, as well, and her full pink lips wouldn't ever
need lipstick if she didn't want to wear it. I think the focal point
·of her face is her light brown eyes, which possess a hint of sadness. Makeup free, the girl is a stunner, and I'm sure I'm not
the only one who notices.

"You didn't have to switch seats, Sister Yvonne," Eva whispers.

"Well, I want to sit next to you, and you didn't seem like you
wanted to sit up front."

Eva's face lights up with a smile. "I didn't want to sit up there.
I don't have on the right clothes."

"Jesus doesn't care what you're wearing, girl."

We take a seat at one of the rear tables. I notice that Eva's
Bible is very old and very worn, but when Pastor Brown tells us
to turn to the book of Ephesians, she has trouble finding it.
Someone wore that Bible out, but it sure wasn't Eva.

Eva seems very preoccupied during the lesson. She fidgets
with her hands and absentmindedly flips pages in the Bible. I
place one hand over hers and whisper a prayer to myself.

Then I say to her, "Whatever it is, it's going to be all right."

Maybe I should've waited until after Bible study to say this to
her, because she bursts into violent tears. When she sees that
she's drawing attention to herself, she claps her hand over her
mouth, grabs her Bible and purse, and rushes out of the gymnasium. I follow at her heels, because even though I said that it
would be all right, her reaction tells me it's worse than I
thought.

Outside, Eva paces back and forth across the parking lot, in
tears and shaking the hand that's not holding her Bible.

"What's wrong?" I ask her. "How can I help?"

"I don't think you can help, Yvonne. No one can help me."

I pause and breathe in deeply. She sounds desperate. "Maybe I can't, but God can. Why don't you tell me what's wrong?"

"I—I don't have the money for my rent. I don't have anywhere to go. I'm gonna be homeless soon."

"Is that all? I most definitely can help with that. We have a shelter here at the church. There are only a few rooms, but it will hold you until we can get you a job. I'll talk to Pastor Brown as soon as service lets out."

"You'd do this for me, and you don't even know me! I could be a murderer or something."

"And if you asked God, he'd forgive you. Why do you want me to think the worst of you?"

Eva begins to cry again. "Because nobody in this world thinks the best of me. Why should you be different?"

I encircle her in my arms as her entire body shakes with her tears. "Nobody in this world matters, Eva. God sees the best in you. He does."

"If you knew the truth about me, you wouldn't hold me like you're doing right now." Eva's voice is tiny and sorrowful. The most pitiful thing I've ever heard.

"Whatever you're keeping is between you and God."

Pam rushes out of the gymnasium and over to me and Eva. "Is everything okay?" Pam asks.

"Yes. Sister Eva just had something she needed to get off her chest. I've got this. Can you do me a favor and let Kingston know that I had to leave early? We're supposed to have dinner, but I'm going to help Eva tonight."

"I can help her," Pam says. "Is that okay with you, Eva? Go on your date, Yvonne."

I feel Eva's body tense in my arms, and I hand her a tissue from my pocket. "He'll understand. Let me handle this."

Pam nods. "All right. I'll tell him. Call me later, okay? Let me know if there's anything I can do to help."

"Okay."

As Pam walks back toward the gymnasium, I release Eva from

my embrace. "Have you eaten? You want some dinner? I could go for some seafood."

Eva gazes at me the way a little girl looks at her mama when she hurts herself or gets a scrape and needs comforting. Even though she's not young enough to be my daughter, her facial expression releases something maternal in me. I want to take care of her like, it seems, no one ever has before.

CHAPTER 15

PAM

When I pull into my driveway from Bible study, I see Logan's car parked in front of our house. My first instinct is to pull back out and find somewhere else to go, but the children are tired, and they have school in the morning. I can't drag them around the city just because I don't want to look at my husband's friend.

No, that's wrong. I *do* want to look at my husband's friend, and that is the problem.

I haven't been able to get him out of my mind since we met at Starbucks the other day. I'm afraid that if Troy sees me in the same room with him, he'll know, that is, he'll be able to tell how Logan's flirting affected me.

Before I can make a mad dash for it, Troy comes out onto the porch. He's on his cell phone, and he waves at me to come on in.

I hurry and park and rush the children inside, with my heart pounding the entire time. I go in the back door to avoid walking through Troy's work area. This house is big enough to engulf a small army, so I should be able to get to my bedroom without having to see Logan.

But it's just my luck that Logan is standing in my kitchen, drinking a glass of water and looking like a tall drink of water at the same time. The children squeal with delight. They like Logan, too.

"Uncle Logan!" TJ says as he gives Logan a fist bump.

The girls wave and give him hugs before scurrying out of the kitchen, probably looking for their daddy.

"Hey, Logan," I say.

"Hey, Pam. Get any good writing done today?"

"No, not really."

"Still distracted?"

I take a nervous swallow. How could I not be distracted? The scent of his cologne has a dizzying effect on me. "Uh . . ."

Troy pokes his head into the kitchen. "Come on, man! I just put Aria in the booth, and she's about to knock this song out tonight."

"Cool. Just getting some water."

Troy nods. "You want something else? Pam can get it. Pam, can you fix us some tea or something? Aria might need it for her voice."

How about a "Hello, Pam" or "How was Bible study, Pam?" Troy really gets on my nerves sometimes, and now is so not the time for him to be getting on my nerves.

"Pam doesn't have to get me anything," Logan says. "I'm pretty capable of finding my own snacks."

"That's cool, too. *Mi casa es su casa*. Just hurry up with whatever you're gonna do so we can get this song mixed down."

"I'll be there in a sec."

I put on a kettle of water for tea and take out a tray and fill it with tea bags, cups, and sugar cubes. Logan leans back on the counter and watches me in silence.

"Don't let him treat you that way," Logan says.

"What way? He's just asking for some tea. That's what husbands do. They ask for stuff."

He clears his throat. "Now you're defending him. That's interesting. I'm just making an observation, that's all. I'm sorry if I overstepped my boundaries."

"You've absolutely overstepped your boundaries."

"I'm sorry. I guess I'm just trying to be your friend."

"You're Troy's friend. That's good enough. Leave the rest of it alone."

"Do you really want that? I enjoy talking to you. You're funny, smart, and I admit, I don't have many friends."

"Well, I've got plenty."

I pile a few more items on the tray and grab the tea kettle as it begins to whistle. Logan turns on the faucet and fills his water glass again.

"Is it because you're attracted to me?" he asks.

"Please, get over yourself. I'm not attracted to you." I've never been a very good liar. The quiver in my voice gives me away.

"Well, I am attracted to you," Logan says. "But you are my friend's wife, so I'm ignoring those feelings."

"Good."

I push past Logan with the tray and head down the long hallway to the study, which Troy turned into his studio when he lost the lease on the warehouse he got when we first became millionaires. He's seated at the keyboard, tapping a few keys. Aria is seated at Troy's desk with her head in her hands, gazing at my husband the way she's gazed at him from day one. I keep telling myself it's only admiration, but I fear that it's more than that. Logan comes in right behind me.

"Here's your tea, Troy. I'm gonna be upstairs."

"Thanks, babe. You don't want to stay and watch us record?"

"I really have to get some work done on my book. I've been so busy this week, and now it's already half gone."

"All right. Get that book money, then. I'll be up in a few hours."

"Good night, Pam," Logan says. "See you next time."

"Good night."

"Pam, can I ask you something?" Aria says. "Do you mind if my boyfriend comes over when I record? I know how you are about people in your house around your kids."

Troy says, "I already told you it was okay."

"But it's Pam's house, too, and I don't want her to be mad at me. I think we're finally friends, and I don't want to ruin it."

This is so out of the blue that I don't even know how to take it. Aria and I hardly ever exchange words, and I certainly don't consider her a friend. I am happy to hear that she has a boyfriend, though.

"As long as Troy doesn't mind, I don't have a problem with it."

"Thanks, Pam."

I wave good-bye to everyone as I leave the room. When I get upstairs to my bedroom and close the door, I finally relax.

My cell phone buzzes in my pocket. "Hello?"

"Pam, are you really not attracted to me?"

I hold the phone away from my face in shock. "Logan, what are you doing? Where are you calling me from?"

"I'm outside."

"Well, go back indoors before Troy wonders what you're doing."

"Why would Troy be in my mix like that? I'll go back inside when you tell me the truth."

"Oh well, stand outside, then. I don't care. See you later. Wait. How'd you get my number?"

"I took it out of Troy's phone."

"You what?" Now I'm feeling a bit alarmed.

Then I hear Logan laughing on the phone. "Pam, I'm teasing you! You looked so crazy at me in the kitchen. I wanted to smooth everything out."

"Everything is fine."

"Okay, then be honest. You think I'm hot."

This makes me burst into laughter. "No, I don't."

"You do! It's okay, because most women find me irresistible. I am well aware of the effect that I have on women. Now that we have that out of the way, we're going to be great friends."

"You're pretty conceited."

"Well, then you understand why I don't have a woman. Maybe you can help me with that."

"This is the most juvenile conversation I've ever had with a man. I've got work to do."

"Juvenile? I thought we were having a little fun."

"I don't know what that means, Logan."

"Okay, I'll let you work now."

I disconnect the call and place my phone back into my pocket. I open up my laptop and try to concentrate on my manuscript and ignore the completely warm feeling in the pit of my stomach.

CHAPTER 16

YVONNE

After I had dinner with Eva, I agreed to meet with Kingston for a late dessert at this little bistro on Coventry that also has a live jazz band. I don't think he was happy about me skipping out on our dinner date, but he has to understand how important ministry is to me. Eva needed me more this evening than Kingston did.

I talked to Pastor Brown for her, and Eva will be able to move into one of the church shelters on the first of the month. She also shared that she never graduated from high school, so Pam and I are going to help her study for her GED examination.

"So the young lady at Bible study tonight is your new project?" Kingston asks.

"She's not a project. She's a soul that needs saving."

"I didn't mean it in a negative way, Yvonne. I just noticed that you've been paying her a lot of attention since she started coming to New Faith. That's a good thing. We should always mentor the newly converted."

"She's got a few things to overcome, but she's off to a great start."

"What about us? Are we off to a great start?"

I smile at him and take a small bite of my caramel apple

cake. "I was wondering when the conversation was going to turn back to that."

"You knew that it would."

"I did, but I wanted to see how you would transition. You're pretty smooth."

Kingston strokes his tie and chuckles. "Yes, I am."

"So last time we talked about me. I'm from the South, divorced, been here in Cleveland for twenty years, and now I teach English to a bunch of rowdy, hormonal teenagers. Tell me about you."

"I think you know that I'm from Detroit. I used to sing in an R & B group before I accepted Christ."

"Really? What were you called?" I ask.

"The Operators. We were a local sensation, and we did a lot of shows. We opened up for New Edition once."

"Were you the lead vocalist?"

Kingston nods. "Yes, one of them. I hit the high notes when necessary, and my cousin Joseph did the low parts."

"Oh, so you were out there hitting high notes like a DeBarge, huh?"

"I was better than a DeBarge."

I frown and scrunch up my face. "I don't play when it comes to DeBarge. You better take that back."

"What's your favorite DeBarge song?"

"'Time Will Reveal.'"

To my surprise, Kingston jumps up and walks over to the band. He whispers something to the keyboard player and then takes the stage.

The lead singer says, "I want y'all to give it up for our brother Kingston. He wants to serenade his lady tonight. Some of y'all might know him from church, but this cat here used to have more panties thrown at him than Prince in his heyday."

Kingston laughs and takes the microphone. "Maybe not Prince, but I'll do my best. This is for a real special lady."

I blush as Kingston starts singing one of my favorite songs.

When he hits those high notes, I forget all about El DeBarge. I stand from my seat and dance in front of the table when he gets to the chorus. *I know just how you feel, but this time love's for real.*

Then I'm not only dancing, but also singing along, like we're the only ones in the restaurant. Usually I'd be looking over my shoulder to make sure no one from church was looking at me, but something about Kingston makes me feel so carefree.

When Kingston is finished with the song, everyone in the restaurant gives him a round of applause and a standing ovation, but no one is clapping louder than I am. He walks back to our table with a smile on his face and gives me a chaste hug. Then he waits for me to sit before he takes his seat again.

"I hope I didn't ruin your song," Kingston says. "I did my best."

"You know you were up there blowing! I'm surprised that microphone didn't melt."

Kingston laughs so hard that his shoulders shake. "That was fun. I haven't sung anything like that in a long time."

"It was great. I am really enjoying myself."

"Me too. You know, I almost gave up on asking you out."

"I'm glad that you didn't."

Kingston places one hand over mine. "I'm glad you finally said yes. What would you like to do on our next date?"

"It's up to me?"

I don't even know what to say. I'm used to a man making all the decisions in a relationship. I never had any choices with Luke. It was all about what he wanted, and I was just supposed to submit. I didn't even know what I liked to do until I left him.

"Yes. The next date is your pick."

"Well, I like boats. Do you want to go to Put-in-Bay? We can ride the ferry across at Port Clinton and spend the day on the island."

"That sounds romantic, Yvonne."

"Does it? Oh, I didn't think of it that way. I thought it would just be fun."

Kingston grins and tastes his coffee. "I would love to have a romantic day with you. Don't apologize for dreaming it up. I'm looking forward to it."

Well, now I just feel foolish. I know Kingston is enjoying this teasing, but I am not at all comfortable with being romantic with him. I'm just getting used to being his friend.

"I'm looking forward to it also."

I drag my gaze away from Kingston's beautiful hazel eyes and stare into my coffee cup. I am so glad that he is all the way across the table and has no idea about the way my heart is pounding.

"Is there anything else you want to know about me, Yvonne?" Kingston asks in a non-flirtatious, but still friendly tone.

"Why aren't you already married?"

Kingston raises his eyebrows and turns up his coffee cup, finishing it off. Then he slowly sets it back down.

"Straight to the point, huh?"

"Was that not a second-date question? Was that more like a fifth-date question? Forgive me. I've never dated anyone."

"Not even your ex-husband?"

I shake my head. "If you call coming over to my mama's house after Bible class dating, then I guess so, but it wasn't anything like this."

"That's kind of a good thing. I can pull out every play in my playbook, and it'll be brand new to you."

"I'll still know if you can step it up some. I do have girl-friends, you know."

"I know you do. I'm just glad to get the opportunity."

"Mmm-hmm . . . Now answer the question."

"Oh, well, I've been married twice already. Both times they left me."

Now, this is information to take back to Pam and Taylor for analysis. Two women left him? Either he's really unlucky in love or you can't tell by looking at him that he's got some issues.

"I know what you're thinking now," Kingston says when I don't reply. "You're wondering what is wrong with me."

"I'm just waiting for your explanation, if you want to give one. If not, I won't press you for it."

"The first marriage I was too young. We were both too young. She decided being married to a musician wasn't as fun as it seemed like it would be."

"What happened to the second wife?"

Kingston laughs, even though I'm as serious as a heart attack. "She's happy and healthy in Los Angeles with her second husband. He was her high school sweetheart, and she decided he was her soul mate."

I'm not silly enough to believe that there's not much more to these stories, but at least he is willing to share something private about himself. Everyone in our church knows my story. Luke is an infamous legend.

"So would you get married again?"

"Absolutely! I don't think I've found my soul mate yet."

"Soul mate? I hear people say that all the time, but I don't think I know what it means."

"I think it's that one person that God has picked out for you."

"Well, that's pretty simple."

"I don't think love is supposed to be hard."

"I don't either."

Kingston smiles. "That's a great thing for us to agree on, Yvonne."

"Can we agree on one more thing?"

"What's that?"

"You singing another song?"

If Kingston's almost permanent smile can get any bigger, it does. "Yes, ma'am. But this time I'm not singing DeBarge."

I sit in my chair, brimming with excitement as I watch Kingston talk to the band members. Then he gets on the microphone again, and he winks at me and grins before the music starts.

When I hear the first few notes of the song, I put my hands

over my mouth to keep from screaming like a teenager. It's "Hello" by Lionel Richie—one of my favorite love songs. And as much as I love me some Lionel Richie, I think Kingston's got him beat. The raw emotion in his voice when he sings "Tell me how to win your heart, for I haven't got a clue" scares me a little.

Oh, Lord Jesus. It scares me a lot.

CHAPTER 17

TAYLOR

This is so not the time to have this little meeting with Luke, but he insists on pressing the issue. Joshua has been home with me every day, since he's been expelled for the rest of the school year, and he's on my last nerve. I don't know what I was thinking when I said I was gonna homeschool this boy. And he's got the audacity to still have something of an attitude about Spencer spanking him. I bet he won't fix his mouth to call me out my name again.

Luke wanted to meet at our house, but I wasn't having that. He said it was to make Joshua more comfortable, but I think he's trying not to spend any money on his son. Don't get me wrong. I know it's not just about a check; it's about the relationship, too. Joshua may not be lacking a thing on the physical needs side, but somehow Spencer and I aren't connecting with him like we need to be. Maybe if Joshua sees how much of a loser Luke is, he'll recognize that Spencer is a winner.

To make it easy on Luke's wallet, we're meeting him at Applebee's, and as usual Luke is late. He always wants someone to anticipate his arrival. He may be redeemed or whatever, but he's still completely as self-centered as ever.

Joshua sees him step into the restaurant before I do. It's like my baby has immediate recognition. He has seen Luke before, but I didn't expect him to remember Luke.

"Is that my father?" Joshua asks.

"That's Luke."

I should've just said yes, but I can't bring myself to call Luke his father. Spencer rubs the middle of my back, as if he understands my struggle. I know that he doesn't exactly know how I feel, but he tries to be of help.

Luke spots us at our table and rushes over. His has a big, friendly smile on his face, even though I'm straight up mean mugging. Joshua looks as if he hasn't decided how to feel yet. He's not smiling, but he's not frowning, either.

It's almost like he's in anticipation of something. I know that look. I remember having it when I was a little girl, every time someone said anything about my daddy. My aunties would say, "She looks just like her daddy," and my mother would say, "Even if he don't come around, your daddy does love you." And my brothers and I would get excited, but I think neither of them felt it more than I did.

The older I got, the more that anticipation turned to disappointment, because my father never did step up to the plate. I never even met him; I only saw faded pictures my mother saved. I hope Luke doesn't disappoint my baby. If he does, he's going to have to deal with me.

Still smiling, Luke sits down at our table, across from Joshua. Spencer and I flank Joshua on either side—a protective stance.

Luke extends his hand to Spencer, and Spencer looks at the hand as if it's diseased, but finally shakes it. Luke chuckles at this and doesn't bother to shake my hand or Joshua's.

"Hello, Joshua," Luke says. "I'm Luke Hastings, your father."

Both Spencer and I flinch, but neither of us responds to Luke. We decided ahead of time to intervene only if he says something damaging or hurtful to Joshua. I'll read Luke later, but right now, in front of my son, I'm going to be the bigger person.

"Why haven't I met you before this?" Joshua asks.

I want to jump up, do the cabbage patch, and give my son

two high fives and a fist bump. My baby might have a few anger management issues, but he is not stupid, not by any stretch of the imagination. Luke thinks he's gonna come up in here charming folk. Nope. Not!

Luke clears his throat and looks at the table. Then he stares into Joshua's eyes with a look so intense, it makes my muscles tense.

"I don't have a good answer to that question. I was married to my ex-wife when you were conceived, so that is part of it. Then . . . well, I guess I haven't been a good person. I'm trying to change. I think God has already forgiven me, but I'll have to earn it from everyone else. I'm sorry that I haven't been around, Joshua, but I sure am glad to see you now."

Joshua stares back at Luke, unblinking. "Nice to meet you."

I didn't know I was holding my breath until I exhaled. Joshua stands up from his seat, walks around the table, and encircles Luke with his arms. Luke hugs him back, nearly crushes him with a bear hug. Both have tears in their eyes, and even I feel emotional at this scene.

When Joshua was little, all I ever wanted Luke to do was acknowledge his son in some way, even if he couldn't raise him. I wanted him to place a hand on his head and say, "This boy is mine. He belongs to me." It didn't happen then, but it's happening now.

Although Luke and Joshua's connection is heartwarming, Spencer's expression is heartbreaking. He hasn't had a hug from Joshua in months, but this buster blows in from never-never land and gets all the love and understanding our son can give. I want to stand on the table and demand that Luke stop all this hugging and get current on his child support payments.

My son is a bigger person than I am, it seems.

"Now that I've listened to God and reached out to you, nothing can keep me from you, son."

"Do you like soccer?" Joshua asks. "I play soccer and basketball."

"I love soccer, but I can't play much anymore." Luke points to his eye patch. "But I can watch you with my other eye."

"What happened to your eye?" Joshua asks as he sits in the seat next to Luke. I don't like this. He's moved outside of my protection.

"I was in a fight in prison."

"Did you win?" Joshua asks.

"No, son. I lost my eye and the fight."

Joshua seems disappointed, and I'm surprised. I expected Luke to say something like, "You should see the other guy." None of this is turning out the way I think it should.

"You got him later, right?" Joshua says.

Luke shakes his head. "No, I didn't. I prayed for him."

"What?" Joshua says. "That's lame."

"Maybe it is. But I went to prison because of my anger. I didn't want to stay there because of it."

I can't take this anymore! This saint routine is going to make my head explode!

"Can we order something to eat?" I say. "I'm starving!"

Luke and Joshua snap their heads in my direction simultaneously, both looking annoyed that I ruined their moment. Whatever. And they have the audacity to look like twins, too.

"Mom, next time can I see my dad by myself?" Joshua asks.

"We'll talk about that later, baby."

"Let's talk about it now, Taylor," Luke says.

Oh no, they don't think they're about to double-team me. I don't even think so!

Spencer says, "Luke, we've been cordial and agreeable to you thus far, but you are not in control of this situation. We can let the courts decide if you want to press the issue."

"I don't believe this has anything to do with you, Spencer. My son is not your concern."

"My wife is my concern, and so is Joshua. I've raised him, and I was there when you weren't."

"You don't need to remind me of that. Not a day goes by that I don't think of my son being raised by someone other than me. But I'm back now, and I'm not going anywhere."

My stomach sinks like a boulder in my midsection. I've never seen Joshua this happy, and I've never been more fearful of the future. Luke's declarations sound like threats.

"You're not running anything, Luke," I say.

He shakes his head and sighs. "Taylor, I wish you and your husband had waited until after dinner to threaten me. Arguing before a meal always ruins my digestion."

Looking at Luke and hearing his voice do more than ruin my digestion—they turn my blood ice cold. I don't care how many churches he's started and how many fiancées he has, this man has not changed, and I'd be a bad mother if I let Luke and his demons into my son's life unchecked.

I am a great mother.

CHAPTER 18

PAM

I don't know what Troy and I were thinking when we bought this gigantic house! Cleaning it is more than a notion, especially since we had to let the housekeeper go because we couldn't afford her anymore. The kids help out some, but Troy does absolutely nothing, even though his studio-study area is the worst part of the house.

I haven't given this room a good cleaning since Troy moved all of his equipment in here two years ago. When I almost choked on a dust ball the other day while trying to listen to Troy's new song, I decided to clean it as soon as Troy was gone for an extended amount of time. Aria has a show in Cincinnati, at Kings Island amusement park, for their opening weekend, and Troy tagged along. I would've complained about the trip, except Troy took the kids with him, giving me a couple of quiet days to write.

But first, I have to get this place clean. Just knowing that those dust bunnies are hiding under my furniture and on top of the ceiling fan is messing with my creative process.

I start by removing the first layer of dust from everything. The keyboards, speakers, amps, computer stands, and underneath the couch. Then I remove the couch cushions and get all the candy, chicken nuggets, and spare change—which I should probably put in a jar somewhere for a rainy day. Last but not least, I tackle Troy's desk. His stacks of papers are so heinous that even they're dusty.

I want to throw everything away, but then I hesitate. It would be just my luck if I threw away a contract or receipt or something he actually needs in the midst of his candy wrappers and fast-food bags.

There are three stacks, one for bills—that he probably hasn't paid—one for things that look important, which I'm unsure about, and one for trash. Of course, the trash pile is the largest of the three.

I'm almost done straightening the desk when I find a cream-colored envelope with Troy's name written on the front of it. It's too small to be a greeting card, and the handwriting is curly and pretty—a woman's writing.

I turn the envelope over and over in my hand, wanting to open it, but at the same time wanting to shred it without knowing what's on the inside. Then the scent hits my nose. It's a musky and sexy scent. A familiar scent. I've smelled it for the last eight years.

After swallowing a few times, I carefully open the envelope. I have no idea why I'm trying to preserve it, but something tells me not to rip into it like I want. Involuntary tears roll down my face as I read the words on the page.

Troy,

Happy birthday, babe. You aren't growing older, just sexier. Like wine, you get better every year.

Unfortunately, for every year that passes that we're not together, I feel all my good years being wasted. I want children. You can't imagine how it felt to watch your wife carry your child when I wished it could've been me.

I'm moving on, Troy. My boyfriend loves me. He can't fully have my heart, because part of it belongs to you, but he will be good to me.

*I wish things could've been different, but maybe we'll meet in
another life or an alternate reality where we're both free to love.*
     Yours forever,
     Aria

I drop the letter to the floor when my trembling hands can
no longer hold it. I don't know if I should cry or jump for joy.
It's obvious that Troy didn't return all her affections, but did he
return any of them? Did they sleep together? Is this why he's
worked so hard for her career to take off? Is he planning to
leave me once she blows up so that they can be together?

I close my eyes and breathe deeply, trying to calm myself
down, but there's no calm way to deal with the fact that your
husband might have had a mistress. Might still have a mistress.

The *nerve* of Troy! Even if he doesn't want her, how dare he
have my children around this woman, who obviously is hopelessly in love with him? How dare he have her in my home? I
had thought when Troy and I had our rough patch with his
drinking and driving that it would be the biggest challenge of
our marriage.

But this is worse.

I remember lying on my face, praying for Troy. Praying for
his life and his salvation. Praying that he'd get up out of that
hospital bed and be okay.

And while I was praying, that ho was scheming on my man.

I take my cell phone out of my pocket and call Taylor, but
her phone goes directly to voice mail. She's got enough going
on right now, anyway, without this to add to it. I think of calling
Yvonne, but she is too much of a prayer warrior. Right now I
need my ride-or-die friend. I don't want to pray about this right
now. I want to drive to Cincinnati and pull out every strand of
weave on Aria's head and put my entire foot up Troy's behind.

The clock on Troy's desk says three o'clock. I could be in
Cincinnati by seven, and Aria's butt could be beat by five after
seven. If only my kids weren't there. I can't let my children see
me acting like a fool, no matter how much I want to handle this
the street way.

I wonder if Aria's *love* for Troy is what made him take the kids with him to Cincinnati. Maybe he's trying to keep her from making a move. Maybe he thinks having the children there will keep him honest.

No. He's not getting a pass. If Troy really wanted to be kept honest, he would've told me about this and found himself a new artist.

I call Taylor's cell phone again. It goes to voice mail again. Then I call Troy. He answers.

"Hey, sweetie. Me and the kids are in line for a roller coaster."

"For real? My son doesn't like roller coasters."

"Well, he's gonna ride today! He's tall enough. It's time for him to man up."

"Where's Aria?"

"Oh, I don't know. Somewhere with her fiancé, I think. We won't meet up until it's time for the show."

He doesn't sound like he's cheating on me. As a matter of fact, I've never been surer of anything else. I will interrogate him about Aria, but it can wait. The children haven't had fun time with Troy in a very long time.

"Okay, well, call me later and let me know how the show went."

"I will definitely call you later. I was thinking maybe we could get on Skype and, you know . . ."

I close my eyes and shake my head. I just found a letter from my husband's possible mistress, and he's asking for an Internet peep show. Only in my world does this type of thing happen.

"Maybe, Troy."

"What maybe? I'm your husband, or are you entertaining some other brotha at my house?"

"Of course not."

"Well, then, you better be in front of that laptop in some lingerie as soon as I get those kids to sleep. That's the only reason I got a two bedroom suite."

"Can the kids hear you?"

"No! They ran ahead. I'm for real, Pam. Don't play me out."

"Call me later."

"Okay, babe."

If I'm not going to Cincinnati, I've got to do something to kill the time until Troy gets home. I pick up the letter off the floor, put it back in the envelope, and place the envelope deep in the stack of important papers. Maybe if it's out of my sight, it'll stay out of my mind for a while.

Writing is the only thing that can help move this mess to the back of my mind. I'd rather sort out the lives of my characters than this mess.

I pack up my laptop and drive to Starbucks, looking like someone hit me with the ugly stick. My thick curls are pushed back with a headband, and I'm not wearing a stitch of makeup. My clothes don't even match. These black-and-white zebra pants really don't go with anything, but especially not an orange and pink Aéropostale T-shirt.

And of course, as soon as I take a seat at my favorite table and get set up, I run into someone I know. And not just anyone. It's Logan.

He smiles and waves at me before I can make an escape, so I just sigh and take a gulp of my coffee. Hopefully, this conversation will take only a moment and won't be too painful.

"We keep meeting here, Pam. What does that tell you?" Logan says as he approaches my table.

I watch him sit, uninvited, but not before I take in how his snug T-shirt clings to his abdominal region and shows a hint of the tattoo on his bicep. Good grief, God made this man fine.

"It tells me that you are stalking me."

"I was coming here first."

"I've been coming to this Starbucks for years, man!"

"Okay, I admit it. Ever since I ran into you last week, I've been stopping in, hoping to see you again."

"And that doesn't sound stalkerish to you?"

"No . . . well, yes, but only from your perspective. I call it trying to link up with a friend."

"Mmm-hmmm."

"How's the book coming? Have you gotten much work done since our last encounter?"

Encounter? Logan is tripping. We bumped into each other quite accidentally while both of us were getting coffee. That does not constitute an encounter.

"I've gotten some done. About twenty pages."

"And this is the second book, right? When does the first one come out?"

"January of next year. It was already written when I signed the deal. The one I'm working on isn't due until December."

"So we've got months to keep meeting each other here."

I narrow my eyes at him and frown. "I am going to find a new, *secret* writing spot."

Logan snatches his shirt near his heart and gasps. "What? Why would you do that?"

"Because I am a married woman, Logan. You know the rest."

"Why do you think I'm trying to take you from Troy? Do you want to know the real reason I've been trying to meet you here again?"

I nod. "Yes, and it better be good."

Logan reaches into his inner jacket pocket and pulls out a stack of folded-up pages. He hands them over to me.

"I wanted to ask you to read my writing. I've been writing a novel for about ten years, and you're the only person I know with a book deal."

I smooth the browned and dog-eared pages out on the table. Clearly, he's had these for a long time. From the looks of them, they definitely predate our meeting, so maybe he is being sincere.

Immediately, I'm captivated by his writing style. The passage is about a young woman who works in her grandmother's soul food restaurant and meets a wealthy entrepreneur who shows interest, but he's unattractive. At the end of the seven pages, I want more. I'm already rooting for the characters, and I want them together. How he managed to do that in seven pages leaves me dumbfounded.

"This is really good, Logan. So good that I have no idea what feedback I could give you. I wouldn't even want you to read my writing. I'm embarrassed that I have a book deal and you don't."

"Maybe I would if I ever finished the book."

"You have to! I have to know what happens to Jewel and Rafael."

"It's a romance, so I'm pretty sure they live happily ever after."

"Yes, but it's all about the ride."

Logan grins suggestively. "You want me to take you for a ride?"

"I want you to take readers for a ride. Your writing is incredible."

"You're going to make me blush, Pam. As dark as I am, that's going to be a sight."

"I'm just being honest."

I hand him the pages back, and he refolds them and puts them in his jacket again. "You've inspired me to finish. I never really thought I was that good."

"I can't wait to read it."

"I guess I have some time to work on it since Troy is out of town for a couple of days. We're almost done with Aria's CD, you know?"

The mention of her name turns my mood sour. Why did he have to bring her up? "I know all about *that* project."

"I'm sorry. Did I upset you? I thought you'd want to know since you were calculating how much money Troy is going to make from royalties."

"I guess it's not the project. It's Aria. I've never liked her, so I don't like to talk about her project if I don't have to."

Logan seems genuinely surprised. "Are you serious? Aria is a sweet girl. Why don't you like her?"

I shake my head and take another sip of coffee. Of course he has no idea why anyone wouldn't like Aria. She's too gorgeous for me to dislike. He sounds as enchanted with Aria as Troy is.

"Look at me, and then think about her. Why would I want her around my husband?"

Logan looks confused. "I don't know what you mean."

"Are you kidding me? She looks like a model! She's sexy as all get out, and she sings like Beyoncé, Toni Braxton, and Chanté Moore all wrapped up in one. And plus, she wants my husband!"

"Yes, she's a great singer, and she's gorgeous, but so what? Troy isn't stupid. He knows he has a good woman. And I think all of your worry is in vain. She doesn't want Troy. She's engaged."

"She does! I found a letter that she wrote him!"

Now, why did I tell him that? I wish I could make those words fly right back into my mouth. Speaking of wide-open mouths, Logan's mouth is hanging open in utter shock.

"What did it say?" he asks.

Men are just as bad as women when wanting to know the scoop! "Nothing, really. I hate that I brought it up. Please don't tell Troy I said anything."

"I won't, but what did he say? How did he explain it?"

"I haven't said anything to him yet. I just found it today. I'm going to wait until he gets home from Cincy."

"I don't know what was in the letter, but you are a bold woman to let your husband be in another city with a woman that you have proof wants him."

Now he's got me sitting up here, feeling like a big dummy. I should be on the road, driving to kick that girl's butt.

Logan says, "I'm sorry. I guess you know Troy better than I do. Maybe he's not interested in her at all."

"Am I being stupid?"

"I think you're being a good wife. A much better wife than Troy seems to deserve."

This is the truth, and I'm so tired of trying to convince Troy of what he should already know. We've been together long enough for him to cherish me, and I am not feeling the least bit cherished.

Then it dawns on me. The thing that had been nagging me in the back of my mind since I picked up Aria's note. If Troy didn't care about Aria and her declarations of love, why did he save the note?

"Are you okay, Pam? Did you leave me?"

I draw my attention back to Logan. "I did go somewhere for a moment. I'm sorry. I was thinking about the letter again, and what I might do the next time I'm in the room with Aria."

"I think you're going to be a lady about the whole thing. I don't see any hood rat tendencies in you."

I cock my head to one side and give Logan my best sista girl neck snap. "You don't know me, Logan. You don't know what I'll do."

"Okay, I'll be Aria. You be you. Go."

"You been sleeping with my man?"

Logan shakes his head. "Nope. You sound like Squeak off *The Color Purple*. Talkin' 'bout Harpo is my man!"

I poke out my lips and roll my eyes. "Is your fiancé not enough for you? You have to have my husband, too?"

"Better, but too passive-aggressive. You're giving her too much power here. It's like you're saying that Troy is up for the taking if she wants him."

Now I really stop and think for a moment before trying again. Then I narrow my eyes and say, "I found your letter."

"Really? Which one?"

"Which one? Which one! She better not say that. I will go straight upside her head. And why do you sound just like her?"

Logan laughs out loud. "She wouldn't be bold enough to say that. I'm just messing with you. More than likely, she's going to pretend that she doesn't know what you're talking about."

"Then I don't know what I'll do after that. I don't want to seem like I'm threatened by her."

"Are you threatened by her?"

Deep inhale, long, tired exhale. "I don't know. Maybe. Look at her."

"She's all right. She doesn't have anything on you, though."

I feel my cheeks warm with a blush. "You're just being nice, and I so appreciate that right now. I needed to hear that, even if it isn't true."

"I sure wish you were single, because I'd make you believe how incredible you are."

Is it a sin that I just wished for a flash of a second that I was single, too?

CHAPTER 19

YVONNE

In lieu of our monthly Sister to Sister meeting, I talked a bunch of the ladies into helping Eva move into her new apartment at the church. It's a beautiful evening and a perfect one to move. The weather is so perfect that I could just stand out here on Eva's lawn until the mosquitoes eat me alive.

The church usually lets out the one-bedroom apartments for a short period of time to homeless congregants, but after I told pastor about Eva's lack of education and resources, he agreed to let her have a six-month paid lease while we help her get her life on track.

She doesn't say much about her past, except that she didn't finish high school and that she had a rough childhood. I don't know for sure, but I think that she was into drugs. Why else would she be so secretive about her life?

Pam walks up from her car, which she's parked on the sidewalk. I didn't think she was even coming, because Troy and the kids are at Kings Island and she has the whole house to herself to write.

"Hey, Yvonne," Pam says as she hugs me tightly. On closer inspection, Pam looks worried about something. Her curly hair is in a big Afro puff, which gives her a youthful appearance. The bags around her eyes do the opposite.

"Hey, honey. Thank you so much for coming. Eva is sure going to appreciate it."

"I'm just glad we could help her. I can't imagine not knowing where I'm going to live. Well . . . I can, but I haven't had to worry about that in a long time. Thank God for that."

"Pastor Brown said that he let her in the apartment on my recommendation."

"So is he gonna hold you responsible if anything goes wrong?"

This question never occurred to me. I guess I just assume that Eva's going to do the right thing.

"I don't know, Pam. I don't think so," I say after pondering for an extra second.

"I hope not. I mean, I don't recall her getting saved or anything. . . ."

"You're not serious, are you? You know we don't just extend our charity to church members."

"I'm just saying. You don't even know her story, really, and you recommended her to stay at the church. What if she's on drugs or something?"

Pam's suspicion gives me a little confirmation on my own, but I'm not going to let her know what I'm thinking. She's decided that Eva might be one of the devil's children, and that's not even like Pam.

"I don't think that's the case, but why would you even say that? What's wrong with you?"

Pam reaches into her purse, pulls out an envelope, and hands it to me. Instantly, I'm taken back to a time when I opened a letter that changed my life. I found out about my husband's affair and love child by opening an envelope.

"Go ahead," Pam says. "Open it. I can't carry this burden by myself, and Taylor is missing in action."

I read the note contained inside the pretty, scented stationery, and I feel my heart drop like a stone. Troy can't possibly be cheating! He and Pam have been through too much for him to throw their marriage away. She's been there for him through poorer and richer and then back to almost poorer. This cannot be happening.

I say, "Maybe there is an explanation."

"Maybe there is, and that's why I haven't totally flipped out yet. It sounds like he maybe turned her down, but I can't be sure."

"Well, he has to find another artist, right?" I ask. "I can't see you feeling comfortable with that arrangement after this."

"I hadn't even gotten that far in my thought process, but now that you say it, you're right. I can't imagine her ever being in my home again without me trying to scratch her face off."

"We're not going there, Pam, because you *are* saved, right? You're too big of a person to do that."

"You know, I'm really getting tired of people thinking that I'm just so nice. Logan said the same thing."

Pam covers her mouth like she said something she didn't mean to say. "Logan is Troy's business partner, right? He knows about this?"

"Yes. I happened to run into him right after I found out, and it just spilled out of my mouth."

Pam's demeanor is off. She can barely make eye contact, and she keeps playing with her hands. Is she leaving something out of the conversation? And if she is, what do I say about that? She doesn't have to tell me everything. Lord knows, I don't tell her everything.

"Are you and Logan friends?" I ask. "Do you think he'll mention it to Troy?"

"I don't think he'll tell Troy I told him."

"Men tend to stick together, girl, just like we do."

I want to interrogate her further about this Logan, but Eva bounces over toward us, wearing a snug T-shirt and capri pants. Some of the brothers that I drafted to move the bigger pieces of furniture stop in their tracks when they see her. One brother drops a box on his foot and yelps.

This child's body is darn near obscene. That tiny top clings to her breasts, which look too perfect to be real. Pair that up with her tiny waist and big round behind, and she looks more like a pinup girl than a church girl. But Eva seems oblivious to the attention.

Eva pulls Pam into a big friendly bear hug. "Hi, Sister Pam! Thank you for coming to help. I've got everything packed neatly, and I've been trying to help bring down some of the boxes, but these brothers won't let me lift a finger."

"I bet they won't," Pam says with a little giggle.

If I knew Eva better, I might suggest that she put on a more modest top. Not that what she's wearing is immodest. It's just that her body doesn't really lend itself to modesty. Some of these brothers have wives, who would choke me right now if they knew what I'd signed their husbands up for.

"Well, relax and let them be men," I say. "You'll need your energy for unpacking, anyway."

"Oh, I know. I'm not looking forward to that. It's going to be such a headache. Yvonne, will you stay with me and help?"

"I sure will! I don't have anything to do this evening, so I can help you."

"You know, Eva, I've run a couple of job training and placement programs at the church. How can I help you get into a career? What did you do before you lost your job?" Pam asks.

"Odds and ends stuff, really. Honestly, I went from one boyfriend to the next. They took care of me."

This isn't really hard to believe. A girl who looks like Eva does could absolutely find a man to take care of her. Several men.

"So you've never had any type of hourly or salaried job?"

"I have, but they weren't steady."

"So what do you want to do now?" Pam asks. "You've got to have income."

"Well, I can braid hair and do sew-in weaves. Maybe I could do that until I get back on my feet," Eva says.

Just like somebody gave her a cue, Taylor and her friend Shaquan walk across the street. Taylor loves weaves, so she could be one of Eva's first customers.

Eva runs up to Taylor and hugs her. "Hi, Sister Taylor. Thank you for your help! And you, too, Sister Shaquan."

Shaquan looks Eva up and down before she hugs her, like she's trying to solve a puzzle or something. I'm more mesmerized by Shaquan's outfit than anything. Who shows up in a designer dress for big girls and eight-inch heels to help someone move? And who wears a royal blue hair weave, ever?

"Girl, I love a good moving party," Shaquan says. "They usually have some of my favorite things."

"And what would those be?" Pam asks.

"Muscle-bound men, sweaty men, and handymen. Okay!"

Taylor says, "Shaquan!"

"I was just playing," Shaquan says. She glances at Eva for a second, and she opens her mouth to say something, I guess, but then she closes it again.

"Since the men won't let us help them, is there anything else we can do upstairs? Can we clean anything?" Pam asks.

"Yvonne and I already cleaned everything from top to bottom," Eva says. "It's a small apartment, so there's not much to clean."

"Well, do y'all mind if I go?" Pam asks. "I can be working on my book while I have some peace and quiet. Taylor, call me later. For real this time. No texts."

"Oh no, you didn't just try to put me on blast!" Taylor says.

Shaquan bursts into laughter. "Yes, she did. And she is telling the truth with how you're always texting people when we're trying to have a conversation."

"Well, try having a deadbeat, no-child-support-paying baby father show up uninvited in your son's life, and then tell me how many phone conversations you're going to have. Luke has got me pretty occupied right now."

I shake my head in anger. I can't believe Luke is trying to disrupt their lives! Hasn't he already done enough damage? Why can't he just go into a dark corner somewhere and disappear?

"Taylor, how do you want us to pray about that?" I ask. "As a matter of fact, we need to fast and pray. There is too much coming against our group right now."

Taylor smiles and gives me a hug. "Yvonne, you know how to pray better than I do. I don't even know what to say to God about Luke. Every time I fix my mouth to say something, it sounds like I'm being unforgiving. And you know what? I *don't* forgive Luke."

Eva says, "Don't hold on to that. You'll be the only one hurt. Trust me, I know."

Taylor lifts her eyebrows at Eva. Maybe Taylor got so caught up in her drama that she forgot Eva was standing right there, but it's almost like Eva intruded on a very private moment.

"My bad," Eva says, as if she could sense her comment wasn't welcome. "I've just had some really bad things happen to me in my life, so I understand not forgiving people."

"It's cool," Taylor says. "Looks like you're just right for the Sister to Sister group. We're a wounded bunch."

"Aren't we all in some way?" Eva asks.

Everyone responds to this with a nod. It seems that now, finally, Eva is starting to win my friends over. Pam still isn't convinced, but Eva's more Taylor's speed, anyway. They share a lot in common. They've got that vixen, man-stealer look that makes it hard for them to connect with other women.

Something sings in Shaquan's purse. The noise and the commotion of her digging in her bag break the silence that has fallen over the group. She takes out her phone and furiously starts texting.

"Taylor, I need you to drop me off somewhere real quick," she says.

Taylor shakes her head. "This is why I didn't want you to ride with me! You always need someone to drop you off. From here on out we are driving separately."

"Um, why would we do that? I'm not using up my gas trying to fool with these church outings. It's Friday, and I just got paid, so stop acting like you don't know."

Everyone chuckles.

"Come on, then. It doesn't look like there's much to do, anyway," Taylor says. "I can drop Shaquan off and come back."

"You go take care of Joshua," I say. "If Luke's been anywhere near him, you might need to lay hands on him and exorcise the devil out of him."

"I know that's right," Taylor says.

"Before y'all leave, let's make a point to pray for each other tonight, okay? I was serious about that," I say.

Pam asks, "Are you going through something, too, Yvonne? What do you want us to pray about?"

"Well, I'm spending all day tomorrow with Kingston. We're going to Put-in-Bay. I don't know what kind of prayer I need, but this is a huge step for me."

Taylor gives Pam a knowing glance, then bursts into laughter. "Let's all bow our heads right now and pray for Yvonne. Lord knows it's been a real long time, and we bind all lust and ho spirits in the name of Jesus."

Now everyone is laughing, including me. That is not the prayer I need, I don't think.

Eva says between her laughs, "Yvonne doesn't strike me as having a ho spirit!"

"Okay," Shaquan says. "This is the purest Polly Purebred I've ever met, and I mean that as a compliment, Yvonne."

"Deep down, somewhere in that holy package is a freak waiting to be released!" Taylor is doubled over now and holding on to her belly as she laughs.

"Oh, shut up, Taylor!" I say. "Seriously, just pray that if Kingston is the right man for me, I don't push him away with this Luke baggage."

Pam says, "You got it, honey. For what it's worth, I think that Kingston could definitely be the man for you. You suffered too long with Luke not to have someone wonderful."

"He's got the right name," Eva says. "A king for a queen."

Now that was touching. "Thank you, honey. I hope he's royalty, because my daddy is the King of Kings and Lord of Lords. . . ."

"Can we go before she starts shouting?" Shaquan asks.

"Yes! Bye, y'all!" Taylor says.

Taylor and Shaquan wave as they go back to Taylor's car. Pam gives me and Eva a hug.

"Call me later if you think about it, Yvonne," Pam says.

"Okay."

Pam starts to walk away, and then she turns around and

comes back. She pulls out a scrap of paper and a pen and scribbles something down on it.

"Here, Eva. You can call me if you need anything and you can't get ahold of Yvonne. Let's get to know one another better."

"Okay!" Eva beams with excitement.

When Pam and Taylor have both pulled off, Eva turns to me and smiles with tears in her eyes. "Do you think they really like me?" she asks.

"Of course they do! What's not to like?"

Eva bites her lip and looks at the ground. "I've never had girlfriends before."

"Well, now you do! But not just girlfriends. Sisters in Christ."

I hug Eva to let her know that I'm serious, and I feel her body tremble. When we separate, she has fresh tears on her face.

"Stop all that crying, girl! You do more crying than laughing. We have to change that."

CHAPTER 20

YVONNE

The brothers at our church are better than any moving service! They've got all of Eva's furniture set up and boxes placed in the designated rooms. Not that she has a lot of possessions, but they did a great job, nonetheless. I promise each of them a personalized bowl of my famous banana pudding and send them on their way so that we can get Eva unpacked.

Eva looks around the living room and scrunches her nose. "This is the worst part of moving. The unpacking."

"It is, but you've got help. Let's get started!"

"Okay. Do you want something to drink? I've got some soda and wine somewhere."

"I don't drink wine, but some water would be nice."

Eva covers her mouth, and her eyes widen. "I'm sorry, Yvonne. I didn't know. Is that one of the church rules? No drinking?"

I sit down on Eva's IKEA couch and shake my head. "Girl, our church doesn't have rules. We follow the Word of God, but there aren't any rules. I personally don't drink, but I'm not saying it's a sin or anything like that."

"Would the rest of the church members think it's a sin?"

Before I reply, I think about some of our church members. Rhoda and Rochelle would definitely call it a sin if asked, but I think Rhoda carries a flask of some sort in her purse. Most would probably agree that drunkenness is a sin, but not a glass of wine. I have no idea what Pastor Brown would think, because he's never preached on anything like that.

"It's not really about what everyone else thinks. It's about what God says. And if you read your Bible and don't feel convicted about a glass of wine, then who am I to tell you that you're sinning?"

Eva looks confused. "Convicted? What does that mean? Sometimes I don't understand the church lingo. I'm sorry."

"Convicted is like when you know something isn't right. You feel it inside, we would say, in your spirit."

Eva nods slowly. "I don't know if I feel convicted about anything. That's the problem."

"You will. If you spend enough time feeding on the Bible, God will meet you where you are. He'll speak to your heart."

Eva seems to ponder this silently as she finds two cans of soda and two glasses. I wish I could tell her something more comforting, but I don't know how to explain something I've known my entire life it seems.

"I'm sorry I can't find any bottled water. Is a Coke okay?" Eva asks.

"Yes, that's perfectly fine, honey. One Coke won't ruin my complexion."

Eva laughs. "Your skin is beautiful, Yvonne! I was going to ask you what you use, because I have acne flare-ups from time to time."

"I just drink a lot of water, and I think I have good genes. God blessed the women on my mother's side with great skin and our slim physiques."

"Well, God blessed me with some major curves, so that's some church lingo I do understand."

"Did God bless you with all those curves, or did you purchase some of them?"

Eva's jaw drops. "Do you think my boobs are fake, Yvonne?"

"Either your boobs or your behind. I ain't never seen someone so thin with so much of both!"

Eva bursts into laughter. "They're both real, Yvonne."

I give her a skeptical glance. "That's your story, and you're sticking to it. It's just fine with me."

She walks over to the couch with the Coke and the glasses and sets them on the floor. "You can touch my boobs if you think they're fake! I promise you they're not."

"I'm going to take your word for it. What do you want to unpack first?"

"I guess my bedding and towels and stuff. And the cleaning supplies, although this place is spotless."

"We have a staff at the church that cleans the apartments once a week. We use them for special guests sometimes, so they have to be in great condition."

"I know that I already said thank you, but Yvonne, I have to keep saying it. No one has ever been this nice to me. Not even my own mama."

I listen intently, thinking that Eva may share something about herself. She's never mentioned her family, so maybe this is the beginning of her sharing something with me.

"My mama could be in a ditch somewhere, for all I know," Eva continues. "She chose drugs over me and left me with my grandmother."

"God bless grandmothers. Mine helped to raise me."

Eva frowns. "Mine was okay, I guess. She died a while back. Sometimes I miss her."

Since she seems to have gone to a dark place, I won't press for any more details. This is progress, though, because she's finally peeling back some of those layers.

"Well, let's find those blankets and sheets, then!"

I open my can of soda and pour some into my glass before marching into the bedroom. The boxes marked BEDROOM are there, so I'm assuming that's the first place we should look. Eva is right on my heels and drinking her Coke straight out of the can.

She points to a large box in the middle of the room. "That's the bedding."

I set my glass down and start ripping the tape off the sides of the box. Eva stands there watching me. "Are you going to help?" I ask.

She chuckles and starts attacking the box from the other side. "You seemed like you were having fun, so I didn't want to interrupt."

Eva hums a tune as we unfold the pretty pink comforter and the cream-colored satin sheets. The bedding is the expensive kind. I've never slept on satin sheets, but these feel so luxurious that I might just try them out.

"What are you humming?" I ask. "Your voice sounds pretty. You should be in the choir."

"I've never been in a choir. I don't really know any gospel songs."

"You'll learn them. That's what choir practice is for. Kingston is always looking for another voice."

"I do know one song," Eva says.

"Let me hear it, then."

Eva clears her throat and sings a very moving rendition of "His Eye Is on the Sparrow." Her voice is even more beautiful than I thought it was from the humming.

"I'm about to call Kingston right now! You should be up there doing solos."

"Don't call him, Yvonne. I—I don't think I should be singing in anybody's choir just yet."

"Well, of course not, but once you get baptized and turn your life over to Christ, I think you definitely should."

"I was wondering when we would start talking about this. I want to get baptized, but I'm not sure."

"About what? About Jesus?"

Eva smoothes out the satin pillowcases and places a big feathery pillow inside one. "No, it's nothing about God. It's about me. The baptism water would probably evaporate if I stepped into it."

"I'm sure it wouldn't. God has seen and forgiven much worse than the likes of you."

"You don't even know me, Yvonne. How can you say that?"

"Then tell me, Eva. You keep telling me that I don't know

you. I'm not going to run away from whatever it is that you've done."

Eva stares at me for a long moment. Then she slowly places her pillow on the bed and retrieves a small footlocker from the corner of the room. She puts in the combination and opens the footlocker. She reaches inside and pulls out a handful of DVDs. Then she walks over to me, places them in my hand, sits on the edge of the bed, and waits.

The DVDs are the filthy kind, and I almost drop them on the floor. Even on the covers the people are doing all kinds of things that should be done only in the bedrooms of married couples, and some things that I don't think I've ever imagined.

"What does this have to do with you, Eva?"

She sighs and takes one of the DVDs out of my hand. "This is me."

Eva points to a girl with her body type on the cover. She is completely naked and has a lollipop in her mouth. Judging by the girl's face, she looks absolutely nothing like the Eva standing in front of me.

"That's not you. I don't believe it." "I don't want to believe it" is the more proper response. I put the DVDs down, because just touching them makes me feel like I need to lie on the altar.

"It is me, Yvonne. I have on a wig, eyelashes, a fake beauty mark, and lots of makeup, but it is me." She lifts her blouse to expose a tattoo on her stomach. "See. Same tat. This is why I don't think I should be in the choir or anywhere near the baptism pool."

I close my eyes and swallow and try to find words to say to this girl. As much as I don't want to admit it, I almost agree with her. I know that blood covers all sins, but this is so disgusting that I'd just want her to come and sit in the back of the church in a long dress—away from teenage boys and husbands.

I am ashamed for feeling this. God delivered me from this. I don't judge people anymore.

"Are you still making these movies?"

"No. This is why I'm broke, Yvonne. I left the business. Almost got the package, so I walked away from it all."

"What is the package?"

"HIV, or full-blown AIDS. Same thing to a porn star."

I glance over at the glass I used, wondering if she used the same glass. What if she has some other disease? What if she has herpes of the mouth or something? *Oh, Lord, Jesus, please help me.* I can't do this. Not this. And why did she have to say *porn?* That word sounds like a disease.

"Yvonne, you look ill. Do you need to sit down?"

"No, I-I'm fine. Let's get your bed made."

I start whipping that sheet through the air like nobody's business, and then it occurs to me that she may have done her ungodly acts right on this very bedding. My stomach swirls at the thought of random bodies and bodily fluids all touching this sheet. I drop it in midair and let it fall to the floor.

"Yvonne, I never did it in my own home." Eva's voice trembles. "I wish I hadn't told you! Now you won't be my friend anymore. Please don't tell the others! Please! Just let me find another church."

"Wait a minute. Just wait, Eva. This is pretty heavy stuff to just drop on someone. I need a moment, that's all. I mean, I thought you were mixed up in drugs or something. I wasn't expecting this."

"This is worse than drugs, huh? This is worse than any other sin you can think of, huh? Yes, I got paid for having sex on camera. Nobody paid me when my uncle took it from me! How about his sins, huh? Are his worse than mine?"

Eva falls to her knees and sobs bitterly. I go to her, drop to my knees, too. I should've known something happened to this child to make her do this. I wrap my arms around her shaking body and rock her back and forth. I sweep the hair back from her face and rock her like I would my own child if I had one.

Finally, her crying slows and her breathing becomes calm and even. She sighs and looks up at me. "Thank you."

I smile and kiss her on the forehead. "You're welcome, honey."

Just as I get ready to fix my mouth to pray for her, this child does the unthinkable. She reaches up with both her hands, grabs my face, pulls me close, and kisses me on the lips. It's a lover's kiss, and I nearly vomit thinking of the meaning of this and of all the other lips that have been on hers.

I jump up from the floor and wipe my mouth involuntarily. I grab my purse and dash for the door.

"Yvonne! I'm sorry! I—I thought . . ."

"You thought what? I'm dealing with you like a sister, and you would do this to me?"

"I'm so, so sorry, Yvonne."

I feel my anger rising. I haven't felt this furious since Luke beat me and left me for dead. "I don't kiss women, Eva. And I suggest that you don't try that on anyone else. I won't tell Pastor Brown, because I want you to get back on your feet. But you can stay away from me."

"Are you going to tell Pam and Taylor?"

"Why? You got plans to kiss them, too?"

"No. I know what I did was wrong, Yvonne. It's just that you were so close, and something came over me. It won't happen again."

"You're darn right it won't."

I swing the door of the apartment open and storm out. On the way to the car, I take hand sanitizer from my purse and rub it all over my face, hands, and mouth. I know it's irrational, but I feel dirtied and unclean.

But most of all, I feel like a failure. This was surely a test that I didn't pass. I thought if I could forgive the girl who slept with my husband and had a love child, then surely I must be a child of God.

Hot tears sting my face as I get into my own car and rush away from the church. When I asked Pam and Taylor to pray for me, who knew that *this* would be my trial?

I want to go back and apologize to Eva and tell her that God will throw everything into the sea of forgetfulness if she will just repent. But my skin crawls at the thought of being in the same room with her.

All the way home, I'm praying only one thing. *Lord, please don't let my reaction to Eva's past keep her from you.*

CHAPTER 21

TAYLOR

"I want to go over my daddy's house," Joshua says as soon as I get home from dinner with Shaquan.

Her little meet up with her new potential boo didn't go as planned, so we decided to go and have dinner at Chili's— Shaquan's favorite spot if she has to pay. If she's out on a date, then she'd rather go to a place with no prices on the menu.

We had a good time, and I was able to get my mind off of this mess with Luke, but as soon as I walk through the door, I have to hear about him. Ugh! Most of all, it makes me cringe to hear him calling Luke "Daddy." He started doing this after he talked for hours on the phone with Luke a couple days after his visit with him at the restaurant.

"You're not going over to Luke's house," I say. As far as I'm concerned, the conversation is over.

"Why not? That's not fair, Mom. You've had me all this time, and he just wants to get to know me. I want to know him, too."

I take Joshua's hand and lead him to the couch. "Don't you want to spend some time with Spencer, honey?"

Joshua shakes his head. "He doesn't like me. He only wants to hit me."

"You know that's not true, Joshua. You've been out of pocket lately. He's just trying to help you get back on track."

"Well, I want my daddy to help me. He understands me."

I cringe again. "He doesn't even know you yet, Joshua."

"But he has to understand me, because I'm a part of him. I mean, for real, Mom, we look just alike."

"Spencer came into our lives when you were little, and he loves you just like you were his own son."

"But I *am* my daddy's son. And he wants to be around me, so why are you tripping?"

My blood just went from simmer to boil in the flash of a second. "Luke ain't done nothin' for you! You didn't even have a decent winter coat until Spencer came along."

"So 'cause Spencer got more money than my daddy, that makes him better?"

"Did Luke tell you to ask me that?"

"No, but you keep bringing up child support. So I'm asking because I want to know. If my daddy was rich, would you let me go over his house?"

I am not about to sit up here and defend myself to my own son. This boy is about two syllables away from getting his behind handed to him. Too grown talking to be eleven years old. My mother would've never let me get away with this.

"I think you better take yourself up into your bedroom, look around, and appreciate everything you have. Then later, when you can talk to me like you have some sense, we can discuss Luke and what he means to this family."

"You can't stop me from seeing him."

"Try me. I'm not playing with you, Joshua. I will beat the black off you."

Joshua shakes his head. "Now you and your husband gonna beat me?"

"I swear, you got five seconds to get upstairs!"

The loudness and ferocity of my voice scare me a little. I've never been this harsh with Joshua, but he is trying my patience with this Luke stuff. I don't know if I'm going to be able to get through this. Maybe I can talk Spencer into moving all of us to Atlanta or Dallas. To a place where Luke can't disrupt our once happy home.

Spencer walks in from the kitchen and sits down next to me on the couch. "We've got a problem."

"Yes, I know. Luke just won't let me have any peace, will he?"

"We got a letter from the school today saying that Joshua will have to repeat fifth grade if we don't send him to summer school."

"Well, of course. They made him miss the last three weeks of school."

"Summer school starts next week, and they sent us several locations he can attend, none of which are close by."

"Bump them. I'm going to homeschool my baby."

"Taylor, how are you going to do that and work, too? I thought we agreed that your time off from work was temporary and that you were going back."

I take Spencer's hand in mine and trace my finger across his palm. "I meant to talk to you about that. I think that I should stay home with him for a while and take an indefinite leave of absence from work."

"You think Ellis Financial would be cool with that?"

"I don't care what they think. Are you cool with it?"

Spencer snatches his hand away from me. A bad sign. "I mean, no, not really. I'm not cool with that. We have a lot of bills, Taylor. Living like we do doesn't come cheaply."

"I know, baby, but we've got a lot of money saved up, and it wouldn't be forever. . . ."

"You mean our retirement fund? Joshua's college fund? That's not money I'm willing to touch. Not for this! What if one of us is truly incapacitated and can't work? Then we might actually have to use some of that money to survive. I'm not going to let Joshua's bad behavior mess up our lives."

"So how do you suggest we handle this?"

"I think we should send him to one of these summer schools and get him enrolled in whichever district will have him next year."

"We're going to have to pay tuition."

"It doesn't matter. It won't even touch the amount of money we'd lose if you came off your six-figure-a-year job."

"But, Spencer—"

"This is not even up for discussion, Taylor. I've sat back and let you make decisions that I should be making. That ends today."

"Okay. Since you're running stuff right now, can you please figure out what to do about this Luke visitation scenario?"

"If you had let me handle it in the first place, we wouldn't be in this mess right now. I think we both need to sit down with Luke and his fiancée, without Joshua being present, for a real talk. We need to lay some ground rules, because this chump is not about to come in and turn our world upside down."

"I'll call him and set it up."

Spencer shakes his head. "You won't do anything. I'll call him and set it up, and if he doesn't want to deal with me, he can deal with the court and that small matter of his back child support bill."

"I love it when you take charge, Spencer. It makes me feel protected."

"I love it when you *let* me take charge." Spencer's voice softens. "You have to trust that I want the best for our entire family. I love Joshua just like he came from my own seed."

"I know you do."

"Well, let me deal with this, Tay. I've got this. And Joshua is going to be okay. He's just smelling himself right now. It's a man thing."

"He isn't a man yet. He better watch himself if he wants to make it to manhood."

"He'll make it! And we'll be proud of him when he gets there."

For the first time since Luke reared his ugly head, I feel better about this situation. Spencer is a man of God, and I trust him. He's going to make everything okay.

Spencer stands up and holds out his hand. "I believe we have a meeting scheduled."

"What meeting?"

"The meeting in my bedroom."

I place my free hand over my mouth and giggle. "Okay, but I

have to call Pam first. She's going through something, and I promised that I'd call."

"You've got twenty minutes, Taylor, and then I'm disconnecting the call."

I take the phone out of my purse and quickly dial Pam's cell. "Hello."

"Hey, girl! What is going on with you?" I ask. "You seemed off at the girl's house."

"So much is going on. But before we get on my drama, what do you think about Eva?"

"I don't know what to think. I just know that Yvonne seems really taken with her. She's like a kitten with a ball of yarn. I've never seen her that excited about helping someone."

"I know. She seems nice, but I don't know. I think she's hiding something."

"Aren't we all?"

Pam says, "Yeah, we are. I've got some stuff that's just between me and God."

"You don't have any secrets, Pam! You are way too boring for secrets. And since we're back to talking about you, are you going to tell me what's wrong?"

"I think Troy may have had an affair with Aria."

Big sigh from me. "You back on that again? I remember you were about to lose your mind behind that girl years ago."

"Well, I didn't have proof back then, but now I have evidence. She wrote him a letter saying she was moving on."

"Okay. Maybe she tried to get with him and he told her to step off."

"That's what every person I've asked has said. But it doesn't have to mean that. It could mean that what they had has run its course and it's over. No matter what, he's got to find a new artist."

"I think you are jumping to conclusions, as usual. I know that Troy loves you, and so what if that girl wanted to get with him once upon a time? He's a good-looking guy, Pam, and he's her mentor. Maybe she just got caught up."

Pam gets very quiet.

"Pam?" I ask. "Are you still there?"

"I'm here."

"Look, I'm not sure if Troy's innocent, but you always think the worst of him. Hope for the best, but prepare yourself for the worst."

"I'll let you know what happens after I confront him," Pam says.

"Don't confront him, Pam. Just tell him that you know about the letter, and see what he says."

"And if he admits to it?"

"Then call me right away, girl. I'll help you hide the body."

Pam laughs out loud. "I know you will. But I'd rather you pray for me."

"I'll pray for you both. But I have a feeling that it's going to work out fine."

"Spencer must be in a romantic mood. You always trying to wrap up my problems real quick when your man is frisky."

"You got me, girl. Spence has me on a time limit, but just know that I'm here for you."

"Whatever! I'll talk to you tomorrow. I won't get any writing done while Troy is gone, so we might as well hang."

"Okay. Later."

I let out a sigh as I disconnect the phone call. I want to be optimistic for Pam, but I've been worried about that Aria chick since the first time I saw her perform. She looked at Troy the way I looked at Luke. There was longing in her eyes, like she wanted to take Pam's place. At the time, I never thought that Troy reciprocated, but now I can't be so sure.

I'm always gonna pray for my girl, but I've got something in the natural for Ms. Aria, too. Game recognizes game, and I know a husband stealer when I see one. If she's trying to mess up my girl's happy home, she's going to have to deal with me and God.

CHAPTER 22

EVA

Eva sat on the floor of her new apartment in a daze. She hadn't moved since she'd run Yvonne off by kissing her. Hours had gone by, and she still couldn't figure out what possessed her to do something so stupid.

It had something to do with Yvonne rocking her back and forth as her grandmother had. Eva had told Yvonne about the adult films, and she hadn't pushed her away. She hadn't been disgusted, like her grandmother had been. Eva had felt a surge of love for Yvonne like she'd never felt for anyone.

And now it was ruined.

Eva glanced over at the discarded DVDs on the floor near her bed. Yvonne had been disgusted by them, and now Eva was, too. They seemed demonic. She wondered why she held on to them. It kind of seemed crazy since she was determined to never go back to that life.

It was only a matter of time before Yvonne told someone Eva's secret. She'd promised not to, but how would she be able to keep that to herself? How could Yvonne let someone like her live on her church grounds? She was going to at least tell the pastor, of that Eva was sure.

Eva replayed the day in her mind. Everyone had come together to help her move. The men came and moved all her things, and not one of them had made a pass at her. This was shocking, but it had made Eva feel safe around them.

Then the women had come, and this had warmed Eva's heart more than anything. Her female friends were scarce, no, nonexistent. But they had shown up to help her move, and they seemed happy to be there.

The one girl, Shaquan, had recognized Eva but didn't remember how they knew one another. Eva remembered. Shaquan had worked at a strip club that Eva had tried before she got into the adult film business. Shaquan was the cook, and she fried chicken wings and fries for the men sticking dollar bills in Eva's G-string.

Eva wasn't really worried about Shaquan spilling her secret. Telling everyone would require her to reveal their connection. And Eva also knew that Shaquan did much more than fry chicken wings. She sold exclusive favors in the VIP room, just like the girls who worked the pole.

Eva considered calling Yvonne. When she'd given her the phone number, she'd said to call anytime. She just wanted to say "I'm sorry" however many times it took for Yvonne to forget what she'd done.

Like everyone else that she'd ever cared about, Eva had pushed Yvonne away. And Yvonne had tried to lead her to God. No one else had done that.

Would her life really change when she gave it over to Jesus? What if she was still sad and lonely? What if the sordid things she'd done on those videos continued to haunt her?

What if it did? What if she wasn't, and what if they didn't?

Eva would never know what could happen unless she just trusted and believed God and let Him take control. She didn't even know what it meant to do that. But first, it seemed to require a decision on her part.

Eva didn't know about baptism yet, but she knew the first thing she'd do. She crawled across the floor on her hands and knees and retrieved the DVDs. Then she reached into her toolbox and got out a hammer.

She pounded on the DVDs until they were in pieces all over

the floor. She gathered the pieces together in a pile and wondered where she could dispose of them. She didn't want them in her new home any longer.

After she discarded the pieces in the Dumpster outside, Eva picked up her grandmother's Bible. She flipped through the pages, looking at the highlighted texts and wondering if those would lead her to understand God or salvation.

Eva's grandmother had highlighted many texts in the book of Deuteronomy. It was the most marked, so Eva assumed that this was her grandmother's favorite book of the Bible. Some of them she'd highlighted and underlined in red.

The first underlined text read, *If a man have a stubborn and rebellious son, which will not obey the voice of his father, or the voice of his mother, and that, when they have chastened him, will not hearken unto them: Then shall his father and his mother lay hold on him, and bring him out unto the elders of his city, and unto the gate of his place; And they shall say unto the elders of his city, This our son is stubborn and rebellious, he will not obey our voice; he is a glutton, and a drunkard. And all the men of his city shall stone him with stones, that he die: so shalt thou put evil away from among you; and all Israel shall hear, and fear.*

Eva shuddered. Then she wondered if her grandmother had applied this scriptural verse to her uncle Parnell. Eva wished that someone had taken him somewhere and thrown stones at him. She would've been the first in line to do it.

The next passage read, *But if this thing be true, and the tokens of virginity be not found for the damsel: Then they shall bring out the damsel to the door of her father's house, and the men of her city shall stone her with stones that she die: because she hath wrought folly in Israel, to play the whore in her father's house: so shalt thou put evil away from among you.*

Eva shuddered with fear. It was as if she could feel her grandmother's presence in the room. Her grandmother had called her a whore. Had she wished her dead and stoned, too, just like Uncle Parnell?

In the margin of the next passage, Eva's grandmother had written in red block letters, "RAPE." The passage read, *If a damsel that is a virgin be betrothed unto an husband, and a man find her in the city, and lie with her; Then ye shall bring them both out unto the gate of that city, and ye shall stone them with stones that they die; the damsel, because she cried not, being in the city; and the man, because he hath humbled his neighbour's wife: so thou shalt put away evil from among you.*

This didn't apply to Eva. She had cried out, but no one had listened. No one had stopped her uncle from stealing her innocence. No one had stopped him from destroying everything pure and sweet within her.

Eva closed the Bible and sighed. There was no joy in these passages for her. She wanted to know the God that Yvonne talked about, the forgiving and loving God. Not the one who called for people to be stoned to death. Were they the same God?

Eva was confused, but with Yvonne angry with her, there was no one to call. She whispered a prayer, "God, please don't let Yvonne hate me. Please take these feelings away from me. I don't want to think of women this way. I want a husband, a baby, and a house. Is that too much to ask, God? I want to be like Yvonne, Taylor, and Pam. They say that they're women of God. I am a woman, but I don't know who I belong to. Help me, God, because I don't even know what to pray. I am lost."

Eva clutched the Bible to her chest, hoping that positive rays of hope would come into her heart. She fell asleep on the floor with the Bible in her arms, wishing more than anything for her prayers to come true.

CHAPTER 23

YVONNE

What time is it? I sit up straight in my bed, disoriented and soaked through with sweat. I shake my head, trying to clear the dream haze, because that's exactly what woke me up—a dream about Luke.

I fan myself at the recollection of that dream, and then I immediately feel ashamed. I dreamed about one of our anniversary vacations, specifically our boudoir activities. I snap my legs shut under my sheets and ask God to forgive my lustful thoughts.

Why in the world would I have a sexual dream about Luke? I haven't thought about him that way since he broke me in a way that no woman should experience, not from the man she loves. And it's not like he was ever that exceptional in the bedroom, either. Whenever I heard married women talk about how much they wanted their husbands in that way, I never felt as if I could relate. It was always wham, bam, thank you, ma'am, with Luke.

Then I remember Eva's stolen kiss. Is that what caused me to have this dream? Was I aroused by that? Oh, Lord Jesus, please don't let me be a lesbian.

I glance over at the clock on my bedside table. It's only six in the morning, but I might as well get up and prepare for my date with Kingston. We're going to get on the road early to beat the Sandusky amusement park traffic.

Maybe the dream has something to do with Kingston. We haven't kissed or held hands even, but his lingering gaze has started a slow-burning fire in me. I didn't want to admit it at first, but I find myself thinking about his cologne for hours after we separate.

No. I am definitely not a lesbian, but is Eva?

That kiss seemed so surreal, as if she was in some kind of dream haze herself. Even after a full night's sleep, I still feel bad about how that ended, but I have no idea how to fix it, or if I should even try. I could end up making it worse.

My cell phone buzzes on the nightstand. I pick it up and squint at the number in the caller ID. It's Eva. I must've thought her up this morning. I hesitate before answering, but I suppose I can either deal with this now or later.

"Hello?" I say, trying to sound as chipper as I possibly can, seeing that I haven't even brushed my teeth yet.

"Oh, I didn't think you'd answer. I was just going to leave a voice mail message."

"Well, I'm awake, so you don't have to do that. What did you want to say to me?"

There is a long pause before she speaks. "Yvonne, please say that we can still be friends. I'm so sorry for what I did."

"I do forgive you, honey . . . I mean Eva . . . but I don't know so much about the friend part."

"I understand why you don't want to be my friend, but I really want to change. Sometimes I feel like I'm out of control when it comes to my sexuality."

"Are you a lesbian?"

"No. I mean, I have been with women on film, but I am attracted to men."

I think about this response, and I don't know what to think. How could a woman have sex with another woman on film and not be attracted to her? I don't know how it works, and I don't even know what I believe about how people become homosexuals. Some people say they are born that way, and some don't.

"How could you do it, then?" I ask.

"It was like I was outside myself when I was filming. We'd use Ecstasy or marijuana, and everything would just kind of run together. Once I did it the first time, it was easier the next time, and the next time and the next."

"I'm going to be honest, Eva. I don't think I can be friends with you. You violated something when you kissed me, and I really wish that you hadn't."

"Okay." I can hear the sadness in her voice. She sounds so pitiful that I could just cry with her.

"But I promise to try as long as you promise to keep your lips to yourself."

"I will! I will! Can I ask you something else?"

"Sure."

"I want to be free of all this. I want salvation, too. God spoke to me when I promised Him I wouldn't do adult films anymore. But I don't know what to do. Can you tell me where to read in my Bible? Where can I find something for me? I keep reading about Israel and the apostles, but I feel lost when I pick up the Bible."

Hmmm . . . what Bible verse would speak to Eva? Then I smile, because I think of the perfect one.

"Try the Gospel of John, chapter four. It's about a woman who Christ met face-to-face. She had a past that she was ashamed of, I think."

"Thank you so much, Yvonne. Will I see you at church on Sunday?"

"I'll be there." I try to sound non-committal, but not mean. Even if I can't put the horrible feelings out of my mind, I still want this girl to meet Christ.

"Okay, then. See you tomorrow."

I breathe a huge sigh of relief as I disconnect the phone. Even though I reacted badly, she still hasn't been soured on Jesus. I would've felt guilty if that had happened.

I jump out of bed, feeling much better, and ready for my date with Kingston. I do all my bathroom rituals, including soaking in a bathtub full of perfumed soap. I've found a new fragrance I like that smells like sweet rose petals. It's soft and sexy. Well, I guess it's sexy. I have no idea what kind of scent a man finds arousing.

And do I even *want* to be sexy? After that dream, I'm not so sure! What if Kingston kisses me and I just start pulling clothes off like I don't have good sense? Lord, help!

Then I pick my outfit. I want to be comfortable, so I pick a jean skirt and flats and this halter top that Taylor forced me to buy last summer. It is very pretty, and Taylor has great taste in clothes.

My hair is easy. I just got my bob freshly cut and styled, so it falls into place perfectly and is soft and bouncy.

I've never been one for a lot of makeup, but I've been taking man-catching lessons from my vixen friend Taylor. She says that I need mascara and at least lip gloss. I can do the lip gloss but not the mascara. I always end up almost putting my eye out with the mascara wand.

When I am totally assembled, I look in my full-length mirror to give myself the once-over. Not bad, if I do say so myself. I'd ask myself out, I think. I may not have all the killer curves of some of the sisters I know, but I am shapely. There are a few gray streaks in my hair, but if I dyed them, I could be mistaken for a woman in her early thirties. Black don't crack, baby! Thank the Lord for good genes and a healthy dose of melanin.

While I'm waiting for Kingston to show up, I put on a pot of coffee and warm a bagel for breakfast. It's not like I can actually eat anything. I'm too excited about our date.

Right on time, at nine, I hear Kingston's car pull into my drive-way. I stop myself from running to the door. That would look desperate, I think, even though I am very eager to see him.

I peek out of the front window as he walks up. He's wearing a peach polo shirt and some khaki shorts. With his sunglasses and baseball cap, Kingston looks younger than his years, too.

I force myself to wait until he rings the doorbell, and then I take slow and measured steps to the door. Finally, I swing it open, wearing a smile on my face. Kingston stands there with his hands in his pockets and a crooked grin.

"Making me wait, huh?"

"No, no! Not at all. I was having a cup of coffee. Do you want one before we get on the road?"

"Sure, especially if you've got some coffee cake to go with it."

"Will homemade almond pound cake suffice? It goes well with coffee."

Kingston steps inside my town house. "I'm sure if you made it, it's delicious. You know you're a legend at New Faith with your baked items."

"I am? Well, I've had a lot of practice at that. When I was growing up down South, it seems like somebody baked something every day."

I lead Kingston into my kitchen and motion for him to sit on one of the bar stools. I pour a cup of coffee and sit it in front of him with cream and sugar.

"I think my next wife is going to be a great cook. I've never been blessed to find that in a woman."

This makes me laugh as I place a big hunk of cake on a plate and slide it next to Kingston's coffee cup. "Oh, really? So who cooked during your marriages?"

"With my first wife, it was spaghetti three days a week and hot dogs the rest of the week." Kingston takes a bite of his cake, closes his eyes, and smiles. "My second wife was too much of a diva to cook. Yvonne, this cake is incredible."

"Thank you. I've got to say, I like a man who knows his way around a kitchen, too. Do you like to barbecue?"

"That is one thing I never mastered. I'm more of a shrimp scampi guy. I could whip you up a spinach soufflé before I could grill a slab of ribs."

I scrunch my nose. "I've never had a spinach soufflé. It sounds bourgie."

"It is. If you want, I can take some barbecue classes before I propose."

"Aren't you getting ahead of yourself?" I ask.

"Nope. I'm right on schedule. I've been trying to win your heart for two years. It's not my fault you only just got on board. You've got some catching up to do. I already know what I want."

I feel my cheeks grow warm at his frank admission. "Um . . . let me use the restroom before we leave."

I rush out of the kitchen and into the bathroom. Clutching both sides of the sink, I breathe in deeply and exhale slowly, trying to slow my racing heartbeat. I look in the mirror and notice that my cheeks are slightly reddened, which is hard to see with my brown skin.

Kingston is coming on strong, and it scares me. I want to get caught up in the whirlwind with him, but does the fact that I'm dreaming of Luke mean that I'm not yet ready to move on? It's been eight years since I've shared my life with a man. If I'm not ready now, maybe I'll never be.

When I feel like I've regained my composure, I go back out into the kitchen. Kingston has finished his coffee and cake. He's washed his dishes and mine and placed them in the rack to dry. This brings a smile to my face. Luke never once helped with chores. He'd rather have an enema than wash a dish, vacuum a floor, or even pick up his dirty underwear and socks. I hated picking up behind him, but over the years I got used to it. Now that I live alone, I'm used to cleaning only my own messes, so if I did decide to take the marriage plunge again, he'd have to be neat.

Kingston is fine, romantic, and he cleans up after himself? He's ahead by a lot more points than I want to admit. I don't know if I deserve him! He seems too perfect.

"Are you ready to go, pretty lady?" Kingston asks.

I nod. "Yes, I am."

"It's a nice day, so we can ride with the top down if you want."

"Sure!"

Kingston claps his hands. "A woman who doesn't mind messing her hair up in the wind. Yvonne, I think you are perfect."

All I can do is grin. He thinks I'm perfect, and I think he's perfect. How perfect is that?

CHAPTER 24

PAM

Since I have another free day before my family gets home, I decide to have a spa day. It'll take my mind off Troy and Aria. Especially since I can't do anything about it right now, save driving down to Cincinnati like a madwoman, which I almost did more than once. I had to force myself to follow Taylor's advice and stay put.

I get dressed in my comfortable light blue Baby Phat jogging suit and flip-flops, pull my hair up into a curly ponytail on the top of my head, and throw on my sunglasses. This is my "I absolutely do not care" look. And I don't care today. I'm about to get my fluffy body rubbed from head to toe and to drink licorice tea and cucumber water.

When I step out on my porch, Logan is parked in front of the house. He's standing outside and leaning against his car, as if he's waiting for me. I take my sunglasses off and stick them in my hair as I walk down the path to greet him. He's wearing athletic clothes, so I wonder if he's on his way to the gym.

"Hi, Logan. What arc you doing here?" I ask.

"I was out and about, running my Saturday errands, and I thought about you. Just checking to make sure you're okay. You were a bit of a mess when I saw you yesterday."

"I'm fine. Thanks for checking on me."

"You sure you're fine? You haven't booby-trapped the house to choke Troy out as soon as he walks in the door, have you?"

"No, not yet. I'm still hoping that the only thing he has to explain is hiding the note from Aria or, better yet, not throwing it away."

"Okay, okay, I believe you. Where are you off to? No laptop, so you're not going to Starbucks to write."

"Very observant. I'm not going to write. I'm going to get a full-body massage by my girl KeKe at Sassy Femmes."

"If you needed a massage, you should've let me know. I would've taken care of that for you. You wouldn't even have to tip me."

"Logan, you are out of order."

He folds his arms across his chest and nods. "I am out of order. I apologize."

"Forgiven. Thanks for seeing about me. I'll see you later."

"I was hoping so. I was thinking that we could talk about my book career over an early dinner."

Dinner with Logan doesn't feel safe to me. Not with him standing here, looking like a chocolate-dipped Greek god. He might be an aspiring writer, but he's also trying to get extra close to me.

"How about a late lunch?"

"I'd love that. P. F. Chang's sound good?"

Nope. That place is too dark, and there are too many intimate corners inside, even during the day.

"Not in the mood for Chinese. Plus, that place is kind of romantic. It wouldn't look right if any of my church friends saw me there with you."

"How about my place, then?"

Now I crack up laughing. "You didn't seriously ask me that, did you? Let's just scrap all the meal plans, okay? I can help you with your book when my husband gets back home. We can all do lunch together."

"Why do you think I'm up to no good, Pam? I've not made any advances toward you. This isn't fair."

Okay, how about telling me that he's attracted to me, showing up at my house when he knows my husband isn't home, asking me out to dinner? His advances might be subtle, but they are certainly real.

"Maybe it's not you. Maybe it's me. I might not be able to resist you."

"Now, that's what I'm talking about. To thine own self be true."

"Oh, please."

"Wasn't that a writer-like thing to say?"

Now the cute banter is starting to annoy me. "I've got to go. I'm gonna be late for my appointment."

"Sure, Pam. Do you want me to come back later to tuck you in?"

"Logan!"

"I'm kidding!"

He waves as he hops back in his black convertible Benz. Troy probably drooled when he first saw this car. It is exactly the kind of ride I'd expect Logan to have. It's dark, fast, and dangerous. Just like he is.

CHAPTER 25

YVONNE

"Why are you getting off at this exit? This is the Cedar Point exit. Port Clinton and Put-in-Bay are a few exits up."

Kingston smiles at me and says, "Change of plans. Let's stop at the amusement park for a few hours, ride some rides, eat some cotton candy, and then go to Put-in-Bay for dinner."

"Caramel apples."

"Is that a yes?"

I nod. "Only if we're getting some freshly dipped caramel apples. With nuts. That's my favorite thing to eat at Cedar Point."

"Oh, I've got so many favorite things to eat there, but my ultimate favorite is the Pierre's butter pecan ice cream on top of a warm funnel cake."

My stomach growls as Kingston describes some of the yummy treats waiting for us inside Cedar Point. I haven't been to the amusement park in years, not since I volunteered to chaperone the youth ministry a few years ago for their end-of-the-school-year outing.

"It shouldn't be too crowded this early, and the Memorial Day traffic is next weekend," Kingston continues. "So we should be able to get some rides in before it gets too hot outside."

"It tickles me that you like to ride the rides. That's for the young people."

"We are the young people, Yvonne! We're far from old."

"I guess so. I haven't ridden a roller coaster since I was in my twenties."

"You never forget how. Buckle up and scream."

I chuckle as I reminisce about roller coasters. "You mean, close my eyes and then scream."

Kingston pulls into the Cedar Point parking lot, which is about half full. I'm glad I decided to wear my walking shoes. If I had gotten too cute, this would not have been a positive adventure.

As we walk to the front gate of the amusement park, Kingston's hand brushes against mine from time to time. Kingston doesn't seem to notice the contact, but I do. Each touch sends a little warm shiver up my arm. By the time we reach the front of the amusement park, I'm ready for Kingston to just go ahead and take my hand in his, but he acts totally oblivious to what I'm feeling. It has such an effect on me that I wonder if he's doing it on purpose.

"Oh no," I say as we get up to the window to pay. Do Rhoda and Rochelle have some type of radar gun that tells them where Kingston and I are going to be?

"It's our friends," Kingston says with a giggle.

"Your friends."

I notice that Rhoda and Rochelle are wearing the same T-shirt, long jean skirt, white socks, and thick gym shoes. They even have matching sun visors with see-through blue, red, and green screens. I didn't even know that they made those anymore.

"Well, look who we keep running into," Rhoda says.

Rochelle says, "It must be God. You know, they say you can leave the church grounds, but you can't get away from church folk."

"Who says that, Rochelle?" I ask. "What are y'all doing out here today?"

"It's a free country, Yvonne, but if you must know, we are here for my family reunion," Rhoda says.

"That's great!" Kingston says. "Are y'all barbecuing?"

Rhoda nods. "Yessir. We've got ribs, burgers, steaks, sausages, hot dogs. Anything you want. And the side dishes are delicious, too. I made them myself."

"Good. Maybe Yvonne and I will stop at your family's pavilion when we get hungry," Kingston says.

I narrow my eyes slightly at this suggestion. I have no intention of spending my date with Rhoda's country, pig feet– and hog maw–eating family.

Rochelle says, "Good! Y'all can sit with me and my boyfriend."

Now, this is news! Rochelle hasn't had a boyfriend that I know of since she's been at New Faith. I am a little bit curious about his identity, and I wonder why she'd bring her new man around Rhoda and her family of crazies.

"He ain't your boyfriend," Rhoda says. "He's your future husband. That's what God told me, so I'm going with that. Plus, he's my cousin and I know him. He needs a good woman to take care of him."

What in the world? I'm about to put Rochelle's silly self on my prayer list. This heifer has completely lost her mind, letting Rhoda hook her up.

"Take care of him?" I ask. "What's wrong with him?"

"He got a leg amputated in the war," Rochelle says.

"I'm sorry to hear that. Did he go over to Afghanistan?" Kingston asks.

"No, not *that* war. The war between him and his ex-wife," Rhoda says. "She ran him over with his pickup truck."

I can't take a second more of this. "All right, Rhoda and Rochelle. We'll see y'all later."

Rhoda looks both me and Kingston up and down. "Yvonne, make sure you staying holy, now. Back when we were young, they used to make us have chaperones when we were courting."

"We're both good and grown, Rhoda," I reply.

"Ain't too grown to get a smite from on high!"

Rhoda is obviously affected by her own "anointing." So much

so that she needs Rochelle to dab the sweat droplets on the top of her forehead. I can barely get Kingston away from them before he bursts into laughter.

"You think it's funny now," I say as Kingston and I walk up the main amusement park fairway. "But when she puts your name on the prayer list, in bold, don't say I didn't warn you."

"Nobody takes Rhoda seriously, except maybe Rochelle."

"You're right. Everybody knows that she's cuckoo for Cocoa Puffs, but she's got something on just about every member of our church."

"I'm not worried about her," Kingston says. "You want something to eat? Some French fries or ice cream?"

"It's too early for ice cream, but I will take some fries."

Kingston walks me over to the shaded tables and benches. "I'll be right back. You can rest your feet while I stand in line."

"I look like I need a rest?"

"No, but I plan on wearing you out today, so you better rest while you can."

I watch Kingston walk over to the food counter, and I find myself gazing at how his broad back tapers into his waist. He looks like he spends a good deal of time at the gym. I bet his muscles ripple just right.

Oh my Lord.

This is why I dreamed about Luke last night. I think Eva has loosed some type of lust spirit over me. That's the only thing that could explain the way my mind keeps wandering to things that are quite the opposite of holy.

I sit up straight and look away from Kingston and enjoy people watching. There are cute little families pushing babies in strollers and holding toddlers by the hand. Sometimes I wonder what it would've been like to have a child to call my own. I enjoy teaching, and of course Pam's and Taylor's children are like nieces and nephews, but it is not the same as having your own.

My stubborn eyes travel back over to Kingston, and I notice he's talking on his cell phone. His arm is waving in an animated fashion, almost like he's having an argument. When he turns toward me with the tray in his hand, he is clearly not wearing his usual smile anymore.

He places the cell phone in his pocket and walks back to the table, where he sits down across from me. His eyebrows are pulled together in a frown.

"Is everything okay?" I ask.

He nods. "Yes. It was my sister. She wants me to loan her five hundred dollars for my nephew who is in jail for the third time this year."

"It's only May."

"Exactly! She thinks my initials are ATM. It's hard being the only successful one in the family."

"I don't really have much immediate family. I've got some second cousins down South, but my mama was an only child and so was I."

"You should be glad that you don't have anyone hounding you with their problems."

I don't say it, but I actually wouldn't mind hearing about or helping with someone's problems. If it wasn't for my church family, I'd be incredibly lonely. Thank God for the Sister to Sister ministry.

"Can I ask you a question?"

Kingston nods while he stuffs some greasy fries into his mouth. "Shoot."

"What is your impression of Eva?"

"The new sister at church?"

"Yes. What do you think of her?"

Kingston swallows and wipes the excess grease from his hands. "I don't really know yet. She's so quiet, but she seems friendly."

"She is. Do you sense anything else?"

"No. Is this a test? Should I be discerning something about her? What are you trying to say?"

"Do you find her attractive?"

Kingston's eyes widen. "So this *is* a test. I suppose she is an attractive woman, but I haven't really thought about it one way or the other."

I wonder if Kingston or any other man could tell by the way Eva carries herself that she's led a rather loose life. After she kissed me, I started to doubt my own discernment. But if there is some mark on her, some identifying evidence of her movies, then Kingston doesn't see it, either.

"She made a pass at me," I say and wait for Kingston's reaction.

His jaw drops in shock. Then he quickly snaps his mouth closed, because it's full of food. "Are you sure?"

I nod. "She kissed me."

"Wow. What did you do? Throw some holy oil on her and recite some Bible verses?"

"You think you're funny," I scoff, "but that's exactly what I wanted to do. Or something like it. The pitiful child called me this morning, apologizing again, but I don't know what to do about that."

"Forgive her, and move on. Obviously, she misinterpreted something from you. I wouldn't dwell on it too long if I was you."

"Really? What if it was you, and what if Eva was Evan and he kissed you? What would you do?"

"After I knocked him out cold?"

"Exactly."

"I'd pray for him, and I would make it clear that our relationship wasn't a sexual one."

"What a calm answer," I say.

"I'm a levelheaded kind of guy."

"So you're okay with me continuing a friendship with her?"

He shrugs. "Yes. I don't see a problem with it."

"I'm going to be honest. I don't know how I'd feel about you being friends with a gay man who is attracted to you."

"It's different with women."

Now I'm the one with furrowed eyebrows. "What does *that* mean?"

"You all are always looking at each other naked, comparing body parts and all that."

I lean back and burst into laughter. "No, we don't!"

"Okay, maybe not, but I think you should still be nice to that girl. She's young, and she has latched on to you for a reason. Maybe you need to show her how to be a true sister in Christ."

"Maybe . . ."

"Can we talk about this after we ride the Raptor?"

My stomach flops at the thought of the twisty, twirly upside-down roller coaster. "Can I ease back into the rides? I was thinking the Blue Streak or the Wildcat maybe."

"They tore the Wildcat down, and the Blue Streak is for toddlers."

"Wah, wah."

Kingston grins. "Okay. We'll do the Blue Streak first and then the Raptor. Ladies' choice."

"Thank you!"

A sense of dread fills me as we head toward the wooden contraption. Kingston says we're young, but a part of me is feeling real senior like as I watch that tiny car fly over those tracks.

I whisper a silent prayer that this will be as fun as Kingston thinks it will be.

"I told you I hadn't ridden a roller coaster in years."

Kingston holds an ice-filled plastic bag to the back of my neck to cure my nausea. I had second thoughts about that Raptor ride as soon as I clicked the lock on that overhead restraint, but Kingston was doing so much whooping and hollering that I kept quiet.

I shouldn't have.

When we stepped off the ride, I couldn't stop the sky and everything else from spinning. My vertigo was so bad that I had to sit down. But the first available seat was in the now-blazing sun, which made it infinitely worse. As much as I wanted to keep them down, those French fries found their way into the garbage can next to the bench.

"I'm so sorry, Yvonne. I didn't think you'd get sick."

"Me either! I guess I'm just too old for this."

Kingston sits down next to me and moves my hair out of my face. "You're not too old, Yvonne. You're just out of practice."

I can't help but think that I'm out of practice with every-thing, not just amusement park rides. Kingston may have a slow learner on his hands.

"We can ride up to Put-in-Bay now if you want," Kingston says.

The thought of getting in a car right now makes my stomach flip. "Maybe not yet. Can we just rest awhile?"

"We sure can."

I close my eyes and take deep breaths as Kingston holds the cooling ice pack to my neck with one hand and massages my hand with the other. His touch is very calming right now, evok-ing nowhere near the excitement I felt earlier.

After about ten minutes of this tender loving care, I am ready to leave the park. "Let's go." I say. "I'm ready now."

"Are you going to be okay on the ferry?" he asks, apparently not wanting a repeat of the vomit.

"I should be. I feel better."

"Great. We can do some sightseeing on the island and have dinner later. Does that sound tame enough for you?"

I can't tell if Kingston is teasing or not. Has my weak stomach caused him to not be attracted to me anymore?

"I don't need tame. I just need it to not flip upside down."

Kingston laughs as he takes my hand and leads me toward the amusement park entrance. On our way out he casually pulls me close and brings my hand up to his mouth for a soft kiss. I guess this answers my question about the attraction.

"Come on, lady," he says. "May the rest of our day be as ad-venture packed as the morning!"

Whether he means it to be funny or not, this is a laugh riot to me. I will take anything but adventure at this point. I will take a calm and peaceful day with my new friend. Or should I say new man?

Kingston is my new man. Umph, umph, umph. I wonder what Mr. Luke would have to say about that. Actually, I don't care what Luke would say. He is the past, and Kingston is defi-nitely the future.

CHAPTER 26

TAYLOR

Spencer decided that it was best if we didn't wait too long to confront Luke about his reappearance in Joshua's life. So I had my brother come over to chill with Josh, and we're on our way to meet with Luke. He asked us to come to his *church,* which is currently in the recreation center of his apartment complex. I'm not happy about meeting on his terms or his turf, but Spencer agreed to it, so I don't say a word.

When we get to the apartment building, I almost don't want to get out of the car. It isn't in the best neighborhood, and there are some questionable-looking men standing in the parking lot. I'm glad that Spencer is here, because I would've turned right back around and gone home.

"Let me do all the talking, Taylor," Spencer says in a somewhat stern voice. I don't know who he thinks he's talking to. I am not Joshua. He better fall back with all that testosterone.

"Really, Spencer?"

"You know what I mean. He likes to focus in on you and ignore me. It's not going down like that today. He's going to respect me, or he's gonna have the courts decide whether or not he's fit to spend time with his son."

"Okay."

I follow closely behind Spencer as we walk up to the building. The glass in one of the doors is cracked and held together with duct tape. Looks like Luke's congregation needs a building fund.

Once we get inside, we're greeted by two women about my age wearing Sunday morning dresses. They're both very pretty and very shapely. They seem like exactly the type of women that Luke's trifling tail would evangelize.

"If you're looking for the Church of the Redeemed, you've found it!" This woman's squeaky voice doesn't match her sexy look.

"Are you having service?" Spencer asks.

The other woman says, "No, not for a few hours, but the prophet is in prayer. We pray with anyone who comes in between now and our service. Do you have a prayer request?"

"No, but you can let Luke Hastings know that I'm out here," Spencer says. "He's expecting me."

Both women look at one another, as if confused. Squeaky Voice says, "But the prophet doesn't like to be disturbed while he's entreating the Lord."

Just as I am about to rip this girl a new one, Luke emerges from behind a door. He's wearing all white—a dress shirt and some slacks. Prison must've made him tacky. Who wears all that white before Memorial Day?

Luke extends his hand to Spencer, and this time Spencer shakes it with a firm grip. They have some extended eye contact, which I'm sure is full of many manlike messages. I wouldn't be surprised if they started beating their chests with their fists and grunting.

"We can go to my office," Luke says. "Thank you, sisters."

The two women nod their thanks, like they're in awe of this buster or something. I wish I had some of the police photos of Yvonne's face after their prophet took his time whaling on it. Then I wonder how much reverence they'll give him.

In Luke's office there is another woman, also wearing all white. She's seated at a table and has a fake-looking smile plastered on her face.

"Who is she?" I ask.

Spencer cuts his eyes at me, and I shrug. I'd forgotten his command that quickly. I'm letting him do all the talking.

"You didn't mention we would have a guest," Spencer says. "Taylor and I would rather this meeting only be between interested parties."

"She is an interested party. Spencer and Taylor, meet my fiancée, Naomi. We're going to be married next weekend, so she wants to be a part of the discussion. She's going to be Joshua's stepmother."

My breathing becomes rapid as I clutch Spencer's arm.

"You should've mentioned she would be here," Spencer says.

Luke chuckles. And in that brief laugh I hear the leftovers of the evil man he used to be. Like I said before, he ain't changed.

"Spencer, I want this to be a friendly discussion. You're a big dude, but you don't have to go throwing your weight around."

Spencer looks self-consciously down at his healthy midsection and frowns. "Let's get this over with."

"But you just got here!" Luke says. "Would you like some coffee? Soda?"

"We're not thirsty," I say as Spencer and I sit down at the table, opposite Naomi.

Luke sits down and folds his hands on the table in front of him. "So you two wanted to talk about Joshua. So let's talk."

"You decided to show up at a really inopportune time for Joshua," Spencer says. "He's going through some very sensitive situations, and how we handle them will probably impact the rest of his life."

"I know exactly what's going on with my son. He's been expelled from school, but the two of you had no intentions of telling me that."

"How do you know about that?" I ask.

"I have friends who give me information, because even if I haven't been around, I still care about him. I care about my blood, no matter what you think."

"But you didn't care about him when he was walking around the church with too few clothes on, huh?" I reply.

"I was a different man then. I have changed, but you're convinced that I'm the same."

Spencer says, "It does matter to us who is giving out confidential information about our son."

"*Our* son?" Luke laughs his evil laugh again. "You know what? I'm not even going to take that away from you. You've done your part. You've raised him thus far, but you need help. My son is just like me. Hitting a teacher is something I would've done at eleven. Stop shutting me out, when we could raise him together."

"I have a degree in early child development," Naomi says. "I want to help with Joshua, too. It takes a village."

If she says one more thing, I'm going to explode on her, and this isn't even her fight to wage.

"Right now it feels like there are too many people in the village. I'm cool on the village," I say.

"Let me talk to him—alone," Luke says. "And if he doesn't open up to me, we can go back to your supervised visits. Trust that I only want to do right by him."

Trust and Luke don't even belong in the same sentence.

"We've got to pray on that, Luke," Spencer says.

"I'll be praying, too," Luke says. "That both of you stop being stubborn and come to your senses."

"On to the second matter," Spencer says, cutting me off before I even speak. "How do you plan to resume your financial obligations to Joshua?"

"Well, I'll probably be in arrears until he's an adult. Isn't that right, Taylor?"

I open my mouth to respond, but Spencer nudges me hard in the ribs. I'm gonna get him back for that.

"We're going to petition the court to forgive your arrears if you will start paying going forward," Spencer says.

Can this even happen? I don't know who my husband has been talking to, but I have never heard of anybody's child support bill being canceled. And why we letting this fool off the hook, anyway? Even if he doesn't have it right now, he owes *me*.

Not Spencer. He's taking this "I'm in charge" thing a little bit too far.

"Well, my money isn't exactly coming in the way I want it to be, but I am willing to make a sincere effort."

Luke is such a liar. He was a successful CPA before he went to prison. I know this fool still has some clients. He's doing his stuff under the table now.

I lift Naomi's hand and examine her ring. "This is *nice,*" I say. "You could've gotten my son some nice shoes and some outfits with what it cost to buy this."

"We bought this on credit," Naomi says as she snatches her hand away.

I lean back in my seat. "Hmmm . . . well, at least you still have good credit, Luke. Why don't you charge your son something for his birthday? It's in June, you know. He's turning twelve."

"Taylor, Joshua will have everything he needs on his birthday," Spencer says. "Let's discuss the visitation arrangements."

"I would be fine with every other weekend in the beginning," Luke says, "but eventually I want joint custody."

I burst into laughter. "You're never getting joint custody, Luke. Get that out of your head."

"Every other Saturday to start," Spencer says. "Let's work up to weekends."

"You said you were going to be reasonable."

"This is about Joshua and what's best for him. He's going to take some time to get used to this new arrangement," Spencer replies.

Luke folds his arms and sighs. "Next weekend. I want . . .would like to have my son at the wedding."

"I think we can do that," Spencer says.

"I'd like you two to come, as well. It would send a strong message to Joshua that we're getting along."

I stare at Spencer with one eyebrow up. If he can't tell what I'm thinking with this look, then he doesn't know me at all.

Spencer says, "I don't think my wife would be comfortable with that."

I fold my arms across my chest and give Luke an attitude-filled glare. "I would not, and my son ain't coming, either."

"It's not healthy to carry all that hate around," Naomi says as she takes Luke's hand. "You should read *Let it Go,* by Bishop T. D. Jakes, because you really need to free yourself."

I sigh and give Spencer a weary "Can we go?" look. I have had enough of Luke for one day. Who am I kidding? I've had enough of Luke to last a lifetime.

I stand to my feet when I can't take another minute or another second. "I'll let it go as soon as Luke stops holding his grudge against child support."

I spin on one heel and stomp over to the door. I don't care if Spencer wants to stay in here and play patty-cake with Luke. I'm not gonna be able to do it.

In a half second, I hear Spencer following right behind me. I knew he wouldn't leave me hanging.

Once we get out to the car, I stand like I always do at my door and wait for Spencer to open it. He ignores me and goes around to his side, unlocks the car, and jumps in. When he starts the car, I realize that he's not going to open my door.

I knock on the window. "What's wrong with you?"

"I don't open doors for men. Get in the car."

Oh, he has lost his ever-lovin' mind. "I'm not a man."

Spencer throws the car into reverse, so I quickly hop in before he leaves me. The last thing I want is to get stranded at Luke's *church* and then have to ask him for a ride home.

Spencer glares at me when I get in the car.

"Stop looking at me like that," I say.

"I asked you to just be quiet and let me talk, but you had to just keep running your mouth."

"And I don't understand why you think I shouldn't have anything to say!"

"Luke doesn't take you seriously. He is a male chauvinist. He doesn't value women at all, especially his former mistress. I've got a strategy when it comes to dealing with him, and I need you to just follow my lead. No questions asked."

I cross my arms and glare out of the car window. Spencer wants me to be quiet and do what he says. That's what Luke demanded of me. Silence and obedience. Looks like I traded one male chauvinist for another.

"Taylor, you know I value your opinion, and I always want to hear what you think. But this time . . . this time trust the man that you married. I love you and Joshua, and I want us to be whole no matter what Luke does."

"Joshua is not going to Luke's wedding."

"Let's talk about it later, after you've had time to think about it."

"No. I'm done talking about it. He's not going."

Spencer floors the gas pedal and grips the steering wheel as he drives off. I guess he's supposed to be angry or something. But he hasn't seen fury until he's seen a mother scorned. And neither has Luke.

CHAPTER 27

EVA

After talking to Yvonne, Eva felt much better. Things were not lost with Yvonne, and Eva thought that maybe they could still be friends.

When Eva's cell phone buzzed in her pocket she thought it was Yvonne calling to chat, but she hadn't read that Scripture passage yet, so she hoped that Yvonne wouldn't ask about that. Eva just couldn't open her grandmother's Bible again. She'd just gone out and purchased a new one so that she wouldn't see the punishments underlined, highlighted, and ready to jump out at her.

"Hello."

"It's about time you answered your phone."

Eva swallowed hard. It was Roe from the strip club.

"How did you get my number?"

He laughed. "You should be wondering how I got your address."

Eva shuddered. "You don't know where I live."

"I do. And you better believe, I'm coming to collect what you owe me. That little sucka move you did at the club wasn't right, but I'm gonna let you apologize to me real nice and easy."

Eva disconnected the call. She'd had enough. Why would her friend give Roe her cell phone number? The last thing she needed to worry about was him showing up at her doorstep. No one from that life knew where she lived.

No one from that life would have any more information about Eva, because she was leaving it behind.

Eva took the plastic wrapper off the new Bible and ran her hand over the deep burgundy cover. The salesperson had offered to engrave her name on the front, but Eva had turned that down. Putting her name on the Bible might offend God, considering how much wrong she had committed.

After a bit of page flipping, Eva located the text that Yvonne had suggested. The passage was long, so she stretched out on the floor on her stomach and placed the Bible in front of her.

When therefore the Lord knew how the Pharisees had heard that Jesus made and baptized more disciples than John (Though Jesus himself baptized not, but his disciples), He left Judaea, and departed again into Galilee.

And he must needs go through Samaria. Then cometh he to a city of Samaria, which is called Sychar, near to the parcel of ground that Jacob gave to his son Joseph. Now Jacob's well was there. Jesus, therefore, being wearied with his journey, sat thus on the well: and it was about the sixth hour.

There cometh a woman of Samaria to draw water: Jesus saith unto her, Give me to drink. (For his disciples were gone away unto the city to buy meat.)

Then saith the woman of Samaria unto him, How is it that thou, being a Jew, asketh drink of me, which am a woman of Samaria? for the Jews have no dealings with the Samaritans.

Jesus answered and said unto her, If thou knewest the gift of God, and who it is that saith to thee, Give me to drink; thou wouldest have asked of him, and he would have given thee living water.

The woman saith unto him, Sir, thou hast nothing to draw with, and the well is deep: from whence then hast thou that living water? Are thou greater than our father Jacob, which gave us the well, and drank thereof himself, and his children, and his cattle?

Jesus answered and said unto her, Whosoever drinketh of this

*water shall thirst again: But whosoever drinketh of the water that
I shall give him shall never thirst; but the water that I shall give
him shall be in him a well of water springing up into everlasting
life.*

*The woman saith unto him, Sir, give me this water, that I
thirst not, neither come hither to draw.*

Jesus saith unto her, "Go, call thy husband, and come hither."

The woman answered and said, I have no husband.

*Jesus said unto her, Thou hast well said, I have no husband:
For thou hast had five husbands; and he whom thou now hast is
not thy husband: in that saidst thou truly. The woman saith
unto him, Sir, I perceive that thou art a prophet. Our fathers worshipped in this mountain; and ye say, that in Jerusalem is the
place where men ought to worship.*

*Jesus saith unto her, Woman, believe me, the hour cometh,
when ye shall neither in this mountain, nor yet at Jerusalem, worship the Father. Ye worship ye know not what: we know what we
worship, for salvation is of the Jews. But the hour cometh, and
now is, when the true worshipers shall worship the Father in spirit
and in truth: for the Father seeketh such to worship him. God is a
Spirit: and they that worship him must worship him in spirit and
in truth.*

*The woman saith unto him, I know that Messias cometh,
which is called Christ: when he is come, he will tell us all things.*

Jesus saith unto her, I that speak unto thee am he.

Eva read and reread the verses several times. The first time
she read them, only one thing jumped out at her. The woman
had had five husbands, and she was living with a man who wasn't
her husband. Eva didn't know what that meant back in biblical
times, but she was sure that if this woman went to a church, she
wouldn't be head of the women's ministry.

The second time Eva read the passage, she noticed that the
woman asked Jesus for the water so that she wouldn't have to
come back to the well. It reminded Eva of herself. She'd come
to God because she didn't have HIV and because she didn't
want to do the films anymore.

The third and last time Eva read the Scripture, she marveled at the fact that when the woman told Jesus that she wasn't married, He didn't judge her. He didn't tell her she would be punished. He didn't tell her that she was going into hell's hot fires.

He told her how to worship God, revealed that He was the Messiah, and He offered her life. He didn't care what she'd done. It had nothing to do with who He was.

Something inside Eva gave way, and the tears flowed freely. These, however, were tears of joy. She picked up the Bible and hugged it to her chest.

This was the God that Eva had been searching for. She had found Him. Or He had found her, just like He found that woman at the well. That woman was in the middle of doing everything wrong, and Jesus fixed her.

For the first time in her life, Eva had hope that her future would be different.

CHAPTER 28

YVONNE

When Kingston and I step off the ferry at Put-in-Bay, I don't feel sick anymore. I actually feel energized and ready for fun. I don't know if Kingston has anything in mind for us, but I already know where I want to go.

"Have you ever been to Perry's Cave?" I ask.

"I don't think so," Kingston replies. "Is that where we're going?"

I nod as Kingston absentmindedly takes my fingertips in his hand and leads me away from the ferry's dock.

He turns to me, smiles, and repeats, "Are we going to the cave?"

I'm so caught up in the tingling taking place in my fingers that I almost forget to answer him. "Y-yes. There's a butterfly house next to the cave, and we can look for precious jewels in the cave."

"I've already got a precious jewel right here, but I'll go look for more if you want."

I never know how to react to Kingston's flirtatious compliments. Should I say thank you? I end up making a nervous sound that is halfway between a chuckle and a hiccup.

"You okay?" Kingston asks. I guess it sounded more like a hiccup.

"Yes, I'm fine. There's the butterfly house up ahead."

Kingston leads the way and pays our admission. As we walk into the house, I inhale the fragrant scents of the bushes and flowers that they placed in strategic areas just to attract the butterflies.

"I love this place," I say. "When I was going through some rough times, I would come out here and the butterflies would remind me that transformation is a good thing."

"It is a wonderful thing. You've metamorphosed, Yvonne?"

I stoop down next to one of the bushes and peer at a pretty black butterfly with turquoise circles on its wings. "I believe I have. I hope so. I'm definitely not the same person I was ten years ago."

"What's different about you?"

"I care more about myself. I never made myself a priority before. Now I take care of me."

Kingston stoops down next to me, and the butterfly escapes into a small tree. He says, "Would you be open to someone else taking care of you, too?"

"Honestly, I don't know. This is all very nice. The dates, I mean. But I'm not sure I want to go the whole distance."

Kingston's gaze becomes serious. I know that wasn't what he wanted to hear, but I had to be honest. I'm trying to picture forever, but I just can't wrap my head around that.

"Why aren't you sure? Do you want to be alone?"

His questions hit home. Of course, I don't want to be alone. Every now and then I think about that, but I don't *mind* being alone, and that makes all the difference.

"I enjoy your company, but I don't know what I really want in a relationship," I explain. "I know what I don't want, but I can't define what I desire or need."

Another black butterfly joins the first, and they fly in little circles around each other as if they're dancing. "Look," Kingston says, "I think they're giving us a show."

"Do you think they even notice us? Sometimes I feel like they completely ignore us, and they're just going about their daily business."

"You may be right, but I choose to believe they're performing."

Kingston takes my hand again, and we walk along the man-made path, enjoying the butterflies as they either perform for us or live their butterfly lives.

When we leave the butterfly house, we head to Perry's Cave. Hand in hand, we enter with our tour guide. Almost immediately, I realize that my flimsy top isn't warm enough for the cave's temperature. It can't be more than fifty degrees in here.

Kingston takes advantage of the situation by pulling me in front of him and wrapping both his arms around me. It's hard to walk this way, but we take our time so that we can remain intertwined.

We stop at the incredible underground lake. This is my favorite part of the cave, because I find it so fascinating that there is a lake beneath the ground and surrounded by rock. I always, for some reason, think about God making water come out of a rock for the Israelites. Something refreshing out of a dry place.

"This is really nice, Yvonne. I'm glad you brought me here," Kingston says.

"I'm glad too. I've never been here with anyone. It's been my hideaway for a while."

"Thank you for sharing it with me."

"You're welcome."

"Even if you don't want forever."

I snuggle against Kingston's body and sigh. "Let's not think about forever right now. Can't we just enjoy what we're feeling right now?"

Kingston bursts into laughter. "You sound like a man trying to weasel his way out of a relationship."

"I guess I do, but I'm telling the truth."

It suddenly becomes darker inside the cave, as if someone switched off the night-light. The tour guide says, "They said there would be a storm this afternoon. I didn't think it would come in this early."

"My weather report said scattered showers," I say. "It didn't mention anything about storms."

"It was updated this morning. They're thinking it might get pretty rough for a few hours and then calm down this evening," the tour guide replies.

Kingston says, "It's a good thing we did our roller-coaster thing this morning."

The tour guide says, "Come on, folks. You don't want to be trapped in the cave when it starts raining. It can get pretty chilly in here."

By the time we leave the cave and get halfway to the seafood restaurant we've chosen, the downpour has started. Once we make it to the restaurant, we settle in and order a late lunch.

"You must be pretty hungry, Yvonne," Kingston says. "Surf *and* turf?"

I laugh out loud. "Yes, I am. I purged all of my food from earlier."

"Order anything you want. Dessert, too, if you have room for it. I want you one hundred percent satisfied."

I narrow my eyes at Kingston and shake my head. It feels like there was some innuendo in that "one hundred percent satisfied" comment. I'm not the kind of woman to trade flirtations of a sexual nature.

"You're getting a little bit too comfortable, aren't you?"

Kingston chuckles. "Don't close up, Yvonne. Don't throw that wall back up. I'm just having a little fun."

"Mmm-hmm. As long as you remember that it's just fun."

As if punctuating my thought, the sound of a loud thunder crack rocks the room. This really makes Kingston laugh.

"I guess God is on your side, huh?" he says with a laugh.

I nod. "Yes! Now, pull yourself together."

Then there is another thunderous sound, and all the lights in the restaurant go out. Seconds later a generator kicks in, but it lights only the emergency exit signs and the baseboards along the floor.

"Can you tell God I apologize for flirting?" Kingston asks. "The power outage is a bit much."

"You are silly!"

The manager of the restaurant walks out to the center of the dining room and says, "Ladies and gentlemen, our generator power is only enough to keep the food refrigerated. During an outage, we don't have the luxury of being able to prepare your food. We hope the power is restored soon, and we apologize for any inconvenience this might cause."

I place a hand over my stomach as it grumbles in response to the manager's words. Guess I won't be getting my surf or my turf.

When the rain slows down just a little, Kingston and I take our chances and quickly run back to the ferry loading dock. Maybe we'll be able to get back to the mainland and find something to eat.

"How soon after this rain stops will the ferry go out on the water?" Kingston asks the ferry attendant.

"We won't go out if we're under a tornado warning or a tornado watch," the young man behind the glass says.

I ask, "Are we under either of those?"

"We're under both."

"Until when?" Kingston asks.

"Until eleven o'clock tonight. This storm is big and moving slowly. It's not expected to move out of the area until tomorrow."

"So how are we supposed to get back to our car? Back home?" I ask.

The young man shrugs. "Do you want to see a list of the hotels on the island?"

"I'll take it," Kingston says.

While we stand inside the dock shelter, the rain and wind kick up again.

"I can drive you guys over to the Put-in-Bay Resort if you want," the young man says. "Nothing's going to be happening here."

I look down at my very cute and very drenched outfit. "Is there anywhere we can get a change of clothes?" I ask.

"You can get sweats at the resort gift shop. I'm afraid they won't have undergarments, ma'am."

Kingston grins as I feel my neck heat up with embarrass-
ment. "Sweats will be fine," I say.

"What's your name, bro? I'm Kingston, and this is my lady,
Yvonne. We sure are pleased to meet you."

"I'm Chad, sir. Nice to meet you, too."

"Were you raised in the South, Chad?" I ask.

"Yes, ma'am. I was born and raised in Mobile, Alabama."

I knew it! He is way too polite to have been raised in Ohio.
"And you moved all the way here?" I ask.

"Yes, ma'am. I was in college at Kent State, and then I just decided to stay up here," Chad says as he shows us to his car—a
rusty Ford Escort.

We pile into the car, with Kingston in the backseat and me
riding shotgun. Chad has to try a few times to get his not so
gently used car to turn over, but once it does, it roars to life
with the energy—or at least the noise—of a much larger auto-
mobile.

"This weather is pretty bad," Chad says. "We haven't seen a
storm like this in a while."

I wonder if this is a bad omen for me and Kingston. Maybe
God is trying to tell me that we're moving along too quickly.

We pull into the Put-in-Bay Resort's parking lot as another
fierce downpour starts. I give up on my hair looking like anything other than a wet fur ball, but Kingston doesn't seem to
mind. He's still grinning at me every chance he gets.

When we get into the hotel lobby, it's packed with other
stranded vacationers. Everyone looks damp and grumpy.

"We are getting separate rooms, right?" I ask as we get in at
the end of the line.

"Of course. Unless—"

"Kingston!" I slap Kingston on the arm.

He chuckles. "I'm joking. Don't you see the smile on my
face?"

"Mmm-hmm. It's an impish grin, though."

This makes Kingston throw his head back and laugh. He's so
handsome when he laughs that it makes my breath catch in my
throat. I could listen to him laugh all day.

"May I help you?" the desk clerk says when it is finally our turn.

"Yes. Can I have two single rooms for one night? We'll check out in the morning," Kingston says.

The clerk taps on her computer keyboard. She frowns, clicks some more, and then frowns again. "We don't have any more single rooms. I'm afraid we're booked up."

"So what kind of rooms do you have?" Kingston asks.

"The honeymoon suite! It's our very best room, and since it's the last minute and all, we'll give it to you for the same rate as a double."

"Absolutely not," I say. "Let's go, Kingston."

"Ma'am, everywhere on the island is booked because of the tornado warning and the ferry not running. But I can call and see if anyone has two rooms if you like."

"Or . . . we could just take the room. Don't worry, Yvonne. I will be a perfect gentleman."

Me and Kingston in a honeymoon suite. I don't think that's a good idea at all. I stare blankly at him, trying to communicate my disagreement to him without opening my mouth.

"I promise, Yvonne. I'll behave."

I'm sure he will, but he's not the one waking up from steamy dreams in a cold sweat. No. The question isn't, will Kingston behave? The question is, will I?

CHAPTER 29

PAM

It is Sunday morning, so I should be getting ready for church. But instead, I'm sitting on the couch, waiting for my husband and children to come home.

I tried to write last night, but I couldn't focus. I kept thinking about Aria knocking on Troy's hotel room door in the middle of the night, him leaving my children in that room by themselves and going with her back to her room. Dangerous thoughts, I know, but I can't keep myself from having them.

In my mind, Aria's fiancé doesn't exist; only her professed love for Troy is real to me. That's what happens when you leave a writer alone to ponder. I can create all kinds of scenarios in my mind, but for some reason, I don't see a happy ending in the future.

My stomach turns when I hear Troy's car pull into the driveway. I look down at Aria's letter in my lap. The scent of the faded perfume wafts up to my nostrils, giving me another sensory reminder that this is real. I wonder how many times Troy held the letter to his nose and inhaled. One time is too many. Twice is grounds for divorce.

My family barges into the house in a flurry of noise. Everyone is two shades darker from roasting in the summer sun all weekend. They look like perfectly bronzed turkeys on Thanksgiving.

Troy hugs me and kisses me on my neck as the children plop down on the couch next to me. I quickly cover the letter with my hand. I don't want to have this conversation in front of my children.

"Hey, Mommy!" TJ says. "We had Cracker Barrel for breakfast."

"You did?" I ask, trying to hide the tremble in my voice.

"Pam, are you all right?" Troy asks.

I shake my head, because I'm afraid if I open my mouth to speak, the tears are going to come spilling out. With Troy here finally, and knowing that I'm about to confront him, this is now too real. All weekend there was a chance that all of this would disappear into dreamland, that I'd wake up from this nightmare.

"Kids, y'all go upstairs. We'll go to the movies later. Maybe Mommy will come with us."

Gretchen and Cicely aren't fooled one bit. They know me well, and they usher TJ out of the room with looks of concern on their faces.

"What's wrong, Pam?" Troy asks once the children are safely up the staircase. "Did something happen when I was gone?"

I hand him the letter without hesitation. If we're going to have this conversation, I want to get it over with. As soon as Troy recognizes the letter, he frowns deeply and sighs.

"I thought I threw that away."

I swallow a mouthful of saliva. Troy's answer is completely unacceptable. He knows it, and he knows that I know it.

"That's how you want to address this, Troy? Really?"

"It's two years old. She gave this to me right before she got serious with her fiancé."

"And you didn't think I'd want to know about it?"

"I didn't think you needed to know about it."

All I can see is red. Troy's cavalier attitude about another woman's declaration of love is out of line.

"I didn't *need* to know that Aria is in love with you?"

"Was. She said she was in love, but she's not anymore."

"How do you know, huh? She's in my house, around my children, in *your* face."

"She's getting married. She ain't thinkin' 'bout me," Troy scoffs.

Something about Troy's tone worries me. Like Aria might not be thinking about him, but he just might be thinking of her. Did Troy turn Aria down because he didn't love her back or because he didn't want to disturb his home? I don't need him to stay with me out of obligation. That is not the marriage I want.

"Are you . . . are you in love with her?" I ask, unsure if I want to hear the answer, but desperately needing to.

"I can't believe you just asked me that."

"Are you?" I repeat.

Troy jumps up from the couch, and the letter falls to the floor. He paces back and forth angrily. He's angry. I'm angry. His emotion is all wrong. He should be apologetic. He's the one keeping secrets.

Troy stops in front of me. "Your jealousy is going to destroy this marriage."

"No! Your dishonesty and secrecy are going to destroy this marriage."

"I was going to tell you, but I knew you would read it this way." Troy sits down again and takes my hand in his. "There is nothing to worry about. I don't feel anything for her."

Troy plants little kisses all over my face. Is this supposed to make my hurt and jealousy disappear? He's trying to kiss this away like I do one of TJ's boo-boos. But this isn't a scratch on my knee. This wound is deep. It's as if Troy's taken a dagger to my chest and touched my heart with the tip of it. This won't go away easily, but I know how to start the healing process.

"I'm glad you don't feel anything for her, because then it won't hurt at all for you to find another artist," I say.

I feel Troy pull away from me. The quickness of his gesture

communicates shock, but I can't, for the life of me, understand why he'd be surprised.

"What do you mean, find another artist?"

"You know what I mean. Aria's time is up. She's getting old, anyway. It's time for you to discover a new star."

Troy shakes his head, then drops it down and holds his face in his hands. "We are right on the cusp, Pam. You can't ask me to do this. The last time we had a big break for Aria, you'd found out you were pregnant with TJ."

"And what does that have to do with anything?"

"It shows that you always put a monkey wrench in the plans when it comes to Aria. I think you've been jealous of her since she started, even before she decided to develop a crush on me."

"What I read in that letter was not a crush. That was passion. I know the difference, and so does Aria."

Troy sighs again. Why does he keep sighing? Is he sick of this conversation? I can keep having this conversation all night, until he agrees with what I'm saying.

I clear my throat and say, "I'm not asking, Troy. I'm telling you. I'm pulling the wife card."

"What wife card? There is no wife card. This is my dream we're talking about, Pam."

I remember when it used to be *our* dream. I have no idea when Troy got so possessive about the music.

"So are you saying that you're not going to find a new artist?"

Troy shakes his head. "That's not what I'm saying. If you want to come to our music sessions to make yourself feel more comfortable, then do it."

"I won't feel more comfortable until Aria is nowhere near my family."

Troy stares at me and then shakes his head. "I'm not letting her go, Pam. I hate that you insist on being a drama queen on this. I hope you come to your senses."

"Just answer one question, Troy."

"Don't ask me anything, Pam."

"Did you sleep with her?"

Troy inhales and exhales slowly but says nothing. Why is it taking him this long to answer me?

"Pam . . ."

"Tell me the truth, Troy, or so help me God, I'm going to leave you this instant!"

"One time. Years ago, before TJ was born. It was only once, Pam."

Something inside me shatters.

"I wish you hadn't asked," Troy says. "It didn't mean anything to me."

"You know what it means to me? It means you're a liar," I say. "You lie, you lie, you lie! And she came into my home after sleeping with my husband, as if she would ever be welcome under my roof. That slut is not welcome here! If you bring her here, I don't know what I'll do."

My body literally quakes with a combination of anger, pain, and shock. Troy tries to hug me, and I want more than anything to be able to accept his touch. But it is tainted now.

"Don't touch me!" I shout. "You keep away from me!"

"I love you and the kids. I. Don't. Want. Her. She is nothing but a meal ticket. The only reason I still deal with her is because she's going to make *us* rich."

Before I can respond, Troy exits the room and leaves me sitting on the couch. I glance at the letter on the floor, and I feel my fury escalate. I scramble off the couch on my hands and knees and snatch the letter up into a balled fist.

I take my cell phone out of my pocket and dial Taylor's number. She answers on the first ring. "Taylor, c-can I stay with you for a couple of days?"

"Pam, what's wrong? Did Troy do something to you?"

"No, but I can't stay in this house. I might do something to him."

"You showed him the letter," Taylor says.

"Yeah. And he admitted to sleeping with her before TJ was born."

Taylor pauses for a long moment. "Oh my God. Stay right where you are. I'm coming to get you."

"Okay," I say in a tiny shaking voice.

"Don't hang up the phone, okay? Just leave it on while I drive over. I'm leaving right now."

I listen to Taylor pray victory over my marriage. I hear her plead the blood over my mind and heart. I only feel numb.

"Mommy, what's wrong?" It's Cicely.

I don't want her to see me like this. "Baby, go on back upstairs."

"But, Mommy . . ."

"I said go!"

She scampers out of the room, and my sobs take over. How could Troy do this to our family? Why did he tell me the truth? Why did he pick today to stop lying?

Why didn't he take it to his grave?

I will never, ever believe that it was only one time. I remember when my intuition first alerted me to Aria. I can recall the day, the hour, the very moment even, when I knew she had designs on my man. I remember walking into Troy's studio and seeing her sitting on his desk like the hood ornament on a luxury car.

I let everyone tell me what a good, good man Troy was, and how much he loved me. I pushed every little doubt and every little fear out of my mind. Told myself that Troy would drink, he might even smoke marijuana, but he would never, ever give himself away to another woman.

Even then, I knew. I *knew!*

Taylor says, "Pam, honey, I'm outside your house. You can come on out."

I look down at what I'm wearing. A nightgown with a robe and slippers. And I need my purse. I didn't think this escape through really well.

"I need you to come in, Taylor. Please, come in."

I drag myself to my feet and go to the front door to open it. Taylor runs up the front stairs and catches me in her arms as I start to crumble again. It seems that my legs just don't want to hold me right now.

Taylor walks me over to the living room couch and helps me sit.

"Troy!" she yells.

Troy appears at the top of the stairs. "I wondered if it would be you or Yvonne."

"Can you please pack her a bag?"

"Where's she going?" Troy scoffs. "She's got three children to look after."

Taylor narrows her eyes at Troy. "Don't do that. Don't. Let her have some space."

Troy laughs out loud. "And you should be the one she runs to? 'Cause you just really know how a married woman feels when her man steps out on her, huh?"

"Yeah, actually, I do. I know too well the damage my sin caused. So can you please get her a bag?"

"She can get it herself."

Troy walks away from the stairs and slams the door at the end of the hall. That is his entertainment room—his man cave. I guess he's letting me know that I can get what I need from our bedroom in peace.

I look up at Taylor. "I'll get the bag. Do you think I should bring the kids with me?"

She shakes her head. "No, ma'am. You are gonna leave them crumb snatchers right here with their daddy. He doesn't have a job."

My first thought is to defend Troy. He does have a job—music is his job. But I don't open my mouth. He doesn't deserve my defense.

"You know what, I think I might need my car while I'm at your house," I say. "Can you just follow me?"

"Do you think you'll be okay to drive?" Taylor asks.

I nod as I ascend the stairs. When I get to the top of the stairs, Troy opens the door to his man cave. "Pam, please don't leave. We can get past this."

I give him an unblinking stare, take in everything I love about the way he looks. His strong, broad chest and, almost, six-pack. His arms. The warmth in his eyes. Then I imagine Aria loving the same things.

"I really wish you hadn't told me."

"I'm telling you the truth. Doesn't that mean anything to you?"

"Too many years have gone by since I first asked you about Aria. I don't know if I can get past this."

"So you're leaving your family."

"If I do leave for good, my children come with me."

"If you leave."

I nod slightly. "I need some time. But don't bring that home wrecker in my house while I'm gone."

"We've already got her vocals done for this project. I won't need her to come here."

I shake my head. He still has no intentions of dropping her as an artist, even with me packing my things to leave.

"Don't *ever* bring her here."

Troy sighs and looks at the floor. "I can't promise you that."

I spin on one heel and storm into our bedroom. The bed we share is neatly made, with Troy's stack of pillows on his side. I shudder at the thought that I may never share this bed with Troy again.

This could be the end of my marriage to Troy, the end of my family unit. Because if he can't promise not to bring Aria into our home, then in my mind he can't promise to stay out of bed with her. And if he can't assure me of *that*, then I can't and won't promise to stay.

CHAPTER 30

EVA

Eva glanced around the church and frowned. None of her new friends were at New Faith this morning. Yvonne hadn't mentioned not showing up at church, and with Pam and Taylor being out, too, it made Eva self-conscious. Had Yvonne told them all about her, and did they not want to even worship in the same sanctuary now?

Eva shook her head and took a seat near the center of the sanctuary. She didn't want to be in the back anymore. Before she read that passage in her Bible, Eva hadn't felt worthy to sit anywhere but in the back of the church. But after she read about herself in her Bible, she felt like she was right where she belonged.

Service was going to start soon, so Eva got settled in for praise and worship, her favorite part of the service. Rhoda and Rochelle sat down on the pew in front of her. They didn't say hello or even acknowledge Eva. She didn't mind. She had absolutely nothing to say to them.

"This is just downright scandalous," Rhoda said. "They ought to be ashamed of themselves."

Rochelle said, "They just bold with it. I mean, even after seeing us in Sandusky, they didn't come to church? You would think that they would've got convicted in their spirits once they saw the saints of God."

Eva tried not to pay attention to Rhoda and Rochelle's conversation. She wasn't a gossiper. But they were talking so loud that she couldn't help but overhear.

"Yvonne has been acting like she lost her Holy Ghost ever since she divorced Luke," Rhoda declared.

Eva's jaw dropped. They were talking about Yvonne? She leaned slightly forward, feeling incredibly guilty for eavesdropping, but not guilty enough to stop.

"She has!" Rochelle said. "And did you know that Brother Kingston has been married, like, five times?"

Rhoda shook her head. "I knew it. You just be glad that the man God has for you is pure. He's never even been with a woman."

"He hasn't?" Rochelle asked. "Didn't he used to be married?"

"Yes, but they never consummated."

Rochelle's eyes widened. "I wonder if Brother Kingston would be interested in me if things don't work out with him and Yvonne."

Eva slapped her hand over her mouth to keep from laughing. She leaned back in her seat and focused on the pulpit. The praise team, minus Yvonne and Brother Kingston, came out and started singing an upbeat worship song.

Eva wanted to burst into laughter at how Rhoda and Rochelle seemed so caught up in worship. Their arms were raised into the air, and Rochelle's eyes were closed. From where she was sitting, Eva couldn't see Rhoda's face, but she imagined that Rhoda was glancing from left to right, checking out people's outfits to judge if they were church appropriate.

The music was good, but not nearly as good as when Brother Kingston led the praise team. His voice was incredibly deep and rich, but he could hit high notes so clear that he sounded like a soprano.

Eva listened intently to Pastor Brown's sermon as he talked about how God answered prayer. It was a sermon she could relate to. God had answered her prayer. She'd asked Him for direction, and she'd wound up at New Faith.

Eva lifted a silent prayer of thanks. She didn't know if she could take the next step. The step that meant she was giving her life to Christ. She wanted to but wondered if she could live up to that life.

Then Pastor Brown said something that stirred Eva's spirit. He said, "If you could be holy all by yourself, then you wouldn't need salvation. The thing is, you can't be holy without God's spirit dwelling on the inside of you, and it is a gift. All you have to do is repent of your sins, be baptized, and ask Him to fill you."

Eva stood to her feet. This made so much sense. She couldn't resist the urges that came up in her mind, because she didn't have God's spirit inside. She stepped down to the end of the row and sighed. It was time.

Maybe it was fitting that none of her friends were at church that morning. Repenting to God was something that she needed to do on her own. She'd never wanted to admit her sins to anyone before, but she kept thinking of Jesus and that Samaritan woman. He knew all of the Samaritan woman's sins, just like He knew all of Eva's.

Eva walked down the center aisle, stepping in time to the worship hymn. With so many eyes on her, she felt like a bride on her wedding day. As she approached the altar, she heard applause but tuned it out. All she could think of was all the things she'd done in her life.

The lady minister at the altar hugged her. "You ready to give your life to God, baby?"

She nodded. "Yes, ma'am."

"You know what that means, right?"

"I think so."

The minister smiled. "It means that all your sins will go into the sea of forgetfulness. It's like they never happened."

Eva shuddered and collapsed into the woman's arms. She broke into tearful sobs, but they were cries of joy! Even if she couldn't quite forget her sins, at least God would.

If this was her wedding to God, Eva's heart said, "I do."

CHAPTER 31

YVONNE

Since the weather has finally cleared, Kingston and I are driving home. It's too bad we couldn't make it to church this morning. There's no telling what gossip Rhoda and Rochelle have dreamed up. It's a good thing they don't know about the honeymoon suite. I would never be able to convince them that no sin took place in that hotel room.

And nothing sinful *had* happened. Not quite.

I accidentally caught a glimpse of Kingston's abdominal region when he was changing his shirt, and I felt my heart rate quicken. For a split second I imagined him with his shirt completely off and me running my fingers over his washboard stomach.

The thought of that makes me glance over at Kingston even now. He hums as he drives, and that ever-present grin has not left his face since we got on the road.

"Did you sleep well, Yvonne? You've been awful quiet this morning."

I did not sleep well at all. I was concerned that I might do something embarrassing in my sleep, like snore or pass gas. Normal things that real live people do. Well, real live unladylike people.

The room was nice, even though the rose petals on the bed

made things kind of awkward. Kingston let me have the bed, while he slept on the sofa, and I kept peeking over at him to see if he was looking at me.

"I slept fine," I finally respond.

"You did? Well, I didn't. I tossed and turned all night," Kingston says.

"Was the couch uncomfortable?"

He shakes his head. "Nope. But there was a beautiful woman in a bedroom with me. I am a man, Yvonne. A man who hasn't had any in a good long time. I spent half the night praying."

Kingston has a dead serious expression on his face, so I have no idea why this tickles me so much. I crack up laughing.

"You're the one who wanted the honeymoon suite!" I say. "It's not my fault there was no honeymoon taking place."

"Laugh if you want," he says. "I'm just being honest with you. Don't get hemmed up with me in any more hotel rooms. I can't be held responsible next time for what I might do."

"Am I that irresistible?" I ask while still laughing.

Kingston looks me dead in the eyes. "You are, Yvonne. To me, you are."

Did it get hot in here all of a sudden? I fan myself with my hand and look away from Kingston's demanding stare. He looks back at the road again and drums his fingers on the steering wheel.

"Yvonne, can I ask you something?"

"Go ahead."

"Would you mind if we started seriously dating?"

I swallow nervously. We've had only three dates. I don't know what "seriously dating" even means. Does that mean he'll want to propose soon? This feels like it's going at warp speed, and I think we need to slow it down a notch.

"And what comes after seriously dating?" I ask. "Because I'm not sleeping with you, just so you know."

Kingston's giggles fill the car with the sound of his richly deep voice. "Yvonne, why do you think I'm trying to take your virtue?"

"I don't really think that, I guess. I'm just afraid of this."

"Afraid of dating, afraid of me, afraid of falling . . ."

"*Terrified* of falling."

I leave "in love" off the end of the sentence, but I think we both know that's what I mean.

"You think I'm secure about all this, Yvonne? I've been married twice. You can't be more afraid than I am."

"So we should quit while we're ahead, right?" I ask. "Maybe it's not a good idea."

Kingston nods slowly and briefly turns his gaze on me. "That's what you want?"

Good Lord, this man is fine. The intensity in his eyes scatters my thoughts like a handful of confetti in the wind.

"I don't know what I want."

"Well, why don't you stop trying to figure out what you want? Why don't you focus on what God wants for you?"

I nod slowly and consider this. When I got ready to divorce Luke, I asked God for direction. I prayed and I cried. I cried and I prayed. Until something happened. Until I felt peace in my spirit about leaving Luke, moving on, and finding myself. I need to spend some time talking to God about Kingston, because he sure doesn't seem to be going anywhere, and I have no idea what to do with these feelings.

"What do you think God wants for you?" I ask.

Kingston gives me a beautiful smile full of longing. "God wants *you* for me, Yvonne. I'm just waiting on you to get the same revelation."

I can't think of any kind of answer that would sound like it makes a lick of sense. So I say nothing and let Kingston wonder what I'm thinking. Maybe it'll buy me some time to sort it all out.

Maybe . . . something will be revealed.

CHAPTER 32

PAM

"You know you can stay here as long as you want, right?" Taylor asks as she hands me a pillow with a fresh pillowcase on it.

I plop down on Taylor's guest-room bed and exhale loudly. I know that I can stay here long. What will my children do without me at home? Luckily, school is out for the summer, and I don't have to worry about them getting themselves ready for school. Troy should be able to handle meals, and if he can't, then my child will stand in the gap for me.

"I wish I didn't have to be here at all."

"You don't. You can confront Troy and tell him to leave. That's what I would do," Taylor says.

I know she's just trying to help, so I refrain from telling her that she's not helping. Confronting Troy again is not the answer, of this I'm sure. I told him to get rid of Aria, and that's the only solution that I can agree with. So if he refuses, does that mean he's choosing Aria over me and our family?

"He slept with her, Taylor. I remember years ago thinking that he had, and you convinced me that he hadn't."

Taylor's eyes widen, as if she recalls that conversation we had. "I asked you if things had changed in the bedroom. I never, ever said for sure that Troy wasn't cheating."

I shake my head and hug the pillow to my chest. It's not Taylor's fault, no matter what she said at the time. The fault lies with Troy and Aria for doing what they did, and with me for not making him lose that girl a long time ago. I should've known better. Should've followed my first mind.

"Are you going to be okay in here?" Taylor asks as fresh tears wet my cheeks. "I'm going to make some lunch before the boys come home from church. Do you want some tea?"

"No thank you. I think I want to write."

"Okay. I'll leave you alone, then. Let me know if you need to talk, cry, holler, go and beat Troy down, go and beat that heffa down, or any of the above."

This makes me laugh. It's a weak, sad, and downtrodden laugh, but it's still better than bursting into tears.

Taylor hugs me tight. "It's going to work out. God didn't bring you and Troy this far to leave you."

I nod, although I don't know if I agree that our marriage is going to work out. Cheating is and always has been a deal breaker for me. Troy broke our vows, he gave what belongs to me to another woman, and he wants me to pretend that it's nothing!

When Taylor leaves the room, I take out my cell phone. No missed calls, meaning that Troy hasn't called. In romances even when the guy messes up, he comes after the girl. Troy hasn't come for me.

I check my text messages to be sure, and there is a message from Logan. **Talked to Troy. You okay?**

Troy told Logan about our drama? Why would he do that? He's probably just trying to get someone on his side about all this.

I type a one-word response. **No.**

Want to talk about it?

I shake my head. Why would I want to talk about the demise of my marriage with a dangerously handsome brand-new friend who just happens to be attracted to me?

I type the same one word. **No.**

I take out my laptop. I'm not sure if I'm going to be able to write anything, because I can't stop thinking about Troy and Aria. *Ugh.* I have to remember not to put them together. Not even in my thoughts.

My phone buzzes again. **You don't have to talk about that, but can we talk about my book? Meet me at Starbucks?**

I start to type the same thing a third time. Another negative. But, then again, I could use Logan's company right now. He makes me laugh, and he makes me feel beautiful. I definitely need humor, and my self-esteem has taken a hit since Troy betrayed me with Aria.

Okay. See you in thirty minutes.

I jump out of the bed and stand in front of the mirror. I look a hot, stinking mess. My hair is completely unruly, and my face is tear streaked and swollen. I don't usually go anywhere looking like this, but I have no intention of getting all dolled up.

I snatch my curly mane up into a high ponytail, wash my face, and put on facial moisturizer. A second glance in the mirror tells me that I haven't improved much, but it's the best I can do. Besides, my sad look matches the melancholy that I feel.

On the way to Starbucks, so many thoughts are going through my mind. My favorite one is that this is all a nightmare and I'm going to open my eyes and none of this will have happened. Not the note, not Troy's admission of cheating, none of it.

As I pull into my regular parking spot, I notice that Logan's car is already here. He steps out as soon as I get out of my car, and for some reason, I don't remember him being this tall. He's got a little brown bag in his hand and that incredible smile on his face.

The sight of him makes me burst into tears.

He runs over to me and encircles me in a hug. I feel my body crumple against his as he strokes my ponytail and makes little soothing sounds. I don't know why I thought I could get through this. I can't. Troy has destroyed me . . . us.

"Come on, Pam. Let's go inside. All of Cleveland doesn't need to witness your grief."

"Just the people inside Starbucks, huh?"

He chuckles. "They won't be paying attention. They're too busy sipping their expensive drinks."

"What's in the bag?"

"Oh, this? Well, I brought you a cupcake. I know how you like them. You can have it with your coffee."

A cupcake? This man sure knows the way to my heart. Every time I pick up anything sweet or delicious, Troy tells me that I should be juicing or some mess like that.

"Thank you," I say as Logan hands me the treat bag.

"Something sweet for someone sweet."

Even though Logan starts walking toward the Starbucks, I stop in my tracks. I look inside the bag at the beautifully decorated miniature cake and sigh.

"Are you real?" I ask.

Logan spins on one heel. "What do you mean?"

"Come on. You are single, gorgeous, thoughtful, and celibate. You can't be real. All those qualities can't be in one man."

He throws his head back and laughs. "Thank you for all the compliments. But I have to disagree with you. I'm not really all that thoughtful." He motions for me to follow him into the coffee shop. I shake my head and make my feet move.

I sit at my favorite table, while Logan orders our beverages. He's got the girl at the counter charmed so much that she might just hand him her panties right along with our coffee. It should be a felony for a man to be this fine and chocolate. It's like he's walked out of every one of my chocolate dreams.

He sits and hands me my cup. "Enjoy, my friend."

I close my eyes and sip, letting the liquid elixir warm my throat and my insides. Good coffee is just about as good as a good man, but since my man is the opposite of good, this coffee is the best thing I've got going for me.

"You didn't bring your laptop," Logan says.

I shrug. "You didn't bring yours, either."

"That's because I didn't really come to work. I've been dishonest with you."

"Really?"

Logan cracks up at my incredulous tone. "Really. I just wanted to get you out of the house."

"Technically, I was out of the house. I'm staying at my girl Taylor's home until I sort all of this out."

"I see. And the children are with Troy?"

I nod. "I thought that would be for the best for now. If I do decide to leave him, of course, my babies are coming with me."

"So you're thinking of leaving?"

"I think so. Especially if he won't drop Aria. I can't trust him after that."

"I understand Troy's reluctance to drop Aria."

"What? He should be doing whatever it takes to hold his marriage together."

Logan picks up his coffee and takes a long gulp. "Well, Reign Records out of Atlanta wants to sign her. They think she's the answer to Mystique."

"Who in the world is Mystique?" I ask.

"Only the biggest R & B star in the world right now. I know you've heard of her."

Logan jumps up from the table and does a little booty shimmy dance and snaps a finger in the air. Then I immediately know who he's talking about! The girl on the perfume commercial. Aria doesn't have anything on her.

I laugh at Logan's dancing. "I'm gonna need you to sit down and never, ever do that again."

"What?"

"I think you just broke multiple man laws all at once. I'm pretty sure they were class A felonies."

Logan sits back down and laughs at himself. "I agree. But you know who I'm talking about now, right?"

"I do, but what does that have to do with Troy?"

"They like all the songs we've done so far, and they want to give her a full album release with fifteen songs. Troy will write most of them, but they've got some young songwriting duo to do about three or four. This will be a huge payday for y'all, and they've got enough money to put behind the project that it'll go at least platinum."

"So are you saying that I'm wrong? He shouldn't drop her?"

Logan shakes his head. "Not at all. If you were mine and I'd messed up as badly as Troy has, I'd drop her like a bad habit. I'm just saying I understand his reasons."

I sit back in my seat and cross my arms over my chest. All Troy has ever thought about since we've been married is how he could blow up. I guess he's finally decided to put it ahead of our entire family.

"Let's change the subject," Logan says. "How's the new book coming? What's it about?"

"It's about a mistress who sleeps with a prominent minister and has a child by him. An updated version of *The Scarlet Letter*. Then she meets her fairy tale prince, but she's pretty jaded by then. Jaded and angry."

"Sounds interesting. I'd want to read it."

"Good, even though you're not in my demographic."

"I should be in your demographic. I like to read."

For a brief instant I imagine Logan and me sitting on some tropical beach, in beach chairs, each of us reading a book. He looks exceptionally fine in his swimming trunks, and I am incredibly thin.

Then I snap back to reality and push the cupcake away from me. My ever-present fluffiness is the only reason why I'm considering staying with a cheater. If I was thin and fabulous, I'd leave in a heartbeat.

Logan takes my half-eaten cupcake and bites it. He grins while doing so, looking just like a mischievous child.

"This is really good. Are you sure you're done?" Logan asks. "I can finish it off for you."

"Be my guest. I'm not in a cupcake-eating mood."

"What are you going to do, Pam?"

I shrug and sigh. "I don't know. I really love Troy. This would destroy the children. I don't know."

"For what it's worth, I believe Troy," Logan says. "He said it was once, years ago. In my opinion he shouldn't have told you about it at all."

I narrow my eyes in anger. "What do you mean, he shouldn't have told me? Are you saying that he should've continued his charade?"

"What did telling you accomplish? He thought that by telling you that it was once and that it was over, you would actually believe that. He doesn't know women."

"Even if he doesn't know all women, he ought to know me."

Logan nods in agreement. "He should know you, but he clearly has a lot to learn. Telling you about Aria was stupid. He should've taken that to his grave. Secrets like that only hurt. They never heal."

"What if I would've found out on my own, huh? Then what?"

"You wouldn't be any more furious than you are right now."

"So that's what you do with your women? You keep secrets and lie behind their backs? No wonder you're by yourself."

"I don't cheat. Believe it or not, I was cheated on by the last two women I loved. Both of them cheated with former flames."

This is unbelievable. Two women, loved by this incredible man, chose to be with someone else? That doesn't sit right with me—at all. It doesn't make any sense. Maybe he's not that great in the bedroom. Is this why he's celibate? Or maybe there's something about him I don't know or that you can't tell by looking at him.

"But I just feel that there is someone out there who will be faithful. I won't rest until I find her."

"I don't know how this conversation turned into us examining your woman problems. We're talking about me," I say. "What's your vote? Do I leave or stay?"

Logan tosses his hands up and shrugs. "I am hopelessly biased, Pam. My opinion doesn't matter."

"You're biased because you are friends with both of us? I get it. I'm sorry for putting you in the middle, Logan."

"I'm biased because, like a fool, I have fallen for another man's wife. I can't tell you to stay with Troy, because I wouldn't mean it. I want you to leave him and come with me."

"Fallen for me? Logan, you barely even know me. How can you say that?"

"I just know. Everything about you, the way you approach problems, the way you chase your dreams, the way you're still considering Troy after everything he's done to you . . . Your heart is gold, Pam."

Logan's intense gaze is making me feel a bit uncomfortable, so I look away from him. Why did he have to come into our lives now? Why couldn't he have shown up when Troy and I were happy? He's here now, when it's all falling apart, promising to be faithful and understanding—everything Troy is not.

My cell phone buzzes. It's Gretchen texting me. **Mommy, Aria is here. TJ is sitting in her lap.**

I slam the phone down with enough fury to rattle the table. "She's in my house."

"Pam, don't jump to conclusions. `. . .`"

"He's got her in my house, playing with my son. I asked him to keep her out of my house."

"But that's where his studio is," Logan says.

I wish he would be quiet with his little defenses of Troy. "Can you just stop? Troy doesn't need your help!"

"I'm not trying to help him. I'm trying to help you. You're driving yourself crazy. I don't like seeing you this way."

I stand up from the table. I can't take another kind word or pitiful glance from Logan. Plus, I need to call Taylor so we can go and get that chick up out of my house. I might be leaving Troy, but I haven't left yet.

"Thanks for hanging out with me, Logan, but I've got to go."

"Do you need me to come with you? You're going to your house, right?"

I shake my head. Me showing up with Logan would be like throwing a match into a vat of gasoline. I suspect that Logan knows that, too, which makes me wonder about his motives.

"You want me to leave Troy, don't you?"

"I already said that I did," Logan says.

"I don't know that I'm flattered."

"It is what it is. Do what makes the most sense to you, and if that's leaving your husband, just know that you don't have to go far to find the next man in your life."

I give Logan an unblinking stare. My mind travels back to the embrace we shared before we came into Starbucks. Those muscular arms, currently straining against the snug cotton fabric of his T-shirt, made me feel safe. I haven't felt safe in a long time.

I shake my head, jostling myself out of that quick fantasy. I don't know what the future holds anymore, because too many things have happened too quickly. But I do know that today I am married, so I put all thoughts of Logan's muscles out of my mind.

"Let me walk you to your car," Logan says.

"No, don't get up. I want you to stay right here."

Logan looks confused. "Will you be okay?"

"Yes. As soon as I get finished regulating."

I walk out of the Starbucks on a mission. Two things I know are true. By the end of today, Troy will have to make a choice—his marriage or that heffa. I'm giving him one more chance to do the right thing. I can't let the night fall on this thing. I can't go to bed not knowing if my forever is through.

CHAPTER 33

TAYLOR

When my girl Pam told me to meet her at her house, because Troy brought Aria over as soon as she left, I got straight into the car, no questions asked. I mean, really? He must've been itching to get that tramp over there. He couldn't even respect Pam's wishes for one day? I have lost all respect for Troy, when I used to cheer for him to get his stuff together.

And Aria! I can't wait to get up in her face. I know I used to be a mistress, so I shouldn't judge, but it's one thing to wreck a happy home and quite another to sleep with a man who is going to leave his wife, anyway. Both are wrong, very wrong, but there's something cruel about what Aria is doing.

Oh, who am I fooling? Being a mistress is cruel business no matter the reason, no matter the marital status, because at the end of the day somebody is gonna get hurt. Adultery has got to be one of the most selfish sins there is. It was a true move of God that Yvonne was able to forgive me for what I did with Luke.

When I pull up to Pam and Troy's house, Pam is already storming toward the house, looking like a madwoman. I hurry to park so that she won't be going in alone.

"Pam!" I shout as I jump out of my car. "Wait!"

Pam spins around, and I get to see the look on her face. First of all, she's beet red, and the look of rage is unmistakable. She must've thought of nothing else but Aria being in her house all the way over here.

As Pam stands there waiting for me, I can see her chest expand and contract as she takes deep breaths. I hope that extra oxygen is calming her down, because she's making me think this is about to be an episode of *Snapped*.

Pam points at Aria's car. "She's still here. She's gonna wish she wasn't."

"I know, girl, but let's not lose it. We have to be strategic about this."

"Strategic? My only strategy is to go straight upside Troy's head and snatch that weave out of Aria's head. Bringing her up in my house after I know the truth? If that ain't bold, I don't know what is."

I hug Pam close and whisper, "Calm down, sweetie. Let God fight your battles."

"You're right," Pam says as she pulls away. "God give me the strength to whip Troy's behind."

Obviously, I'm going to have to be the prayer warrior here. And later I'm going to have to remember to ask Pam why she smells like men's cologne. DKNY Be Delicious, in fact. It's a distinct scent that I like, but Spencer doesn't. And neither does Troy. Pam's been hugging on some other mister.

We storm up to the front door, and Pam whips out her key and walks in. We don't have to go far for the confrontation, because Troy and Aria are standing right in the foyer, laughing like they are the best of friends. Aria is wearing a pair of almost sheer black leggings and a fitted T-shirt. The outfit, even on her perfect body, looks obscene. She looks like she's about to turn a trick or flip around a pole or something.

"Pam!" Troy says. "This isn't what you think. Aria left the tracks she needs to practice here. . . ."

"What *does* she think, Troy? I know your wife doesn't think there's anything between us," Aria interjects.

Troy's eyes widen, and he gives Aria a shut-up signal, which she totally misses, because she keeps talking.

"I do have a man, Pam," Aria says. "Maybe one day you'll stop accusing me of taking yours."

"I've never accused you," Pam says.

"Not out loud, but you've always thought I was trying to hook up with your husband. I am too good for that. I don't want to share with someone else. Troy is here to get my music career off the ground. That's it."

"So you're in the habit of screwing your producer for tracks?" Pam asks. "Because you're not about to stand up here and lie to my face."

Aria turns to Troy. "What does she mean, Troy?"

"Just stop, Aria. She knows," Troy says as he rakes his hand over his head.

"Yes, I know you slept with my husband."

Aria, now looking a little bit uncomfortable, says, "That was a long time ago. I was young, and I—I wanted Troy to put my career first. I thought that if he loved me, he would."

I say, "You can save that mess, girl. There is no excuse for what you did. You, either, Troy."

"Ms. Pam, I am so sorry," Aria says. "I never meant for you to find out, if that means anything at all."

"It means nothing. Get out of my house, and never come back, unless you want my foot so far up your fake behind that you'll be hiccupping Nine West."

"But what about . . . ?"

"Your music? We'll see about that. If Troy wants to throw away all these years of marriage and take you to Reign Records or wherever, then I guess you'll be hearing from him."

Troy frowns. "How do you know about Reign Records? You left before I could tell you about that."

Pam rolls her eyes. "Don't even think about questioning me. Aria, you got five seconds to get out of my house before me and my girl jump on your whorish self."

Aria quickly looks from me to Pam, and I guess we look like we're about to stomp that tail, because she runs out of the house without another word to us or Troy.

Pam follows her out with a glare, sending all types of darts and daggers with her eyes. If I were Aria, I'd stay gone from here. Troy ain't all that, and if she can sing, then somebody else will help her blow up.

"What you gone do, Troy?" Pam asks.

"We already had this conversation, Pam. So if you aren't coming home to stay, you might as well go on back over to Taylor's house. Reign Records is about to make me a millionaire again. I'm not passing that up."

"Then, since you about to make so much money, you better ask them for an advance so you can find a place to live, because you got to go!"

Pam's roar is so impressive that I believe her. I almost want to tell Troy he can come and stay over our house.

"I'm not leaving, Pam. This is my home as much as it is yours."

"Do you want to leave in handcuffs?" Pam asks.

He narrows his eyes. "You wouldn't."

"Yes, I would! Just like you would lay up with another woman."

"Pam, the children!" Troy exclaims. "Do you think Gretchen and Cicely aren't listening?"

"Listening? Listening! How about what they *see?* Who do you think told me that Aria was here?"

Troy takes a moment to look at me and then Pam. "I don't want to lose you, Pam. You've got to believe that. I'm going, but it's not for good. I'm gonna make this up to you."

"The only thing you can do is cut all ties with that girl." Pam's words are so pointed and direct that I know Troy has to understand that she's dead serious.

"I can't do that, Pam."

"Then go."

Troy leaves with nothing. Not even an overnight bag. This is a man that plans on winning his wife back. I hope he doesn't think he can do it with money, though. My friend is a lot more complex than that.

"He'll be back, you know," I say after I hear Troy's car pull out of the drive.

"I know. And if he won't do what I ask, he can leave again."

"Pam, girl, is there something you want to tell me?"

Pam looks confused. "You already know all my business, and I guess Yvonne will, too. I've got to call her. I need all the prayers I can get."

I pull Pam into Troy's study and close the door. I don't want any eavesdropping children to hear the rest of this conversation. Not if I'm wrong, but especially not if I'm right.

"What is it?" Pam asks.

"Why do you smell like men's cologne? Where did you go when you left my house?"

Pam lifts an eyebrow. "I went to Starbucks, and I ran into an old friend there."

"Oh. I was just wondering if you had you a little something on the side, too."

Pam's jaw drops. "I can't believe you would think that! I'm not like Troy. I'm not a cheater."

"All right, girl. You know I was just checking, 'cause you are still a woman. You aren't a saint."

"None of us are. Thank you for looking out for me."

"You know I got you."

On my way back to my car, I say a silent prayer for my friend. *Lord, protect Pam's mind, her heart. Don't let her block Troy out so soon, and please let Troy come to his senses. You can do the impossible. I've seen it. I'm trusting you to do it again. Pam doesn't deserve this pain. In the name of Jesus.*

CHAPTER 34

YVONNE

The thing I like best about teaching is that I'm free in the summers to do whatever I please. Some teachers complain about the salary, but it's just fine with me. I don't need much, and I'm perfectly comfortable. As long as I have enough to put together a Sunday dinner, then I'm all right.

Lately, I've taken to starting my day with a walk around the neighborhood just after dawn. My neighborhood is quiet, and I can get some meditation time in with the Lord. It's the perfect way to start my day.

This morning I open the door to my condo and find a bouquet of flowers. Yellow roses. I smile, knowing that they must be from Kingston.

I pluck out the little card and open it up, but as soon as I start reading, I drop the vase to the ground and it breaks in a thousand little pieces.

It's an invitation. To Luke's wedding.

Attached to the invitation is a note that reads. *This weekend I will remarry. I would love to see you there. We spent twenty years together. Not all of them good, but not all bad, either. If you came, I think it would go a long way in healing things between Taylor and me, because I want to be a part of my son's life. I will understand if you don't come, but I really wish that you would. In Christ, Luke*

I notice that my hands are shaking uncontrollably. Why would he invite me to his wedding? He wants to continue tormenting me even now, eight years later. Once an abuser, always an abuser, my mama used to say. Too bad she didn't sniff it out in Luke when she and her biddy friends were busy setting us up. I hope his new wife doesn't have the same problems I had with him.

I look down at the mess on the ground and suck my teeth. Instead of walking, it looks like I'll be cleaning up. I go back inside, still shaking, and get a brown paper bag to get up the pieces.

On my way back out, my cell phone rings. I look at the caller ID and shake my head. It's Eva. This girl has a bad habit of calling at the crack of dawn.

"Hello, Eva."

"Hi, Sister Yvonne. I hope I didn't wake you up. I know it's early."

"I'm an early riser. What's going on with you this morning?"

"I just wanted you to know that I read that Scripture you told me about. The Samaritan woman. And it . . . well, it changed my life. I gave my life over to Christ on Sunday."

"I am so happy for you, Eva. You made the right decision."

After a long pause, Eva says, "You don't sound happy for me. I've messed up our friendship, huh?"

"It's not that. I promise I haven't even given that a second thought after you apologized. I've got something else weighing on my mind."

"Oh, okay. Well, then, I'll let you get on with your day. Thank you for praying for me."

Now I feel bad. She sounds so pitiful that I can't just leave it like this. "You know, Eva, salvation is sure something worth celebrating. Do you want to have breakfast?"

"Yes, yes, I would, but I don't want to come in the way of whatever you have planned today."

I let out a small laugh. "Well, I was planning to take a walk, and that's . . . well, it's ruined, so why not breakfast with a friend?"

"Oh, thanks, Yvonne! It would mean a lot to me." I can hear her smile through the phone.

"I'll pick you up in about twenty minutes, and we can go to Cracker Barrel. Sound good?"

"Yes. See you then."

"Okay, see you in a few."

I quickly clean up the glass and flowers from in front of my condo and toss Luke's invitation in the trash. I don't care what he's trying to accomplish with Taylor. I have no intention of being a part of it.

On the way over to Eva's apartment at the church, I call Pam to catch up. We haven't spoken since my date, and I want to tell her about everything Kingston said.

"Hello." Pam's voice scares me. She sounds strange.

"Hey, girl. I wanted to tell you about the weekend. You up yet?"

"I'm up."

"Kingston and I went to Cedar Point, and we got stranded in Put-in-Bay. We had to spend the night in a hotel's honeymoon suite, girl! Ain't that some mess? And we had the nerve to see Rhoda and Rochelle at the amusement park."

No reaction from Pam.

"Pam?" I ask. "Did you hear what I said?"

"Uh, I'm sorry, Yvonne. A lot of stuff went on here over the weekend, but I am glad you had a good time on your date."

I hear it in her voice. Something horrible has happened.

"Pam, tell me."

First nothing, then sobs. Horrible, gut-wrenching sobs. "Troy's gone, Yvonne. I kicked him out."

"What? Why?"

"He cheated on me with Aria. I asked him to cut ties with her, and he refused. So now he's gone."

I feel so ridiculous sharing the details about my date when Pam is having the worst time ever with Troy. I always suspected there was more to that relationship than what Troy said, but I let it go for Pam's sake.

"You know God's gonna work this out, right?"

Pam chuckles. "That's what I told you when you found out about Taylor."

"If it sounds half as crazy to you now as it did to me then, I'm going to be doing the lion's share of the praying."

"Well, get to it, prayer partner. What are you doing right now?"

"Going to have breakfast with Eva. She gave her life to Christ on Sunday."

"Oh, that's good. I'm glad for her."

"You want to come along?" I ask.

"No, I'd be too much of a drag. But you have fun, though."

I want to tell Pam about what happened with Eva, about how she kissed me, and how I don't feel 100 percent comfortable going out to breakfast with her. But I don't think I need to weigh Pam's mind down with anything else.

"Do you need me to come by later?" I ask.

"No. I'll be fine. I just need to spend some time with God."

Finally, I pull into the church parking lot. It's surprisingly quiet at this time of morning since the staff doesn't show up until eight o'clock. Pastor and First Lady Brown usually get here at about ten, so the parking lot is nearly empty. There is one other car, one that I don't recognize, but it's not running, so maybe someone just parked out here. They do that sometimes when they go to the bar on the corner or the strip club down the street. We've even had to tow abandoned cars off the property.

I call Eva to let her know that I'm downstairs, and she sounds just as excited to be going to breakfast now as she was fifteen minutes ago. There's something about her that reminds me of a little girl wanting approval. I wonder what kind of life she had. It must've been crazy if she ended up doing pornography.

Eva emerges from the building's side entrance and starts jogging over to my car, waving the whole way. Then she sees the other car in the parking lot. A look of terror comes on her face. She stops in her tracks, spins, and runs back toward the church. Two car doors swing open, and big, very big, men jump out of the car and pursue Eva!

I don't know what to do, so I get out of my car and scream at the top of my lungs. Then I call 9-1-1.

"Help! I'm at New Faith on Kinsman. There are two men trying to attack a girl!"

I hear Eva scream, and I grab my umbrella from the backseat and run in her direction. One of the men has Eva in a headlock, and the other one kicks her in the stomach. I let out a war cry and charge at one of the men with the end of the umbrella. I make contact with the side of his head and hear something crunch.

Then everything goes black.

CHAPTER 35

EVA

From her stretcher, Eva looked at the unconscious Yvonne. Roe had sent his goons. Of course he had. It had only been a matter of time until he did, until he got revenge for the whipping Eva had put on him at the strip club. She had expected it to be soon but had hoped none of her new friends would be involved.

Why did it have to be Yvonne? The one she really cared about?

Although the other women had been nice to her, none of them had really accepted her like Yvonne had. Yvonne knew the worst about her, but she came back.

Yvonne didn't deserve to be punched in the side of the head by that fool Roe's henchmen. Eva had gotten in a few good licks after he'd attacked Yvonne, but he had subdued her, as well, and had disappeared before the sirens sounded.

"Is she going to be okay?" Eva asked one of the paramedics that sped by after leaving Yvonne.

"She's got a pretty massive concussion, but I think she'll be fine."

Eva sighed and fell back onto the stretcher. She'd been so worried about Yvonne that she hadn't been paying attention to her own injuries. Something wasn't right with her abdominal region, but the doctors were going to check her out at the hospital.

On another stretcher was the goon that Yvonne took out with her umbrella. He had an oxygen mask on his face and looked like he was still unconscious, too. That made Eva smile. Yvonne had been a beast! She'd taken that umbrella and gone straight upside his head. They would laugh about this later, when Yvonne woke up.

On the ride over to the hospital, Eva heard the paramedic mention something about internal bleeding, but she wasn't in too much pain.

"How are you feeling?" one of the paramedics asked.

"Like somebody beat me up."

"Sense of humor, I see. We're gonna get you all patched up, but hopefully you break up with the guy who did this to you."

"He wasn't my boyfriend."

"I'm so sorry. Most of the time when we see this much damage, it's usually the boyfriend."

"Wait. How much damage?"

"You've got at least four broken ribs. Luckily, your lungs weren't punctured, or any other vital organs, so far as we can tell. And you're conscious. That's always a good sign."

"Four broken ribs. Y'all gonna fix 'em?"

"The orthopedic surgeon at the hospital will."

"Good, because I don't think I'm going to be conscious that much longer."

Eva went in and out of consciousness for the rest of the ten-minute ride to the hospital. As she drifted in and out of her sleep state, Eva thought of her grandmother, Uncle Parnell, and all the horrible things that had happened to her on every movie set. It was as if she relived every violation that had ever happened to her. Then she thought of Yvonne, who'd come to rescue her, even after she knew who Eva was and what she had done.

After a few hours she awoke to a nurse standing over her. "Good. You're awake. Let me take your vital signs."

"Am I all right?" Eva asked. She felt like she'd been hit by a semitruck.

"Yes, ma'am. Your surgery was a success. You'll probably be leaving tomorrow or the next day, at the latest."

Eva was sure that if she had medical insurance, the recovery time would've been a couple more days, but she supposed she could take pain medication at home just as well as she could at the hospital.

In the hallway outside her room were several police officers having a conversation.

"What's up with the police?" Eva asked.

"They're here to arrest your attacker, I believe."

"There were two of them."

The nurse shrugged. "The other one must've gotten away, then. Was he not injured?"

Eva remembered one of the dudes jetting as soon as the sirens sounded. Roe was going to be annoyed that his henchmen didn't finish off the job, but maybe what they had done was enough. Maybe Roe would be satisfied with breaking a bunch of her ribs.

"How's my friend? The lady that came in here with me?"

"She's fine. Nasty bump on the head, but she's just fine. She's got two men out there making a fuss over her."

Eva lifted her eyebrows. *Two men?* Sister Yvonne played the role of the shrinking violet pretty well, but when it came down to it, she was pulling two men?

Eva laid her head back on the pillow and sighed, wondering if her brand-new friendship with Yvonne would survive this. First, Eva kissed Yvonne; then she got her beat up. That definitely felt like two strikes.

Eva didn't know if she could be her own friend after all that! But she hoped deep down inside that Yvonne didn't hold all this against her, because she sure didn't know how to live as a saved person.

All Eva knew about being saved was what her grandmother had preached from her big chair. Holiness or hellfire. She couldn't use any of that in the real world. She wasn't even sure her grandmother had any use for it, other than to torture the rest of the family.

Eva wanted to be grounded in her faith like Yvonne. She wanted to believe that God was going to make everything be okay, even when it looked like everything was a mess. Like Eva's life.

Eva touched her bandages and stared at the ceiling. She started crafting yet another apology to Yvonne. She'd give it as soon as she had the chance.

Eva had a sneaking suspicion that she'd have to lay it on extra thick this time.

CHAPTER 36

YVONNE

Icould just kick myself for not changing the emergency contact on my hospital records. I thought I'd handled everything when I got a divorce from Luke, but that was one little detail I forgot. When I opened my eyes and saw that fool sitting in the corner of my room, I almost passed back out.

"Yvonne, you're awake," Luke says.

I roll my eyes at him and rummage through my purse on the bedside table. I text Kingston, **I'm at University Hospital, in the ER. Please come when you can.**

"So you're just gonna act like I'm not even here?" Luke asks as he strokes his silver goatee. I have never felt more like stabbing someone.

"Why are you here, Luke?"

"The hospital called me and said you had me down as an emergency contact. As a minister of God, I couldn't leave one of His little ones unattended."

I narrow my eyes at him and feel a pain shoot through my head. Guess I'm not all the way better yet. I close my eyes and breathe deeply.

"Are you in pain? Do you want me to call the nurse?" Luke asks.

"I don't want you to do anything." I press the on-call nurse button.

Kingston texts a response. **On my way. You all right?**

Then my phone rings. I knew it would. Kingston and I are too old to be communicating just by text. Our generation likes to hear a person's voice. I find myself getting angry at Pam and Taylor sometimes, because they like conducting entire conversations by text.

"Hey."

"Yvonne, you sound bad. Are you hurt?" Kingston asks.

"I have a head injury, but I think I'm going to be all right."

I hear Kingston gasp. "A head injury? Did you fall trying to change a lightbulb or something? You know you can call me whenever you need anything done around the house, right?"

"It was nothing like that, babe. But please come to the hospital, because I'll need someone to take me home."

Oh no, Luke did not have the audacity to bristle when I said "babe." He's got a whole lot of nerve after all the stuff he's done to me.

Luke says, "I'll take you home, Vonne."

I stretch out in the bed and snatch the covers all the way up to my chin. Luke sitting here is annoying. Him using my old nickname is infuriating. So I cover the phone with my hand. "Can you leave please?" I ask.

"Was that a man's voice?" Kingston asks. "Who is that?"

I suck my teeth. "The hospital called my ex-husband down here, and he showed up because he's a man of God."

Kingston, I'm sure, can hear every last drop of sarcasm that I give with those words, because he immediately bursts into laughter.

"Yvonne, don't commit any felonies," Kingston says. "I am leaving now, and I'll be there in ten minutes."

"I can't wait until you get here."

I disconnect the call and roll my eyes at Luke again. "Can you get out of my room please, before I call the hospital security?"

"So you've got a beau, huh? I didn't think you'd find anyone to fill my shoes."

"Oh, please."

The on-call nurse peeks her head into the room. "Do you need anything, Mrs. Hastings?"

I purse my lips together and shake my head. "I am Ms. Hastings, not Mrs."

"Oh, I'm sorry. The chart said . . . and isn't this your . . . ?"

"Ex-husband. Get out, Luke."

Luke laughs. "Yvonne, stop acting like this. At least let me keep you company until your *beau* shows up."

I don't like the way he says "beau," like it's an insult. I don't like him.

The nurse says, "Ma'am, would you like me to get security?"

"Come on, Vonne. Let me just talk to you for a second. Then you won't have to call security. I'll leave on my own."

"Is there anything you can get me for this headache?" I ask the nurse as she's backing out of the room.

"The intravenous pain meds must be wearing off. Let me ask the doctor what we can give you besides Tylenol or Motrin."

"Thank you."

When the nurse leaves, I turn my attention back to Luke. "You've got two minutes, because my man is going to be here soon, and I don't want to subject him to you."

"Did you get my invitation?"

"Yeah, I got it, and you ain't funny, Luke. You like to get your jollies by mentally torturing people, but I'm serving you notice, devil. You can't touch me anymore."

Luke bursts into laughter. "Devil? Yvonne, it's been eight years, and you haven't changed one bit. But I have. I invited you to the wedding because I thought that if you came, then Taylor might come and bring my son. I want him there."

"Why don't you just leave them alone? Spencer and Taylor don't need you meddling in their lives."

"Because Joshua is my son! I know I haven't done right by him, but I want to. I may have been a womanizer, Yvonne, but I am a good father."

"Yeah, well, Joshua's wanted for a whole lot of things."

"And that's going to change."

Luke stands up from his seat and clasps his hands together. Standing there, in his black suit with his minister's collar, he sure does look the part of an anointed man of God. I know better.

"There is no way in the world I'd come to your wedding, Luke. You wouldn't want me there, anyway. I might just stand up and give my testimony."

"You could do that. It would be evident to everyone around you how much I've changed, no matter how you try to keep me tethered to that old man."

"Get out!"

"You might want to do as the lady wishes." Kingston steps into my room and closes the door behind him.

Luke spins and appraises Kingston. Looks him up and down and scoffs. "Vonne, you're always supposed to upgrade the second time around. Looks like you didn't get that memo."

Kingston chuckles. "She has upgraded. From a cheater and a woman beater to a real man who appreciates a real woman."

"A pretty boy with some slick lines," Luke says. "You should bring him to the wedding. Then you won't look so pitiful."

"Not going to your wedding," I say.

"She doesn't look pitiful at all," Kingston says. "And she wants you to leave, so this is the last time I'm going to say it."

Luke looks Kingston up and down again and laughs. "Well, I would kiss you on the forehead and tell you to get well soon, but that wouldn't be appropriate with your man here. So I'll just say, 'See you next time.'"

I cross my arms and refuse to answer Luke. He strokes his goatee and chuckles as he walks out of the room. I don't say that I hate anyone, not anyone, but I have a serious dislike for this man. I think that I need to go back to the prayer closet again if Luke is just going to be showing up all over the place.

"Kingston, I am so glad you showed up," I say. "Thank you for rescuing me."

"I didn't do anything that hospital security couldn't have done."

I don't know exactly what Kingston is implying by that statement. "Do you think I wanted him here?"

"No, not really, but it had to make you feel special that your ex-husband, who is about to remarry, rushed down to the hospital when they called."

"I don't know if he rushed down, but it also didn't make me feel special. It just made me feel ridiculous for not having named a new emergency contact."

Kingston nods slowly, as if convincing himself of my explanation. "He invited you to his wedding?"

"Yes. He wants me to convince Taylor to come with Joshua, but I don't want anything to do with it."

"Enough about him. How are you feeling? What happened to you?"

"I went to pick up Eva for breakfast, and there were some men at the church waiting for her outside. They attacked her and started beating on her, so I called nine-one-one, and I hit one of them with my umbrella."

Kingston bursts into laughter.

"What's funny?" I ask.

"Your umbrella, Yvonne? Two men are attacking your friend, and that's your weapon of choice?"

I narrow my eyes angrily. "Well, look, it's a big golf umbrella. I hit the guy with the long metal tip on the end. That thing is heavy. I knocked him out, so it must've been the right thing."

"That was a move of God, girl. That's like how God let that little stone slay Goliath. Your arm was anointed if you knocked that guy out!"

As much as my head hurts, this makes me laugh uncontrollably.

"Let me touch your arm!" Kingston says, and I snatch it away from him. He needs to stop teasing me.

"Okay, seriously, I'm worried about Eva. What's going on

with her that she's got goons waiting outside her apartment to beat her up?"

"Does she owe someone money or something?" Kingston asks. "That sounds like a drug deal gone wrong."

"Can I tell you something and you not say *anything*? I mean nothing!"

Kingston lifts his eyebrows with interest. "You can tell me anything, and I won't ever repeat it."

"Well, she used to be in X-rated movies, so maybe it has something to do with that."

Kingston takes this in for a moment and says, "That's not really a career of choice, but, I mean, they usually work for a check. This sounds like more than that."

"Maybe I'll just ask her," I say. "I think I have the right since I got punched in my durn head."

"I agree. But I want you to be safe, Yvonne. You scared the mess out of me calling me from the hospital."

"I did?"

"Yes. You had me rushing down here, and you didn't even say what was wrong. Don't do that to me again."

"I'm sorry! I didn't mean to do that."

"I forgive you."

"Thank you, Kingston. I don't know if anyone's ever worried this much over me."

He clears his throat, and walks over to my bed. He brushes the hair out of my face and kisses my forehead. My skin tingles beneath his lips. Then he kisses each of my cheeks, and I think my entire body shivers. When he places the sweetest kiss ever on my lips, I almost can't enjoy it, wondering how my breath smells after being unconscious.

My eyes get cloudy with tears. It's like I've never been kissed before in my life, but I was married for twenty years.

"Yvonne . . . let me worry over you. Let me pray over you."

"O-okay. All right."

"Yvonne . . ."

"Yes?"

"Let me love you."

I open my mouth to reply, but no sound comes out. I just nod enthusiastically, because what I feel right now feels like the Lord sent it straight from His throne. I feel like how Eve must've felt when Adam told her she was the bone of his bones and the flesh of his flesh.

Is this what love feels like? If so, I've been deprived for way too long.

CHAPTER 37

PAM

Yvonne, Taylor, and I have not had any girl time since Troy left or since Yvonne had her big date with Kingston, so we decide to have lunch at Mallorca, our favorite Portuguese restaurant downtown, before our Sister to Sister meeting tonight. As usual, I get here first and hold the table. I am always the first one to arrive.

Yvonne arrives next, and she's still got a bandage on her head from her run-in with her new friend's enemies. Only Yvonne would've been smack-dab in the middle of that. The one person at the church who's probably never been in a fight—other than with Luke—and she's the one that had to run into the goons.

I wave Yvonne over, and she jogs over to the table and hugs me. She's got a huge smile on her face.

"What is going on with you?" I ask. "You are positively glowing."

"Pam, I have never felt like this before. I think I might be falling in love!"

I squeal with delight. Even though Troy and I are going through the roughest patch ever, I have to celebrate my friend. She's never been romanced properly, and Kingston is just the one to do it, with his fine self.

"So any more details about the date?" I ask. "Did he kiss you?"

Yvonne shakes her head. "Not then. But he did tell me he was up all night because he couldn't stop thinking about me!"

I fan myself and smile. "Wow. You put something on him, Yvonne. That man is sprung."

"At the hospital he kissed me, and it was incredible." Yvonne's eyes glaze over a bit. "Oh, I sound ridiculous, like a teenager or something."

"It's all right, girl! You're still a woman, and he's a man's man, honey. You better go 'head and get yours."

Yvonne looks alarmed. "Get my what?"

"Girl! It's just an expression." I burst out laughing.

"Oh, I thought you were talking about . . . you know!"

I shake my head and keep laughing. "Yvonne, I would never tell you to fornicate. Never, ever."

"Oh, 'cause I thought you were reading my mind or something. I've been having these dreams. I need to take myself down to the altar and let someone cast these lust demons out of me."

"You are *not* lusting! It's called being a human, Yvonne. You were married for twenty years, so it's not like you're a virgin. Women have needs, just like men."

"I guess, but I don't know that Luke was much of a lover. I hear other married women rant and rave about their men, and I have never had anything to sing about."

I am so glad that Taylor is not here for this conversation. Especially since she had lots to sing about when it came to Luke. I guess cheating men go above and beyond with their mistresses and leave their wives wanting more. Ooh, why did I have to think about cheaters? My entire mood shifts, and I feel the darkness come over my face.

"Oh, Pam, I'm sorry. Have you talked to Troy?"

I shake my head. "I don't have anything to say to him, you know? Like, if it was just the cheating, then maybe I could get past it, but he won't cut ties with the girl. Like she's the only way that he has to come up in the music industry."

Taylor finally walks into the restaurant, and she's got an angry look on her face. She sees us before we even get a chance to wave and storms over to our table. She plops down and slams her purse on the table.

"Would y'all be mad if I had a glass of wine? I need to calm my nerves," Taylor says after blowing kisses at me and Yvonne.

"I'm not sitting here with you while you get intoxicated," Yvonne says. "It's bad enough I spent the night with my boyfriend in Put-in-Bay."

Taylor laughs out loud. "Your *boyfriend?* So you claiming Kingston now? It's about time."

"She's in love," I say.

"What? Go 'head, Yvonne! Do I hear wedding bells?"

Yvonne's eyes widen. "No! I don't think so! Not yet. But Kingston is really getting to me, girl."

"Well, why you come in here looking all sour?" I ask Taylor. "Why do you need alcohol?"

She rolls her eyes. "Oh, that fool Luke. He wants Joshua to be in his wedding, and he showed up over at our house with a little white tuxedo. I asked him, what part of my son ain't coming to that wedding do you not understand?"

"He invited me to the wedding, thinking that you might let Joshua come if I did," Yvonne says. "I impolitely declined his invite."

"Impolitely!" I burst into laughter. It takes a lot to get Yvonne to be impolite. If she's nothing else, she's polite.

"Okay, I don't blame you," Taylor says. "Why does he think you want to see him marry somebody new? Luke doesn't have good sense, for real!"

"I think something happened to him while he was locked up," Yvonne says. "Like, beyond him finding Jesus again. I don't know. When he lost his eye, some of his sense fell out with it."

My phone buzzes with a text message. I usually don't even check my phone at the table, because I think that is one of the rudest things ever, but I left the kids at home alone, and I need to make sure that they're okay.

It's a text from Logan. **I hope you're smiling today, Pam.**

I'm smiling right now, I text back.

My phone buzzes again, and Taylor snatches it away from me. "Hey!" I say.

"Who in the world is texting you?" Taylor asks. "You sitting up here grinning and blushing like you got a new man or something."

"Give me my phone!" I lunge forward and try to grab it back.

Taylor swings it out of my reach. "I'm sure it's breathtaking. What in the world? Who are these texts from?"

I pause and grin at Logan's response. **I'm sure it's breathtaking.** I may be enjoying this a little bit too much, but oh well. My husband's current artist is his ex-mistress. Flirting with Logan doesn't even come close to making us even.

"They're from a friend."

"A friend?" Yvonne asks. "A male friend?"

"Mmm-hmm. The friend you were smelling like the other day," Taylor says. "You are straight up tripping, Pam."

I scrunch my nose and lips into a frown. "Okay, first of all, his name is Logan, and he's Troy's producer friend. He's just trying to make me feel better."

"No good can come from this," Yvonne says. "Pam, you know better."

"What? How is it that y'all take up for Troy and he's out sticking his you-know-what who knows where! Telling me we're gonna get past this. Well, what if I don't want to get past it! Why do I always have to do the forgiving?"

"Just because he's out tricking it doesn't mean you have to do the same. You do remember that little thing we call salvation, right?" Taylor asks.

Oh, no, she didn't! No, she didn't! I've never done anything out of pocket in my life! I've always been faithful to Troy, even when I wasn't sure if he was being faithful to me. I didn't steal anyone's husband!

"I didn't forget that I'm saved. But don't we all sin and come short of the glory of God?"

Yvonne looks like she wants to slap me. "I know you didn't just try to use the Bible to justify your flirting. The devil is a lie."

"All right, my bad, my bad! I'm just having fun. Logan is a friend trying to make me feel better. There is absolutely nothing going on, so y'all can cancel the prayer vigil."

Taylor lifts an eyebrow. "What does he look like?"

"Who? Oh, Logan?"

She nods. "Yes. Your *friend*."

"He's about six-three. He's dark, dark like motherland dark, but not ashy, just buffed like a piece of onyx. And he's got this voice that will make you shiver, and the most penetrating gaze." I fan myself again. "He's gonna, um, make someone a great husband one day."

"Someone? Sounds like you want it to be you," Yvonne says.

"He's fine, okay. I admit it. He's ridiculously fine, but I'm not attracted to him." I run a finger through my hair and twirl a strand at the end.

"You lying," Taylor says. "Be careful, girl."

"This is not good," Yvonne says. "He sounds dangerous."

"He's not. He's being a good friend. And if he flirts a little, it's harmless. He actually asked me to hook him up with someone."

"Oh, really?" Taylor says. "What about my girl Shaquan? She's looking for a good brotha, and he sounds right up her alley."

"Um, no. Shaquan is way too ghetto for him," I say.

"Too ghetto? Wow. Well, what about our newly saved member, Ms. Eva? She's sweet," Taylor replies.

I roll my eyes. "No. He's way too sophisticated for her."

Taylor looks at Yvonne. "Are you thinking what I'm thinking?"

Yvonne nods. "Yes. Pam needs to repent."

"No, I don't."

"Are you even thinking about letting your husband come back home?" Taylor asks. "He wants to come back. He keeps calling Spence, because you won't answer his calls. You're too busy chatting it up with your new man."

"When he called Spence, did he mention cutting Aria loose? And where in the world is the waitress? I'm thirsty and hungry."

"You're definitely thirsty," Taylor says. "You need to leave this man alone before you get into a situation you ain't ready for."

"I know it's rare for this to happen, but I agree with Taylor," Yvonne says.

I frown at both of them. "I'm gonna need both of you to stop judging me. Taylor, you've got your fairy-tale prince, and, Yvonne, you're on your way to a happily ever after. And all I have is a broke negro who likes to cheat on me. Don't judge me!"

Finally, the waitress walks up. "Ladies, can I get your drink orders?"

"I will have a glass of Moscato," I say.

Yvonne frowns. "You're drinking now, too?"

"I said, 'Don't judge me,' Yvonne. Make sure you fill that glass all the way up."

The waitress nods as Yvonne scowls at me. I shrug and roll my eyes.

"Well, if she's drinking, then I'm drinking," Taylor says.

"No, you're not!" Yvonne says. "Clearly, Pam needs an intervention."

I stick my tongue out at Yvonne while Taylor orders a Coke.

"Okay, ladies, I'll get those drinks right out for you."

Taylor says, "You know that I'm not judging you, Pam. I just want you to be careful. If this guy is as hot as you say, then you don't want to give the devil room. If you get with him, Troy will never forgive you."

"Right. It's a double standard with men," Yvonne says. "Men want us to forgive them, but they are very unforgiving when the tables are turned."

"You both are jumping to conclusions. I haven't done anything wrong, so I don't have anything to repent about or ask for Troy's forgiveness for. But I don't know if I want to work things out with him."

"Stop saying that," Taylor says. "You have children."

"So I'm just supposed to forget that he slept with that girl? Would you forgive Spencer if he cheated on you?"

"W-wait, this is not about me and Spencer."

"I stayed with Luke," Yvonne says.

"And *that* was the right thing to do!" I say sarcastically.

Yvonne nods. "You're right. Leaving Luke was the right decision. But I only came to that choice after talking to God. I know you haven't taken this situation to the throne, because you wouldn't be texting some other man if you had."

Talk about making me feel convicted. She's right, though. I haven't taken this situation to the altar. I guess I'm mad at Troy and God behind this. Why didn't God reveal this cheating to me before I wasted so many years? He could've saved me the trouble.

"Take it to the throne, Pam. Before you decide, talk to God about it," Yvonne says.

I nod, making a promise to Yvonne. I won't make a decision about my and Troy's future without asking God's help. But Troy better be praying, too. He's the one who needs to get right.

"Did you find out who attacked you, Yvonne?" Taylor asks.

She shakes her head. "No. Eva says she doesn't know the guys, but she thinks she knows who sent them."

"Who does she think sent them?" I ask. "Who's out to get her?"

Yvonne takes a deep breath. "What I'm about to tell y'all is the story she told me. I'm going to preface this with that."

"You think she's lying or something?" Taylor asks.

"Well . . . just listen to the story, and judge for yourself. I don't exactly know what to think."

"This ought to be good," I say. "Do tell."

Yvonne says, "She said that she went to dance at some strip club and that God convicted her before she could go out on the stage. So she didn't end up dancing that night, and the club owner was mad, because he had advertised that she was going to be there."

"Wait, he *advertised* that she would be there. Is she a video vixen or something?" Taylor asks.

"Worse, a former porno star," Yvonne says. "And that's not something for y'all to share."

My jaw drops. "Wow. She used to do adult movies? That's just wow."

"So the club owner advertised that she was gonna be there, and he got angry that she wouldn't dance. He tried to rape her, and she fought back. Because Eva knocked him out, he got mad and sent his goons to find her."

"And you just happened to be in the wrong place at the wrong time?" I ask. "So what's she doing now?"

"Staying at the women's shelter over on Seventy-Ninth, because she's afraid to go back to the apartment at church for now."

"Women's shelter?" I ask. "Nonsense! I've got lots of room. She can stay with me."

"No. You don't want that spirit around your children," Yvonne warns.

"What spirit?"

"I think she might be bisexual."

Taylor's eyes get really huge. "Bisexual? She's bi?"

"I'm not sure, but she did kiss me, and I'm telling you it was a strange spirit. Hopefully, she got delivered from that when she went down in the water."

I shake my head at Yvonne. "First, you judge me for a glass of wine, and now you're judging this girl for her past."

Yvonne says, "She just kissed me a few days ago, Pam. That's almost the present."

"I agree," Taylor says. "A few days ago is pretty darn current."

"Was it before or after she turned her life over to Christ?" I ask.

"Before. A couple days before," Yvonne says.

"Then that's good enough for me. It's the past. She can stay at my house."

"I'm not judging her," Yvonne says. "I wouldn't still be her friend if I was. I just didn't want you to open Gretchen and Cicely up to anything, you know?"

"I pray over my children all the time. Can you call her and tell her she can stay with me?"

Yvonne jots the number on a piece of paper. "You can tell

her at the Sister to Sister meeting tonight. It might seem strange if I do it."

"Why? Because you could've offered her a place to stay yourself?" I ask.

"No. I just don't want her to think we're sitting around talking about her."

"We are, though," Taylor says. "Once she gets to know us, she'll understand that it's not gossip, and that we're just trying to find out folks' prayer requests."

Taylor, Yvonne, and I burst into laughter at Taylor's joke. Taylor hated the Sister to Sister meetings when she first started. She called them gossiping sessions. And there is definitely gossiping going on.

The waitress shows up with our drinks and sits the glass of wine in front of me. Yvonne stares with a scowl on her face.

"Are you *really* going to drink that before we go to church? The sisters will smell it on your breath."

I sigh loudly. "Please take this back and bring me a Coke."

Yvonne grins victoriously. "Thank God!"

Well, since I can't have any wine for my nerves, I'm gonna get my grub on. Paella and warm, crusty parmesan bread sound right down my alley. And bump a salad. I need extra bread. No man, no alcohol . . . I might as well have my carbs.

Thank God for carbohydrates.

CHAPTER 38

YVONNE

The Sister to Sister meeting is packed today. I figured it would be. Anytime some drama pops off at the church, everyone shows up. I even warned Eva about it on the way here. Rhoda and Rochelle, who are usually unfashionably late, are front and center, and it looks like they've even brought the refreshments.

Rhoda rushes up to me and Eva as we join the circle of chairs. She gives me a tight hug and murmurs something in my ear that sounds like an unknown tongue.

"Sister Yvonne, God has truly got His hand on you. You have been beaten twice by big burly men and survived to tell us about it." Rhoda has her "deep" facial expression on. It takes every bit of restraint for me to keep from rolling my eyes.

"Thank you, Rhoda. I know that I'm a child of God."

Then Rhoda looks Eva up and down. "And you! I'm putting you on the prayer list indefinitely. I'm glad you went down in the water, because I've heard some shocking reports about you. But it's covered under the blood, so we're not gonna talk about it here."

Eva looks at me with an alarmed expression on her face, and I shrug. I have no idea where Rhoda may have gotten her information, if she even has the correct story. Sometimes she's on reconnaissance missions to see what kind of scoop she can collect by acting like she already knows.

Taylor's friend Shaquan pushes past Rhoda and hugs Eva. "Congratulations, girl, on getting baptized and all. You inspired me."

"Really?" Eva asks. "Did you get baptized, too?"

Shaquan laughs. "Well, I've been baptized a couple times already."

"A couple?" Taylor says from her seat in the circle. "Girl, Shaquan done been down in the water at least a dozen times since we've been grown."

Eva covers her mouth and giggles, and Shaquan gives Taylor the hand. "Listen at that hater here. I get baptized again every time I turn my life back around. It takes some of us longer than others to get all the way right."

"Well," I say, "the Israelites did walk around the wilderness for forty years. Where's Pam?"

Taylor lifts an eyebrow at me. "She went to make a phone call."

I shake my head, because I gather from Taylor's expression that Pam's talking to her new friend. Part of me wants to call Troy and tell him myself that he needs to handle his household, but loyalty to my friend keeps me from doing so.

Carmisha must've come upon some money, because she's got on a new outfit. It's a jean jacket and skirt with patches of light blue jean and patches of black. Her hair is slicked down and gelled into a little mound on the top, and then there is an explosion of weave on the top. It looks like a weave waterfall. She's also got on a full face of makeup and a set of sparkly acrylic nails, each one a different color.

"Hey, Sister Yvonne," she says as she hugs me. "I heard you done turned vigilante. That's what's up! I know who I want with me walking down a dark alley."

"It was nothing, y'all!" I say. "My sister was being attacked, and I jumped into the fray. I'm afraid I didn't think of what I was doing."

Pam emerges from outside with a huge smile on her face.

She immediately wipes it off when she sees me looking at her. She takes a seat next to Taylor in the circle after waving to Eva and Carmisha.

"Let's get started," Taylor says. "I've got some prayer requests."

Rhoda says, "Come on, Rochelle. Set yourself on down so I can call this meeting to order."

Rochelle hustles her ample behind over to the center. This poor child has gained so much weight since she became Rhoda's protégée and partner in crime. Probably all those after-church visits to the buffet restaurants.

"Bless the Lord, oh my soul, and all that is within me!" Rhoda sings. She gets everyone to join her in singing Myron Butler's version of "Bless the Lord," one of my favorites. Everyone except Pam, that is. Pam has a pensive expression on her face as she gazes out the window.

"Thank God on this evening for waking me up in my right mind! For starting me on my way. For being a fence around my family, including my future cousin-in-law twice removed, Sister Rochelle. Thank you, oh, Lord."

I am so bad. I just chuckled to myself about Rhoda thanking God for being in her right mind. I hope Eva didn't see that. I don't want her to form opinions of the sisters based on what I think. I've got plenty of history with Rhoda that lets me know she's absolutely in her *wrong* mind, but bless the Lord anyhow.

Taylor stands up to signal to Rhoda that it's her turn to speak. You have to do that with Rhoda, because she'll take up the entire time testifying and getting her weekly breakthrough.

"I need y'all to pray for me, Spencer, and Joshua. You know I don't usually tell my business, but I need y'all to pray for my son. He's going through so much these days, just trying to figure out the kind of man he wants to be, and his biological deadbeat now wants to be in his life. I can't see it."

Shaquan rolls her eyes. "Luke needs to go somewhere and fall off the face of the earth."

Taylor shakes her head at Shaquan, to quiet her down, I suppose. "What?" Shaquan says. "Everybody don't know that Luke is Joshua's father?"

"I mean, we *suspected*," Rochelle says. "Since he look just like Luke and everything. But no one actually confirmed."

"Oops, my bad!" Shaquan covers her mouth with her hand.

"I don't care if everyone knows," Taylor says. "Yvonne knows, and we've moved past all that. So I don't care if everyone else knows."

Eva raises her hand, and Rhoda acknowledges her. "Um . . . I—I need you all to pray for me. I'm staying at a women's shelter right now, and I just hope that I can find a job so that I can get a place of my own."

"Well, I can help with that!" Pam says. "You can stay at my house for as long as you need."

Rochelle says, "Your husband is okay with that?"

Pam clears her throat and ignores Rochelle's nosy question. She's probably already heard that Troy isn't staying at home. I don't know how Rhoda and Rochelle do it. They always manage to know the scoop. I bet they hang out in the bushes or the treetops with binoculars and bags of potato chips, because Rhoda doesn't go anywhere without a snack.

"I also want y'all to pray for me about some spiritual issues," Eva says. "Before I got saved, I did some . . . um . . . unsavory things. And for some reason, the devil keeps calling them to my mind."

Eva sits down quickly, as if uttering those words sapped all the energy from her. She looks at the floor and not at everyone else, but Rhoda's and Rochelle's eyes look like they're about to bug right out of their silly heads. I want to slap the both of them.

"I think we should do a twenty-four-hour prayer circle for Sister Eva," Carmisha says. "They did that for me when I just couldn't stay away from my last baby daddy. It was like I could feel the Holy Spirit covering me."

"I think we should start a twenty-four-hour prayer circle for our entire ministry," Rhoda says. "The devil is sure busy. We've got leadership not showing up on Sunday mornings, secrets coming out left and right, and Pastor Brown has a spot on his lungs."

I narrow my eyes at Rhoda for her little dig at me and Kingston. I was wondering how she was going to work that into the conversation. I've got something for her.

"Y'all put me on the prayer wheel, too," I say. "There's a man in my life."

Rhoda and Rochelle lean forward, bug-eyed and slack jawed. Heffas.

"And he says he just can't stop thinking about me," I continue. "Ask the Lord to help me keep my virtue."

Shaquan bursts out laughing. "Yvonne! You were married for a long time, right? I don't think you have any virtue left!"

Pam and Taylor join her laughter. I hold mine in, although it's hard, because Rhoda's entire gelatinous body is shaking like it's about to explode. I think she's got gossip overload. She's gonna pop if she doesn't get to share these stories.

Rhoda jumps up from her seat. "Twenty-four-hour prayer wheel it is! The Word says that if God's people would humble themselves and pray, He would heal the land. Lord, we need a healing!"

Rochelle goes down on her knees with tears in her eyes. Rhoda touches her on the forehead, and she falls to the floor. Eva views the spectacle and then looks at me. I give a little head shake.

Rhoda runs over to the cupboard and pulls out a bottle of vegetable oil from the kitchen ministry. "I need to anoint everybody's head with oil."

"That is *not* the anointed oil, Rhoda!" Taylor says. "That's for the catfish dinners on Friday."

I jump to my feet. I feel like I started all this, so I better bring the focus back on God, for real. Especially since Taylor and Eva need to see a real move of God. Pam too.

"Come on, y'all. Let's join hands and pray," I say.

"What about the oil?" Rhoda says.

"We don't need it. It's just symbolic of the Holy Spirit, and we can have that if we get together on one accord in the name of Jesus," I reply.

Rhoda sets down the bottle of oil and joins the circle. I start off the prayer. "Lord, we come to you humbly, asking for for-giveness for foolishness and for anything unlike you." I say that part for myself. I shouldn't have poked Rhoda and Rochelle.

"We have some real issues, here, oh, God. Some real strong-holds that need to be broken. We pray against bitterness and unforgiveness. No matter how many times we learn that lesson, Lord, it isn't enough. Teach us how to forgive."

I squeeze Eva's hand tightly when I say this. I want her to know how much I forgive her. I hope she hasn't thought me judgmental, because then I'll have to ask her to forgive me.

"Dear God, make us to know that when we submit ourselves to you, you will help us to withstand every urge from the enemy. Even if they're called to mind, you will be able to neu-tralize them. By your stripes we are healed. In our minds, our bodies, and our spirits. We thank you in the matchless name of Jesus."

When we open our eyes, Eva is shaking and has tears rolling down her face. She hugs me and holds on for dear life. Then she pulls me away from the circle to a corner of the room.

"Y-Yvonne," she whispers, "my uncle raped me when I was lit-tle, and no one saved me, not even my grandmother. Thank you for praying about forgiveness. I know now that I don't for-give them."

I stroke Eva's hair and hug her again. "Do you want to talk to your grandmother about it? I'll go with you if you like."

She shakes her head. "My grandmother is dead."

"Your uncle too?"

"No. He's dying, though. My cousin said that he caught the package about five years ago, and now he's in hospice."

Eva breaks down again and falls into my arms. I'm so glad we decided to have real prayer in here. Sometimes I don't think we take this group seriously enough. There's nothing funny about prayer.

"Eva, honey. I know Pam offered you her place, but why don't you come and stay with me for a while?"

She stares at me, blinking tears, which spill all over her face. "Are you sure? I mean after—"

"I am not concerned about that. That's under the blood. We're going to get your stuff from that shelter, and you are going to stay with me."

I never had a daughter, a goddaughter, or a niece, but I think God has placed this girl in my path for a reason. Maybe she's not the only one who needs a breakthrough. Maybe I need one, too.

CHAPTER 39

PAM

For the first time in a long time, the Sister to Sister meeting actually felt like a prayer group. Yvonne put her foot in that prayer, and I think she got her own blessing, too. I hope that little bit about unforgiveness wasn't about me and Troy, though. God doesn't require me to accept cheating from my husband. No matter what they say or think, I have grounds for divorce.

I walk through my home, straightening up, although there's not really much to straighten. Over the past few days, with Troy being gone, there's not been much of a mess. He's the one who tears everything up. The children are ridiculously neat. I guess they get that from me.

Troy left me a voice-mail message to tell me where he's staying. At the Fairfield Inn about five minutes from our house. I don't respond. I have nothing to say until he tells me that Aria has been erased from our lives.

The doorbell rings, and I know we're not expecting company. It better not be Troy, because that is a violation of this trial separation we got going here. I don't care if his name is on the deed, I will call the police with a quickness.

I take a peek out the window and notice that it's Logan. He's got a huge smile on his face and a box of cupcakes in his hand.

I shake my head and inhale deeply. I exhale and then open the door.

"Logan, I don't think—"

He holds a finger to my lips, shushing me. "It's just cupcakes, Pam."

I take the box from his hands and take the sight of him all the way in. He's wearing a snug T-shirt and jeans, and the scent of his cologne immediately tickles my nose. As always, his best accessory is his smile.

"Thank you, Logan."

"Were you busy?" He points to the scarf on my head. I quickly snatch it off and toss it on the floor behind me.

"Just doing a little cleaning, that's all."

"Want some company?"

I look over my shoulder and up the stairs. Me having a guy here won't look good to my children.

"I don't think so. It's not a good time."

He steps a little closer. Into my personal space bubble. The danger zone. I think his cologne has got crack in it or something, because I'm already addicted.

I put one hand on his chest. "No, not this evening. Thank you for the cupcakes. I could sure use the carbs, but not the company."

"I just came by to tell you that I spoke to Troy today about Aria. I thought you'd want to hear what he has to say."

Shoot. I can't just leave him standing out here so the whole neighborhood can see a man that's not Troy all up in my face. I do want to know what Troy said, though.

"Come on in, Logan. But just for a little bit. I don't want my babies to get the wrong idea."

"Why would they get the wrong idea?"

"They're not used to me having male company over, so I just don't want to alarm them, especially with their daddy not being here."

"I'll be quick, then."

"Come on into the kitchen."

I put the cupcakes on the counter and take out a carton of milk. "Want some?" I ask. "If I didn't know any better, I'd think you were trying to fatten me up with all these cupcakes," I say. "Are you a chubby chaser or something?"

Logan laughs out loud. I frown and shush him, and he gets much quieter. "I am not a chubby chaser. I think you look fine. You're just thick."

"Anyway! Enough of that. Tell me what Troy said about Aria."

Logan takes a seat on one of the bar stools. "I asked him if he was going to drop her, at least after the Reign Records deal goes through."

"And?"

"Well . . ."

I forget about my rules and slam my hand down on the kitchen counter. "Tell me!"

"He said that you aren't running nothing, and that he was going to ride this thing all the way through and see how much money he's going to make."

"He said *what?*"

"He thinks you'll eventually come around, because you want the money, too, especially since Aria is getting married."

I can't believe this. While he's begging through Spencer to come back home, he's being all big and bad with his homeboy, talking about how I don't run nothing! Well, maybe I don't, but I do decide whether or not he comes back up in here, at least tonight.

"Do you think you'll stay separated?" Logan asks. "He says that he misses you."

"He doesn't miss me enough, and he doesn't love me more than he loves money, so I don't know what's going to happen with us."

"You are too beautiful to be treated this way, Pam."

I chuckle. "Like, does it bother you to be two faced like this, Logan? You're going back and forth between me and Troy."

"I am kind of caught in the middle."

"Only because you want to be! You don't have to be my friend, Logan. I appreciate what you've done so far, but you are Troy's friend. You don't have to betray him."

Logan takes one of the cupcakes out of the box and takes a bite before getting up off the bar stool. "Are you saying you don't want to be my friend?" He walks toward me while waiting for my answer.

"I—I don't know."

"Because I'd rather be your friend than Troy's. Other than the music, Troy and I don't have anything in common. But you and I, well, we've got our writing, our humor, and our love of cupcakes."

Logan takes a finger full of chocolate buttercream frosting and holds it close to my lips. I gulp and close my eyes. *Don't take the bait, Pam! Don't do it!*

My mind is screaming at me, but his cologne has got me severely twisted, and his lips are so close to mine. His warm chocolate-scented breath is right beneath my nose.

Then he kisses me, and all thoughts cease. It is a "get you weak in the knees" kiss, an intimate kiss, the kind I've only ever shared with Troy.

I push him away. "Logan, I think you should go."

"Your mouth is saying that, but I think your body is saying something else."

Logan pulls me close with one arm and kisses me again. This time it doesn't feel sweet. It feels invasive and forced. And his hands are groping where they shouldn't grope.

Now his kiss muffles a scream as he unhooks my bra in the back and yanks my shirt up so that he can violate me further.

"Logan, stop!" I scream as I finally yank my face away from his lips.

"Stop? Pam, you've been teasing me since the day we met. You heard me say I was celibate, and you've just been tempting me and flirting with me."

"I don't believe you're celibate!"

Logan yanks me close again. "You're right. I'm not. But stop fighting me, Pam. I'm gonna make you feel so good, you're gonna forget all about Troy."

Then I hear something that sounds like a roar as Troy storms through the kitchen. Logan has only a half second to respond, and it's not enough time, because Troy is on him like white on rice. Troy punches Logan in the stomach, and it makes him drop to his knees.

"Hey, man! Your wife let me in. She wants me. Don't get mad 'cause she got revenge on you."

"Troy, that's not true!"

Troy points at me and says, "Pam, shut up and go upstairs."

"What are you gonna do, Troy?" I ask, my voice trembling.

"I heard my wife scream." Troy kicks Logan under the chin, and blood spatters across the floor.

"Troy!" I scream. "You're gonna kill him! I don't want you to go to jail!"

This seems to sink in with Troy. He stops his assault. "Fool, you got about ten seconds to get out of my house."

Logan crawls out of the kitchen on his hands and knees. I grab Troy when he looks like he's going to attack him again.

"Don't! Just let him go, please. I just want this to be over."

Troy turns and looks at me with disgust. "Next time you want to spend time with a man, don't have him over here. Isn't that what you requested of me?"

"He wasn't over here for that, Troy! He said he's been talking to you. I didn't know he was going to do that."

"Well, I don't want to get any more texts from my daughter that a man is in our home."

Gretchen! Normally, I would be mad about her snitching to her daddy, but this time I'm actually glad that she did that. Who knows what Logan would've done if Troy hadn't come in?

"You won't, Troy."

"Did he tell you that after this project I'm dropping Aria? Is that how he got you in a lip-lock?"

My eyes widen. "He said the opposite. He said that you had no intention of dropping her."

Troy slams his hand down on the counter. "I knew he was

feeding you information. I saw his number come up on your text logs. But I had no idea he was telling you lies."

I frown deeply. "You're checking my text messages?"

"Not really, no. I just scan the bill from time to time."

Mmm-hmm. Sounds like I need to be checking his messages while he's following up behind me!

"So are you letting me come home?" Troy asks.

"No. I'm still mad."

"What if Logan comes back and gets the rest of what he wanted?"

I fold my arms across my chest stubbornly. "I can handle him."

"No, you can't. Look, even if you don't want me in the bedroom yet, I'm staying downstairs. This is my house, and I might have to bust a cap in somebody tonight."

I don't like the idea of Logan coming back, so I stop arguing with Troy. I just want to wash his handprints and touch off my body. How could something so sweet turn into something so terrifying and sour?

"All right, Troy. I'm going to take a shower and get in bed."

Troy nods. "I'm going to try not to wonder if you led Logan on or not, Pam. He doesn't seem like the type that would just take it from a woman without provocation."

No, he didn't. "Okay, well, I'm going to try not to wonder if you really slept with Aria only once, because she seems like the type to come back for seconds."

"I told you it was once."

"You heard me scream."

A stalemate. Because trust has been shattered on Troy's side and questioned on mine, neither one of us is willing to give the other the benefit of the doubt.

"I'm going to bed, Troy."

"Are we going to make it through this, Pam?"

He's going to drop Aria. That's the first step, but it's certainly not a fix.

"Talk to me in the morning. Let's just get past tonight, okay? I'm exhausted."

As I leave the kitchen, I turn to watch Troy. He goes into the refrigerator, gets out the cold cuts, mayonnaise, cheese, tomatoes, lettuce, and pickles. Then he goes into the pantry to get his hoagie rolls. Totally on autopilot, he goes back to doing what he does on a nightly basis.

Troy belongs here. This is his home. But I have no idea if I can let him back into my heart.

I go to my—no, our—bedroom, and finally it hits me. I was nearly raped. A man that I let into our home almost violated me in the worst possible way. With my children upstairs.

My stomach lurches, and I barely make it to the bathroom before I vomit up the contents of my stomach. It annoys me that I can still taste those cupcakes in my mouth afterward.

I rinse my mouth and wipe the tears from my eyes before I undress and stumble into the shower. I don't even mind the rush of cold water as I turn both faucets on full blast. I stand immobile under the stream, letting the finally warming water purify my body—even if it can't cleanse my spirit.

Why God? I clutch my washcloth to my chest and sob. Why is this happening to my family? I've loved Troy for so many years, and he's loved me back. Why is God allowing the devil to put a wedge in our union?

Then something in my spirit says, *Repent.*

Repent? Of what? I was attacked by Logan. I didn't ask to be fondled! This is not my fault. Rape is never a woman's fault.

What do I have to repent about?

I tilt my head back in the shower and let the water wash over my face. No. The attempted rape wasn't my fault. Not at all.

But did I let Logan get too close to me? I connected with him. I opened myself to him. Made myself vulnerable to him and shared my discontent about Troy with him. I didn't ask to be raped, but I did invite trouble to my front door.

"Lord, forgive me," I cry out in the shower. "Please, Lord! I beg you to restore me, and restore my union with Troy! Strengthen us! Cause all distrust to be forgotten. Oh, Lord, make me trust my husband again. Remove Aria from us, God!

Remove the stain of what has transpired. Lord, God . . . I beg you!"

My amens are tears and sobs. I have recognized my sin and have asked God to forgive me, and I know that He is faithful and just to do that. But what about Troy, and what about me? Neither one of us is as faithful as God.

Neither one of us has been faithful at all.

CHAPTER 40

TAYLOR

"Spence! Where's Joshua?"

Spencer opens his eyes and tries to focus. I know he's trying to take a nap, but I just got home from shopping, and my son is nowhere to be found.

"I don't know," Spencer says. "Maybe he's outside or at the basketball court."

"No and no. I just came from outside, and he's not at the court."

Spencer sits up in the bed. "Bike riding maybe?"

"No. His bike, skateboard, and scooter are all in the garage. So none of the above."

"Did you call his friends' mamas? I don't know where he is."

My eyes widen, and I ball my hands into fists. "He was home with *you*, Spencer. The least you could do is act like you care!"

I storm out of the bedroom and grab my car keys off the hook in the hallway. "Where are you going?" Spencer asks.

"Where do you think? To find my son!"

"Wait. Let me put some clothes on. You are running around like a banshee, and he's probably just down the street."

See, these are the times when I wonder if Spencer would act differently if Joshua was his biological son. I go out in the morning to get groceries, and my son is still asleep. I get back later, and he's missing. Something is wrong with that picture. Maybe Spencer doesn't have the same parental instincts that I have, because he doesn't have any biological children—yet.

I think that I'm pregnant, but I haven't mentioned it to Spencer or anyone. I want to be sure before I say anything. But now that I see how he's acting with Joshua, I ask myself if he is going to be different when his child gets here. Is he gonna want to spank his biological child, or will it just be mine catching the belt?

Spencer comes out of the bedroom in sweats. "Okay, where do you want to look?"

"At both parks and up at the school. Sometimes they play ball up there."

"You don't think he went over to Luke's house, do you?"

My eyebrows go up in surprise at the suggestion, then go down into a deep frown. "He wouldn't dare."

"I think he might. Get Luke on the phone."

I dial Luke's cell phone number, and it rings a few times before going straight to voice mail.

"He's not answering."

"Well, do we know where he lives?"

"No. I just know about the church," I say.

Spencer says, "After we check the parks, that's where we're going."

After driving all over our neighborhood with no results, Spencer drives us to Luke's church.

"I swear that if he has my son, I don't know what I will do to him," I mutter.

"Calm down. If he has Joshua, he'll be coming home with us. No need to get all bent out of shape."

I stare at Spencer incredulously. "Are you kidding me? If he's got my son without me knowing, that's more than enough reason for me to get bent out of shape. Actually, that's cause for me to act one hundred percent crazy and deranged. He betta hope my son ain't up here!"

Spencer can barely park the car before I'm out and storming

toward the entrance to the apartment complex's recreation center. No one asks me where I'm going or who I'm there to see. I guess I look like I'll take somebody's head off, because at this point I can practically breathe fire.

I throw open the door to the gymnasium/sanctuary, and there is Luke and what looks like his bridal party. And guess who else? My baby!

It's about to go down.

"I hear it's bad luck to walk down the aisle during the rehearsal, but we don't believe in luck at this assembly. God cancels every curse." Luke doesn't even notice me standing at the door.

I yell at the top of my lungs, "He cancels every curse, but he sure ain't about to cancel the arrest warrant I'm about to whip out on your behind! You think you can kidnap my son and get away with it?"

Luke looks at me and then looks at Joshua with questions on his face. I stride over and snatch Joshua by the arm.

"Joshua," Luke says, "you didn't tell your mother you were going to be here? Who dropped you off? I thought you said she was bringing you."

"My friend's mom brought me," Joshua says. "Mom, my dad didn't kidnap me!"

"Somebody better tell me what the heck is going on before folk start going to jail," I say. "'Cause I'm getting real irritated at this lack of detail."

Joshua snatches his arm out of my grip. "I wanted to come to my father's wedding. He asked me to be a groomsman. I knew you'd act crazy, just like you're doing right now."

"Boy, you ain't seen me acting crazy! Don't make me embarrass you in front of all these people."

"Joshua, apologize to your mother," Luke says. "You can't disrespect her like that."

"Even when she's tripping?"

Luke has a faint smile on his face. I want to slap it right off. "Even when she's tripping. The Bible makes a promise to young men who obey their mothers and their fathers. He promises you a long life."

Joshua looks up at me. "Sorry."

"Taylor, forgive me, as well," Luke says. "I didn't know he was here without your permission. I thought you'd had a change of heart."

"Mom, you're not being fair. I was at you and Spencer's wedding."

I turn to face Spencer, who has finally caught up with me. "He wants to be a groomsman in Luke's wedding."

"I don't see a problem with it," Spencer says. "He's old enough to make that decision."

"Spencer and I are still not coming," I say. "I will drop my son off and pick him up."

"I was thinking I could swing by and get him in the bridal party limo," Luke says.

The only thing that stops me from doing five backward somersaults that end in me putting Luke into a choke hold is the fact that Joshua looks so excited. But someone please tell me how he can afford a hood-fabulous wedding when he hasn't paid child support? He needs to be sending a limo full of tennis shoes and school supplies.

I close my eyes and nod. I can't fix my mouth to agree verbally. Joshua seems very excited, because he hugs me tightly around my neck.

"The rehearsal is almost over," Luke says. "Go with your mother until she brings you in the morning. I'm sure she still has some fussing to do on the way home."

Fussing, screaming, hollering, ranting, and raving. All of the above and then some, but I don't like Luke saying anything that I'm going to do, like we're coparents or something like that. Luke has it twisted. There are no coparents in this situation. I'm Joshua's mother, and Spencer is his stepfather. The others are all temporary, including his father.

"So we'll see you tomorrow, bright and early?" Luke asks.

"Spencer will drop him off and then will wait for him until

he's ready to come home." Spencer looks like he wants to object, but he knows he's on my bad side right now, so he can forget about fussing.

I pull Joshua up out of this gymnasium and storm past Spencer. He follows right behind us and slams the door. When we get to the car, I nearly throw Joshua into the backseat.

"Ow!" he yells as he bumps his head going in.

Spencer stares at me before we get into the car.

"What?" I ask.

"Don't be too hard on him. He was with Luke, not robbing a bank."

I cock my head to one side. "I almost don't know which one I'd rather he be doing."

We get into the car, and I turn around and glare at Joshua.

"Ma, can you stop looking at me like that?"

"You aren't in control of anything, boy. I can look at you however I want. You better be glad I'm not back there beating your behind."

"I'm too old for spankings, Mom."

"No, you're not."

"Are you going to spank me for going to my father's wedding?"

I close my eyes and sigh. "No. I'm not."

"Good, because I really like him, Mom. Don't make him go away again."

I open my eyes and say, "You think I made him go away? Did he tell you that?"

Joshua shakes his head. "No, but you hate him, and of course, Auntie Yvonne hates him. Y'all don't want to give him a chance, but I do."

I let out a huge sigh. I'm going to have to allow this, even though I don't want to, because if I don't, my son is going to end up hating me.

"Don't let him say anything bad about me," I say.

Joshua's eyes light up. "So this means you're not going to stop me from being around him?"

"For now, you can see him. But if I even think he's a woman beater still, I'm getting you away from him."

"Thanks, Mom."

I can remember only a few times where Joshua looked this happy. Ain't that about nothing? I spend his entire life trying to make him content and making sure he has everything he needs, even when I have nothing, and Luke comes in and takes all of his admiration.

What part of the single-mom game is that?

CHAPTER 41

YVONNE

Kingston says that he has a surprise for me, but to be honest, I am afraid of his surprises! Ever since the attack, he barely lets me out of his sight long enough to go home and go to bed. The night after the attack he slept in his car outside of my condo, and he said he didn't care who saw him. I didn't even know he was outside until that following morning. It was a . . . surprise!

Who knows? Maybe it'll be something fun. Lord knows, I need something to break up the endless prayers I've been doing for my friends.

Taylor called and told me that she's letting Joshua go to Luke's wedding. I don't agree with that at all, but she is the parent, and I guess as ignorant as he is, Luke should be recognized as a parent, too. I just wish he would leave them alone. He knows Joshua is being raised right, so why does he even interfere?

"Yvonne, I'm done cooking dinner!" Eva says. "Do you like spaghetti?"

"Who doesn't like spaghetti?" I say. "But I'm going to pass. I don't want something so heavy on my stomach at choir practice."

Eva is the perfect houseguest. She cooks! I am a good cook

myself, but there's something decadent about sitting down and letting someone else prepare your meal.

There's the doorbell, right on time. Kingston has never been late picking me up. We're not even going on a date. We're going to choir practice. I take one last look in the mirror and adjust the purple flower on the left side of my hair. Someone told me once that Hawaiian women wear their flowers that way. Left side for single women, right for married, and in the middle for those who are open to negotiation.

Guess it's the middle for Ms. Pam.

I open the door with a huge smile on my face, because no matter what I'm thinking about, I'm happy to see Kingston. "Hello, you!" I say as I hug him around the neck.

He pulls back and plants a soft kiss on my lips. I think I could go on savoring his kisses for an eternity.

"What is the surprise?" I ask.

Kingston grins and shakes his head. "You are very impatient, Yvonne. You'll have to wait for your surprise."

"Oh, all right. Would you like something to eat before we go to choir practice?"

"No thank you, but I'd like something to eat *after* practice."

"A lady doesn't entertain male company in her home after dark."

Kingston laughs. "Well, it's a good thing you aren't going to be entertaining me. You'll be feeding me."

I punch him lightly on the arm. "You are teasing me."

"Ditto."

This makes me crack up. Kingston keeps accusing me of teasing him, and it tickles me that he's this attracted to me. Luke never treated me as if he desired me. But every intense gaze Kingston sends my way lets me know that he wants to know me in more than the biblical sense.

I know that's how God made men and women, but it still frightens me. Chastity is not optional—it's a requirement with me. I just hope Kingston doesn't try to put me in an uncompromising position. I would be so disappointed, especially since I've decided to give him my heart.

In the car on the way to choir practice, Kingston hums and looks so pleased with himself that I'm curious about what he's thinking.

"A penny for your thoughts," I say.

"They are worth a little more than that, but if you're on a budget, I'll accept your little piddly coin."

"Piddly? You're calling my money piddly?"

"One cent, Yvonne?"

I laugh out loud. "What *are* you thinking about?"

"You."

"Well, I'm right here, so tell me what's going on in your head."

He lifts an eyebrow. "It wouldn't be proper to tell a lady these things."

My jaw drops. "Kingston!"

"Hey, you asked! I wasn't going to say anything at all."

"You're about to minister, Kingston!"

He nods. "I know. Don't you realize that's why ministers usually start off their prayers asking for forgiveness? It's a daily thing for men."

"I'm not going to believe my pastor is thinking about First Lady in a carnal way before he preaches."

"It depends on what First Lady is wearing."

"Kingston!"

"I'm just saying. Pastor Brown is not a saint. He's a man who loves the Lord . . . and his beautiful wife."

We finally get to the church, and not a second too soon. I'm done listening to Kingston say ridiculousness about my pastor. I'm going to choose to believe that he's not thinking about anything other than God's grace and mercy in the pulpit.

I don't wait for Kingston to open the door for me. I just jump out of the car and start walking toward the church. Kingston's feelings seem hurt.

"Why didn't you let me get it?" he asks when he catches up to me.

"Because I didn't want you to rub any of your *flesh* off on me."

Kingston laughs. "Please stop saying things like that! You want me to stay in the spirit, but you keep egging me on."

Kingston casually takes my hand in his as we walk into the church. I look down at his hand and then up at him. "So we're going public?"

"I've already gone public. Every person that asks, I tell them you are the one."

This warms my heart and makes me squeeze Kingston's hand tighter. My only reply is the smile that is plastered on my face.

As soon as we enter the sanctuary, the giggling starts. There are a lot of young women in the choir that I mentor, so I consider removing my hand from Kingston's, but then again, they need to see my fairy-tale prince treat me like the queen that I am.

Kingston leads me up into the choir stand and takes his place in front of the microphone stand.

"How's everybody doing tonight?" he asks.

Everyone answers at once, and Kingston smiles. He does this at the beginning of every practice. After everyone is done with their chaotic hellos, Kingston opens choir practice up with a prayer.

"Okay, I'd like to teach you all a song. It's an oldie but goodie, but mostly a goodie."

I love when Kingston picks out hymns. In my opinion they don't write gospel music like they used to. I don't want to go get it or stomp. I want the precious blood of the lamb! Hallelujah!

Kingston signals to the musicians, and they start playing. This music is familiar, but it is not a hymn. Nowhere near. It's "Time Will Reveal," by my favorite group, DeBarge. I'd know this music anywhere!

Kingston holds the mic to his mouth and sings, "I tell you I love you, but you won't believe it's true."

My face reddens, and I cover it with my hands when I realize Kingston is singing to me.

"More precious than silver, more precious than diamond rings, or anything that I can give you, it wouldn't mean a thing.

If you didn't have my love beside you there to guide you through. Ain't it good to know you do?"

I am thrilled and embarrassed at the same time. Kingston gets down on one knee and pulls a ring out of his pocket.

He keeps singing. "Yvonne, will you marry me? 'Cause this time love's for real. Come spend your life with me. This special love that's deep inside of us will last until the end of time!"

Everyone applauds as I stand here shaking, crying, and nodding yes all at the same time. Kingston keeps singing as he slips the ring on my finger. There are oohs and aahs from the choir at the ring. I wouldn't have cared if he gave me a ring out of a Cracker Jack box!

When he finishes the song, Kingston stands to his feet and hugs me. If I could just freeze this moment in time, I would. I've never, ever been so happy to be alive.

"You've made me the happiest man in this church right now," Kingston says.

I whisper to him, "I can't even describe the way you've made me feel."

"This is nothing, Yvonne. I'm only getting started."

I'll take this as a promise of bigger and better things to come, although I don't know what else God could do that's greater than Kingston. It's like God wanted to make it up to me for enduring Luke by giving me the most tender, handsome, and God-fearing man that He could muster.

"Hallelujah!" I shout. I meant to keep my praise inside, but when I thought about what God had brought me from and where he was taking me, I couldn't help but shout.

The keyboard player goes from playing DeBarge to shouting music, and I cut a rug right up there in the choir stand. The entire choir claps and dances before the Lord with me.

I guess to non-churchgoing folk, we'd probably look like we're doing a rain dance or something. And I would agree with them. A latter rain dance. My latter man is absolutely better than my former man. And if that ain't worth a shout, then I don't know what is!

CHAPTER 42

PAM

"So counseling for you and Troy, huh?" Taylor asks.

"Yeah. What do you think? Would you do it? Would you stay with Spencer if he cheated on you?"

Taylor slams her hand down on my patio table. "The devil is a lie. Spencer would not cheat, but if he did, I wouldn't stay with him. I couldn't."

"And yet you advised me to stay with Troy."

"Yes. Y'all are two different people. It'll work out with you and Troy if you just let it, Pam."

"I don't want to talk about it until we get done with counseling."

There's nothing that I can say that will convince Troy that I never slept with Logan. After he had a chance to think longer and harder about the whole thing, he decided that I was being unfaithful, and that the only reason why Logan tried to rape me was that he had already had a taste.

Yeah, it's going to take a lot of prayer to fix us.

I watch our children splash in the pool. They're happy that Troy is back home, no matter what issues we might have. They love their daddy.

Taylor says, "You think you've got drama? I'll see your marriage counseling and raise you an ain't nobody got time for that. Right now my son is probably walking down the aisle at his father's wedding."

"You've grown," I say. "A couple of years ago we wouldn't be having this conversation."

Taylor shakes her head. "No. I don't know how much I've grown, but at least I didn't hide Joshua in another city when Luke showed up. I considered that, you know."

I laugh out loud. "Spencer would've stopped you."

"Not if I put my mind to it, he wouldn't. He is absolutely no match to my wit."

I need Taylor's humor to keep my mind off my life. Troy and I haven't told anyone about Logan's attempted rape. I wanted to call the police and file a report, but Troy said that it would ruin him in the industry if he did. So we just dropped it and pretended that it never happened.

Except that I can't forget. I feel terror in the pit of my stomach every time I see a man who looks like Logan. I've always thought that I was a good judge of character, but I guess the devil can fool anybody silly enough to go playing with fire.

"I guess we've got a wedding to plan, huh?" I ask, wanting to change the subject of the conversation and the train of the thoughts in my mind.

"We do! Yvonne is going to be a beautiful bride."

"Yes, she will."

Taylor covers her mouth with her hand and chuckles. "Should we invite Luke?"

"Girl, hush!" I say.

"I'm joking. Well, sort of. I think Luke should see how happy Kingston makes Yvonne. Then he'll realize how much of a loser he is."

"No, he won't," I reply. "He'll assume Yvonne is faking her new joy, or that she's going overboard to make him jealous."

"You're right. He's an egocentric buster," Taylor says. "And my baby is right there hanging out with him."

"Do you want to go and make sure Joshua's all right?" I ask. "I can ride with you."

"Wouldn't that be a crazy-lady kind of thing to do? Plus, we're not dressed for a wedding."

I look down at my bummy pair of sweats. "We're dressed for a loser's wedding."

"I don't know. . . ."

"Oh, come on," I say. "It'll be fun. We can be the crackish-looking ex-girlfriends."

"Crackish?" Taylor asks.

"Yeah." I scratch my neck as I reply. "I 'on know why y'all all on this dude. He's so broke, he ain't gave child support since my son got out of diapers. . . ."

Taylor giggles and scratches her neck, too. "Yeah, little Ray-jahnay, Mudfoot, and Bryce don't have new shoes, either."

I burst into laughter. "Rayjahnay? Mudfoot?"

"The ghettoer the better."

"Come on," I say. "Let's do this. I'm in the mood for a laugh."

Taylor bursts into a flurry of belly laughs, and I try to join in. Her laugh is one of someone who's laid their burdens down. Mine is counterfeit. Mine sounds like that of someone whose yoke all of a sudden got heavy.

Taylor notices that I've stopped laughing, and she stops, too. She takes my hand in hers. "Pam, I'm still praying for your situation."

"Thank you."

Taylor says, "I'm not stopping until you get a breakthrough."

And I believe her, because that's what we do. We enjoy each other, and we pray with each other. She is my sister, even if we don't share a drop of blood.

CHAPTER 43

EVA

Eva stood outside the building, unable to walk inside. Yvonne waited patiently beside her, not rushing or admonishing her. Just waiting.

"I don't know if I can do this today," Eva said. "It's like finding out that the bogeyman is real and then going to have coffee with him."

"You don't have to do it today, if you don't want to. I'd be happy to ride out here with you another time."

"No, I've got to do it now, before I lose my nerve," Eva said, although she didn't have much nerve at all.

"Okay, sweetie. I'm here with you."

Eva clutched Yvonne's arm and practically dragged her into the hospice where her uncle Parnell was living out his final days. As soon as they entered the building, a smell of decay accosted Eva's nose. Life was fleeting in this place.

They checked in at the front desk. "I'm here to see Parnell Jacobs," Eva told the desk attendant.

"That's wonderful. You're his first visitor."

"I am?" Eva asked.

"You are. Even though he has a daughter and a son listed here, you're the only one who has shown up."

The desk attendant gave Eva and Yvonne two ragged paper

visitors' passes. They were so worn out that they needed replacement, but the two ladies took them, anyway.

"He's in room two-sixteen," the attendant said.

Once they found the room, Eva stood in front of the door for a second, almost changing her mind. Having Yvonne there helped so much, but not quite enough to make her feel at ease. It was a monster she was confronting and demanding an apology of. A monster who'd stolen her innocence.

God, can you help me through this one?

Eva's short and sweet prayers were coming more frequently now, but was she prayed up enough for this? Yvonne was not going any farther. It was just Eva's turn now.

She gently pushed open the door, holding her breath the entire time. Her exhale rushed out as she saw her uncle lying on the bed. He couldn't have been more than eighty-five pounds, and he was attached to an oxygen tank. His face was barely recognizable, save for the thick glasses he always wore.

"Baby girl," Parnell croaked.

Eva cringed. "Don't call me that. I'm a grown woman."

Parnell pats the seat next to his bed. "Sit down right here."

"No, Uncle Parnell, I just wanted to say that you stole my innocence and everything else from me."

Uncle Parnell looks away from my intense glare. "I did. I'm so sorry about that, baby girl."

"That's it? That's all you have to say for yourself?"

"I was wrong, Eva. Everyone knew it. Your grandmother Susie, your cousins. They all wanted me to die, but you left the scene and made my presence more tolerable for everyone else."

Uncle Parnell's eyes rolled into the top of his head, and his entire body quaked.

"Do you need a nurse?" Eva asked.

Her uncle couldn't answer. He was having a seizure.

The nurses and doctors swarmed around her and pushed her out of the way. They worked on him for a few moments and got him stabilized, but the hopeless looks on their faces told Eva that it wouldn't last long.

Yvonne poked her head in from the hallway. "Are you okay?"

"Yes. I think I'm done here. Can we go to the cemetery now?"

Eva left the unconscious uncle Parnell and left the facility with Yvonne. She didn't know what she expected from her uncle. But an apology had to be far down on the list.

It was a silent drive to the cemetery where Grandma Susie was buried. Eva clutched the big white Bible to her chest, and tears spilled down onto and over the binding. She had never been to the grave site. Wasn't invited to the funeral and had never taken the time to visit it herself.

After Yvonne parked, Eva got out of the car with the Bible and a bouquet of flowers. First, she spread the flowers all over the gravestone. Then she set the Bible down in front of the stone.

"Grandma Susie, I know you can't hear me, but I just want you to know that I did pay for my sins in life. But Uncle Parnell touching me wasn't my sin. It was his. I'm leaving your Bible here with you. I have one, and I've highlighted only words of life."

Eva could barely say the speech she'd prepared through her sobs. Yvonne got out of the car, put her arms around Eva, and squeezed.

"You must think I'm crazy, Yvonne, to be standing out here talking to a gravestone."

Yvonne shook her head. "No, ma'am, I do not."

"Whether you think that or not, could you not tell the other ladies? I want them to be my friends, and they won't if they think I'm crazy."

"They wouldn't think this was crazy, too."

"No, Yvonne! Swear you won't say anything!"

Yvonne smiled at Eva and hugged her again. "Don't you worry about your secret. Go ahead and talk to God, your grandmother, and everyone else you need to address. And, honey, I won't tell a soul."

And Eva believed her.

Eva stood silently in front of her grandmother's grave, now

finished with her declaration. It was so quiet that she could hear her own breathing. She counted the inhales and exhales without thinking.

Her counting was different this time, though. The last time she'd numbered her breaths, it was with the thought that she was getting closer to taking her last. Now her inhales drew strength and her exhales carried power.

God breathed new life into Eva. And she became a living soul.

DON'T TELL A SOUL

Tiffany L. Warren

About This Guide

The questions that follow are included to enhance your
group's reading of this book.

Discussion Questions

1. Pam has made great strides with her writing and now has a book deal. What do you think about Troy's lack of support? Does it justify Pam's later actions? Should a woman pursue a career that might take her away from fulfilling her family's needs? Is this part of being a Proverbs 31 woman?

2. Yvonne's romance comes at a time when she has finally gotten used to and comfortable with her single life. Are her feelings about Luke surprising? Discuss the complexities of dating after being married for many years.

3. If you were in Taylor's shoes, how would you handle Luke's sudden reappearance? Do you believe in Luke's transformation? Do you agree or disagree with Spencer and Taylor's decision regarding Luke's visitation with Joshua? Should Taylor have followed Spencer's lead from the beginning?

4. Eva's journey is not typical. She has her altar-call experience after deciding to change her life. How should the church deal with new members who are not quite finished with their past? Base your discussion on (John 4:4–29).

5. Were you surprised by Logan? Did you like him as much as Pam did? Where did Pam go wrong? Where should she have drawn the line? Was the friendship doomed from the start?

6. What do you think is next for Pam and Troy? Do you think he's really going to drop Aria? Should Pam walk away if he doesn't?

7. Are Rhoda and Rochelle ever gonna get delivered from their gossiping spirit?

Don't miss Rhonda Bowen's

Get You Good

On sale in April 2013 from Dafina Books!

CHAPTER 1

Sydney was never one for sports.

It wasn't that she was a couch potato. She just wasn't one of those women who met the crack of dawn with a pair of Nikes and a bottle of Gatorade.

However as she stood at the center of the Carlu's Round Room, surveying the best of the NBA that Toronto had to offer, she had to admit that professional sports did have its attractions.

"Sydney, whatever you do, don't pinch me."

Sydney grinned and folded her arms as she considered her younger sister.

"Why?"

Lissandra bit her lip. "Because I do not want to wake up from this dream."

Sydney turned toward where Lissandra was staring, just in time to catch the burst of testosterone that walked through the main doors. Brawn, beauty and brazen arrogance wrapped in suits. Who said a girl couldn't enjoy basketball?

Sydney's eyebrows shot up. "Is that . . .?"

"Yes, girl. And our HD TV does him absolutely no justice," Lissandra said, as her eyes devoured the newest group of NBA stars to steal the spotlight. "I love this game."

Sydney laughed. "I don't think it's the game you love."

"You laugh now," Lissandra said, pulling her compact out of her purse. "But when that hot little dress I had to force you to wear gets you a date for next weekend you'll thank me."

Sydney tugged discreetly at the hem of the dangerously short boat necked silver dress that fit her five foot nine frame almost perfectly. It was a bit more risqué than what Sydney would normally wear but seemed almost prudish compared to what the other women in the room were sporting. At least it wasn't too clingy. And the cut of the dress exposed her long elegant neck which she had been told was one of her best features.

"I'm here to work, not pick up men," Sydney said.

"No, we're here to deliver a spectacular cake," Lissandra said, checking her lipstick in the tiny mirror discreetly. "And since that cake is sitting over there, our work is done. It's playtime."

"Focus Lissa," Sydney said, touching Lissandra's upper arm. "Don't forget this is an amazing opportunity to make the kind of contacts that will put us on the A-list. Once we do that, more events like this might be in our future."

"Okay fine," Lissandra said with a sigh, dropping her compact back into her purse. "I'll talk to some people and give out a few business cards. But if a player tries to buy me a drink, you best believe I'm gonna take it."

Sydney grinned. "I wouldn't expect otherwise."

"Good," Lissandra said with a naughty grin. "'Cause I see some potential business over there that has my name on him."

Sydney sighed. Why did she even bother?

"Be good," Sydney said as she lost her sister to a six foot tall brother with dimples across the room.

"I will," she threw behind her. But since she didn't even bother to look back, Sydney didn't hope for much.

Sydney eventually lost sight of her sister as the crowd thickened. She turned her attention back to their ticket into the exclusive Toronto Raptors NBA Season opener event.

The cake.

Sydney stood back and admired her work again, loving the

way the chandelier from above and the tiny lights around the edges of the table and underneath it, lit up her creation. The marzipan gave the cream coloured square base of the cake a smooth flawless finish, and the gold trim caught the light beautifully. The golden replica of an NBA championship trophy which sat atop the base was however the highlight.

She had to admit it was a sculpted work of art, and one of the best jobs she had done in years. It was also one of the most difficult. It had taken two days just to bake and decorate the thing. That didn't include the several concept meetings, the special ordered baking moulds and multiple samples made to ensure that cake tasted just as good as it looked. For the past month and a half, this cake job had consumed her life. But it was well worth it. Not only for the weight it put in her pocket, but also the weight it was likely to add to her client list. Because once everyone at the event saw her creation, she was sure she would finally make it onto the city's pastry chef A-list, and Decadent would be the go-to spot for wedding and special event cakes.

She stood around the cake for a while, sucking up the oohs and aahs of passersby, before heading to the bathroom to check that she hadn't sweated out her curls carrying up the cake from downstairs. She took in her dark chin length locks, which had been curled up for the night, her slightly rounded face and plump pinked lips and was satisfied. She turned to the side to get a better view of her size six frame and smiled. Even though she had protested when Lissandra presented the dress, she knew she looked good. Normally she hated any kind of shimmer, but the slight sparkle from the dress was just enough to put Sydney in the party mood it inspired. Okay, so Lissandra may have been right. She was there for business, but that didn't mean she couldn't have some fun too.

By the time she reapplied her lipstick and headed back the room was full.

She tried to mingle and did end up chatting with a few guests, but her mother instincts were in full mode and it wasn't long before she found her way back to the cake.

She was about to check for anything amiss when she felt gentle fingers on the back of her bare neck. She swung around on reflex.

"What do you think you're doing?" she said slapping away the hand that had violated her personal space.

"Figuring out if I'm awake or dreaming."

Sydney's eyes slid all the way up the immaculately toned body of the 6 foot 3 man standing in front of her to his strong jaw, full smirking lips, and coffee brown eyes. Her jaw dropped. And not just because of how ridiculously handsome he was.

"Dub?"

"Nini."

She cringed. "Wow. That's a name I never thought I would hear again."

"And that's a half tattoo I never thought I'd see again."

Sydney slapped her hand on the back of her neck self consciously. She had almost forgotten the thing was there. It would take the one person who had witnessed her chicken out on getting it finished to remind her about it.

Hayden Windsor. Now wasn't this a blast from the past sure to get her into some present trouble.

She tossed a hand on her hip and pursed her lips. "I thought Toronto was too small for you?"

"It is."

"Then what are you doing here?"

"Right now?" His eyes flitted across her frame in answer.

"Stop that," Sydney said, her cheeks heating up as she caught his perusal.

"Stop what?" he asked with a laugh.

"You know what," she said. She shook her head. "You are still the same."

He shrugged in an attempt at innocence that only served to draw Sydney's eyes to the muscles shifting under his slim fit jacket.

"I can't help it. I haven't seen you in almost 15 years. What, you gonna beat me up like you did when you were seven?"

"Maybe."

"Bully."

"Jerk."

"How about we continue this argument over dinner?" he asked.

"They just served appetizers."

The corner of his lips drew up in a scandalous grin. "Come on, you know you're still hungry."

He was right. That finger food didn't do anything for her – especially since working on the cake had kept her from eating all day. But she wasn't about to tell him that.

Sydney smirked. "Even if I was, I don't date guys who make over $150,000 a year."

He raised a thick eyebrow. "That's a new one."

"Yes well," she said. "It really is for your own good. This way you won't have to wonder if I was with you for your money."

"So how about we pretend like I don't have all that money," he said, a dangerous glint in his eyes. "We could pretend some other things too – like we weren't just friends all those years ago."

"I'm not dating you Hayden," Sydney said, despite the shiver that ran up her spine at his words.

"So you can ask me to marry you, but you won't date me?"

"I was seven years old!"

"And at ten years old, I took that very seriously," Hayden said, his brow furrowing.

Sydney laughed. "That would explain why you went wailing to your daddy right after."

He grabbed his rock solid chest. "I'm an emotional kind of guy."

"Hayden! There you are. I've been looking all over for you!"

Sydney turned to where the voice was coming from and fought her gag reflex. A busty woman with too much blond hair sidled up to Hayden, slipping her arm around his.

"This place is so packed that I can barely find anyone." The woman suddenly seemed to notice Sydney.

"Sydney!"

"Samantha."

Samantha gave Sydney a constipated smile. "So good to see you."

Sydney didn't smile back. "Wish I could say the same."

Hayden snorted. Samantha dropped the smile, but not his arm.

Sydney glared at the woman in her red feathered dress and wondered how many peacocks had to die to cover her Dolly Parton goods.

"So I guess you two know each other?" Hayden asked, breaking the silence that he seemed to find more amusing than awkward.

"Yes," Samantha volunteered. "Sydney's little bakery Decadent, beat out Something Sweet for the cake job for this event. She was my main competition."

"I wouldn't call it a competition," Sydney said. It was more like a slaughtering.

"How do *you* know each other?" Samantha probed.

Hayden grinned. "Me and Sydney go way back. Right Syd?"

Samantha raised an eyebrow questioningly and Sydney glared at her, daring her to ask another question. Samantha opted to keep her mouth shut.

"So this is where the party is," Lissandra said joining the small circle. "Hayden? Is that you?"

"The very same," Hayden said pulling her into a half hug. "Good to see you Lissa."

"Back at you," Lissandra said. "Wow, it's been ages. I probably wouldn't recognize you except Sydney used to watch your games all the –oww!"

Lissandra groaned as Sydney's elbow connected with her side.

"Did she?" Hayden asked, turning to Sydney again, a smug look in his eyes.

"Well it was nice to see you all again," Samantha said, trying to navigate Hayden away from the group.

"Samantha, I can't believe you're here," Lissandra said with a hint of laughter. "I thought you would be busy cleaning up that business at Something Sweet."

Sydney bit back a smirk as a blush crept up Samantha's neck to her cheeks. Samantha went silent again.

"What business?" Hayden looked around at the three women, who obviously knew something he didn't.

"Nothing," Samantha said quickly.

"Just that business with the health inspector," Lissandra said, enjoying Samantha's discomfort. "Nothing major. I'm sure the week that you were closed was enough to get that sorted out."

Hayden raised an eyebrow. "The health inspector shut you down?"

"We were closed temporarily," Samantha corrected. "Just so that we could take care of a little issue. It wasn't that serious."

"Is that what the exterminator said?" Lissandra asked.

Sydney coughed loudly and Samantha's face went from red to purple.

"You know," Samantha said, anger in her eyes. "It's interesting. We have never had a problem at that location before now. It's funny how all of a sudden we needed to call an exterminator around the same time they were deciding who would get the job for tonight's event."

"Yes, life is full of coincidences," Sydney said dryly. "Like that little mixup we had with the Art Gallery of Ontario event last month. But what can you do? The clients go where they feel confident."

"Guess that worked out for you this time around," Samantha said glaring at Sydney and Lissandra.

"Guess so," Lissandra said smugly.

Sydney could feel Hayden eyeing her suspiciously, but she didn't dare look at him.

"Well, this was fun," Sydney said in a tone that said the exact opposite. "But I see some people I need to talk to."

Sydney excused herself from the group and made her way to the opposite side of the room toward the mayor's wife. She had only met the woman once, but Sydney had heard they had an anniversary coming up soon. It was time to get reacquainted, and get away from the one man who could make her forget what she really came here for.

* * *

By the time the hands on her watch were both sitting at eleven, Sydney was exhausted. Plus she was completely out of business cards.

"Leaving already?" She was only steps from the door, and he was only steps in front of her.

"This was business not pleasure."

Hayden's eyes sparkled with mischief.

"All work and no play, makes Sydney a dull girl."

This time her mouth turned up in a smile. "I think you know me better than that."

His grin widened in a way that assured her that he did.

"Remind me."

She shook her head and pointed her tiny purse at him.

"I'm not doing this here with you Dub."

He stepped closer and she felt the heat from his body surround her. "We can always go somewhere else. Like the Banjara's a couple blocks away."

Darn him and his inside knowledge.

"If we leave now we can get there before it closes."

She folded her arms over her midsection. "I haven't changed my mind Dub."

He grinned. "That's not what your stomach says."

Sydney glanced behind him, and he turned around to see that Samantha was only a few feet away and headed in his direction. Sydney wasn't sure what string of events had put Samantha and Hayden together that night. The woman was definitely not his type.

"I think your date is coming to get you," Sydney said, her voice dripping with amusement. "Maybe *she* wants to go for Indian food."

"How about I walk you to your car?"

Without waiting for a response, he put a hand on the small of her back and eased her out the large doors into the lobby and toward the elevator.

"What's the rush?" she teased.

"Still got that smart mouth don't you."

"I thought that was what you liked about me?" she said innocently, as he led her into the waiting open elevator.

"See that's what you always got wrong Nini." He leaned toward her ear to whisper and she caught a whiff of his cologne. "It was never just one thing."

Sydney tried to play it off, but she couldn't help the way her breathing went shallow as her heart sped up. And she couldn't keep him from noticing it either.

His eyes fell to her lips. "So what's it going to be Syd? You, me and something spicy?"

He was only inches away from her. So close that if she leaned in, she could...

"Hayden!"

A familiar voice in the distance triggered her good sense. Sydney stepped forward and placed her hands on his chest.

"I think you're a bit busy tonight."

She pushed him out of the elevator and hit the door close button.

He grinned and shook his head as she waved at him through the gap between the closing doors.

"I'll see you soon, Nini."

For reasons she refused to think about, she hoped he kept that promise.